MASQUES

BOOKS BY BILL PRONZINI

NOVELS
MASQUES
HOODWINK
LABYRINTH
BLOWBACK
GAMES
SNOWBOUND
UNDERCURRENT
THE VANISHED
PANIC!
THE SNATCH
THE STALKER

COLLABORATIVE NOVELS
THE CAMBODIA FILE (WITH JACK ANDERSON)
PROSE BOWL (WITH BARRY N. MALZBERG)
NIGHT SCREAMS (WITH BARRY N. MALZBERG)
TWOSPOT (WITH COLLIN WILCOX)
ACTS OF MERCY (WITH BARRY N. MALZBERG)
THE RUNNING OF BEASTS (WITH BARRY N. MALZBERG)

NONFICTION
GUN IN CHEEK

ANTHOLOGIES
THE ARBOR HOUSE TREASURY OF HORROR AND THE SUPERNATURAL
   (WITH BARRY N. MALZBERG AND MARTIN H. GREENBERG)
CREATURE!
MUMMY!
VOODOO!
WEREWOLF!
THE EDGAR WINNERS
BUG-EYED MONSTERS (WITH BARRY N. MALZBERG)
SHARED TOMORROWS (WITH BARRY N. MALZBERG)
THE END OF SUMMER: SCIENCE FICTION OF THE 50S (WITH BARRY N.
   MALZBERG)
MIDNIGHT SPECIALS
DARK SINS, DARK DREAMS (WITH BARRY N. MALZBERG)
TRICKS & TREATS (WITH JOE GORES)

MASQUES

A NOVEL of TERROR

Bill Pronzini

ARBOR HOUSE
New York

B-2

Library of Congress Catalog Card Number: 80-70219

ISBN: 0-87795-308-2

Manufactured in the United States of America

10 9 8 7 6 5 4 3 2 1

For my mother,
Helene G. Piazza,
with love

Author's Note:

The points of view expressed in this novel are those of the characters, and are the product of a fictional concept. They do not necessarily reflect my personal views. Nor is there any intent to cast aspersions on the city of New Orleans, its people, or its Carnival celebrations. New Orleans, in fact, is one of my favorite cities and I hope to return there many times in the future.

B.P.

PART I
CARNIVAL SATURDAY

It was a voluptuous scene, that masquerade . . . a gay and magnificent revel . . . There were much glare and glitter and piquancy and phantasm . . . There were arabesque figures with unsuited limbs and appointments. There were much delirious fancies such as the madman fashions. There were much of the beautiful, much of the wanton, much of the bizarre, something of the terrible, and not a little of that which might have excited disgust.

—EDGAR ALLAN POE
"The Masque of the Red Death"

ONE

THERE was a kind of madness in the city.

He had felt it yesterday afternoon, when he first arrived in New Orleans; and last night at the Krewe of Hermes, his first Carnival parade; and now again today, in the bright sunshine and the clutter of humanity on Bourbon Street. Others might have called it excitement—the unrestrained revelry of New Orleans in Carnival season, with just a few days left before Mardi Gras. But it did not feel that way to him. It felt like a kind of madness, with undercurrents of violence and tragedy, and it made him uneasy, it made him almost afraid.

He kept trying to tell himself that this was imagination. And nerves—his frayed nerves. He had only been here one day; you could not relax and start enjoying yourself in one day. Give it time, he thought, a little more time. He'd get into the spirit of things eventually. That was why he was here, wasn't it? To start having some fun again?

Having fun was what Mardi Gras was all about. "The Greatest Free Show on Earth," they called it here. A week or so of merrymaking for most visitors, but for the residents, an entire Carnival season beginning on January 5, the Eve of Epiphany, the holy day commemorating the manifestation of Christ to the Magi, and ending weeks later on Shrove Tuesday, the day before Lent. A movable feast. An American tradition since the landing of Bienville in 1699; a New Orleans tradition since the first krewe, the Mystick Krewe of Comus, was organized in 1857. Fun and frolic. *Laissez les bon temps rouler:* let the good times roll.

But he still could not talk himself out of the uneasiness, the nascent fear. Not yesterday afternoon and not last night and not now. The uncontrolled atmosphere seemed more acute on Bourbon Street, as if it were centralized here, or emanated from somewhere in the ten-block expanse they had closed to traffic this morning, as they did every night after dark, and turned into a pedestrian mall. It was in the faces of sharp-eyed hookers like predators hovering on corners, flashily dressed blacks and cowboys in ten-gallon hats, hard-looking young men in motorcycle garb, already half-drunk, swilling beer or Hurricanes from twenty-four-ounce "go-cups," the blank-expressioned fat kid so spaced out on drugs that he kept walking around in circles and muttering senseless incantations to himself. It was in the brightly colored costumes of the early maskers—a big-footed clown here, a leering pirate there, an Arthurian knight down the way wielding what looked to be a real sword—and in the festive decorations on lampposts and the wrought-iron balconies above. It was in the shrill laughter, the shouts of vendors and of shills for the strip and topless shows, the heavy throbbing beat of Dixieland jazz, the counterpoint rhythms of rock, country and western, and the steam calliope playing Stephen Foster melodies aboard one of the Mississippi River steamboats anchored at the foot of Decatur Street. It was in the odors of beer and whiskey, pralines, spice, garbage, marijuana, sweat and urine and old vomit. It was in the refuse in the gutters and in the corpses of huge ginger-colored cockroaches that spotted the narrow sidewalks. It was everywhere in the Vieux Carré, maybe everywhere in New Orleans, and it was inescapable as long as he remained a cell within it. And it would get worse, too, as more and more people flocked to the city for Mardi Gras, as the merrymaking grew even wilder and approached what would be a frenzied pitch on Fat Tuesday. He would either have to adapt to it long before then, blank out its menace real or imagined, or it would overwhelm him and send him hurrying home prematurely.

I shouldn't have come here, he thought. This isn't what I need; this is the last thing I need.

But he had come here and he was going to make the best of it. That was what he insisted to himself, not for the first time, as he turned off Bourbon and onto Toulouse. Stick it out, try to have some fun. He hadn't run away from any of the other unpleasantness in his life, including Lara, and he was not about to start now.

He went straight down Toulouse to Decatur, past Jackson Square, and then up onto the observation platform near the river. He sat on one of the benches. It was better here—not so many people, not so much noise, and a cool crisp wind blowing in from the Gulf. He could see the steamboat *Natchez* berthed nearby; that was the one that had the steam calliope, still blaring in its festive way. People were streaming aboard and standing along her deck rails, getting ready for one of the river tours. He thought about joining them. One of the things he'd planned to do, after poring over the Chamber of Commerce literature his travel agent had given him, and the New Orleans guidebook he'd bought, was to visit the bayou country on one of the old renovated paddlewheelers. But he hadn't brought his Pentax and the rest of equipment with him this morning; it was still back in his room at the Pirate's Head. Besides, he didn't really feel like going for a boat ride. He didn't know what he felt like doing.

Sitting there, he lit a cigarette and stared out at the wide muddy-brown expanse of the Mississippi. Freighters, barges, a passenger liner or two, a few pleasure craft—New Orleans was a busy port even at Carnival time. He wondered where the ships were from, where they were going.

I don't give a damn where they're from or where they're going, he thought.

The cigarette tasted wrong; he dropped it and ground it out with his shoe. He wasn't used to smoking any more. He'd quit twelve years ago—no, thirteen, just before his twenty-fifth birthday—and he'd only started again when Lara filed for divorce. Something to do with his hands, something to help him relax. But it was not much of a crutch. Neither was liquor; he'd started on that, too, after the separation. Or was it after the fire? Well, he would have to quit again one of these days, when he got his head together and his life back on an even keel. The cigarettes and the booze both.

He stood, aimlessly, and went down the far steps, along the boardwalk that led across a line of industrial railroad tracks, and up the stairs to the Moonwalk. Fanciful name, he thought, for what amounted to a long wooden quay with benches strung along it and a short tier of seats like those in a sports stadium, all overlooking the river. Lovers were supposed to come out here at night and walk in the moonlight and be enchanted by the mighty Mississippi. That was more or less what it said in the tourist literature, anyway. There were a few lovers out here already, he saw—some walking hand in hand, some sitting close together, one couple sharing a bottle of wine, another couple talking alternate tokes off a marijuana joint. Anything goes at Mardi Gras time. Nobody gets hassled unless they hassle somebody else.

He started to wander along the Moonwalk, but with all the couples around, the loneliness welled up inside him. Young, middle-aged, elderly, even a pair of homosexual males—all two by two. Maybe it was better back in the French Quarter, after all. At least there you could blend in with the crowd. Intimations of madness and pangs of fear were bad enough, but loneliness was worse. Loneliness was the worst emotion of them all.

His watch told him it was almost noon. The hell with this, he thought, it's time for a drink. He wasn't so far gone that he was drinking in the mornings yet; he'd made a pact with himself—no alcohol before noon and a three-drink limit between noon and five o'clock. After five . . . well, it all depended. On where he was, on how he felt. On how lonely he was.

Walking back toward Jackson Square, he wondered how much one of the hookers would charge to spend the night with him. He hadn't paid for sex since he was eighteen, when he had driven with some friends to a brothel outside Reno; but then, sex wasn't his primary motivation this time. Companionship, that was what he needed more than anything else. Somebody to talk to. Somebody, like in the Kristofferson song, to help him make it through the night.

A hundred dollars? Maybe not that much; maybe as little as fifty. But did he want to pay fifty dollars for mechanical sex and mechanical conversation with someone who would look at him, just as the whore in the Reno brothel had looked at him twenty years ago, as if he were contemptible? No, a hooker wasn't the answer. He'd have to do what he had originally intended: go barhopping, even though he had never liked the singles game much, and hope to pick up a woman somewhere. Christ knew, the city was full of unattached and no doubt uninhibited women; and he wasn't exactly an ogre. He had attracted Lara, hadn't he?

He didn't know much about picking up women—he'd never cheated on Lara once in the fifteen years they were married, and wasn't that a goddamn laugh—but he was personable and reasonably intelligent and had an interesting occupation. Or at least most people thought photography was an interesting occupation. And he knew a fair amount about jazz, an interest which had developed into a minor hobby over the years; a knowledge of New Orleans jazz would make a good conversational gambit. So all right, then. Find a bar, find a woman, find a little companionship. Make it through the night, make it through Mardi Gras. Then go back home and pick up the rest of the pieces. It wasn't an unreasonable equation. Hell, it might even turn out to be easier and more agreeable than he expected.

He made his way along the St. Ann promenade adjacent to Jackson Square. On one side was one of the iron-lacework Pontalba buildings, built around 1850, the oldest apartment building in the United States. On the other side, street artists sat under umbrellas and shade trees, with their paintings arranged on easels and on the park fence behind them. People milled in between, and in front of the cathedral and the Cabildo Museum on Chartres Street. He saw a drunk eating a muffuletta sandwich and dribbling olive relish on his shirt, a man in a clown costume selling phallic-shaped balloons, a teen-age girl either drunk or stoned with her blouse unbuttoned down the front and one of her breasts poking free; he saw two men in black denims and corduroy vests arguing loudly and heard one of them say, "Well, fuck it, man," just as a pair of nuns came by, and when they looked at him disapprovingly, heard the man say, "Fuck you too, sisters." An itinerant jazz band was playing "Bugle Call Rag" and several people were dancing, including one couple whose motions imitated those of lovemaking. The feeling of uneasiness began to crawl over him again. Damn it, why couldn't he come to terms with all this bacchanal? He wasn't a prude, he didn't object to having fun as long as it didn't get out of hand. Why couldn't he get into the mood of it?

At the corner of St. Ann and Bourbon, just as he got there, a black man in a purple suit slapped a mulatto woman across the face and called her a slut. She spit on him. The man caught hold of her arm and dragged her up against him, and she began to scream obscenities at him. Some of the crowd jamming Bourbon stopped to watch, but none of them made an effort to intervene when the man slapped the woman a second time. None of them seemed particularly concerned; a few even looked amused.

He veered away from the scene, at an angle across the street. When he came up onto the *banquette* opposite he found himself staring at a black sign hanging from the overhead gallery, with lettering on it in red and yellow. The sign was made in the shape of a black-cowled woman with strangely staring eyes, and the lettering said: *Voodoo Museum & Gift Shop.* He moved over beneath the sign to the building's narrow doorway. It was raised a pair of steps off the sidewalk, and from the semidarkness within he could smell incense and herbs and something that might have been an exotic perfume.

Voodoo. That was something else that had been mentioned in the guidebook. New Orleans had been the home of voodoo in the United States since the early 1700s, when the first slaves were imported from Haiti and other Caribbean hotbeds of the cult. It was the home, too, of Marie Laveau, the Voodoo Queen of New Orleans for nearly seventy years in the 1800s, who had held outlawed *vodun* ceremonies in the backyard of her St. Ann cottage and in a swamp near Bayou St. John, and who many claimed was an agent of Papa Là-bas—another term for Satan, in nineteenth-century patois. Holy serpents, *mamalois* and *papalois, rada* drums, blood sacrifices, dolls with pins in them, good-luck charms and death charms. Voodoo. A legitimate religion coexisting with Catholicism on the one hand, a lot of superstitious nonsense on the other hand.

He considered going inside, but only for a moment. The images cast up in his mind by the thought of voodoo were disturbingly similar to the Carnival reality that surrounded him—the wild noisemaking, the obscene dancing, the thudding beat of drums, the sudden violence. No, he didn't want anything to do with voodoo. Voodoo was one of the last things he wanted anything to do with right now.

Time for that drink, he reminded himself. And pushed away through the crowd to St. Ann, without looking back to see the figure of the black-cowled woman that hung in the shadows behind him.

TWO

THE Pirate's Head Hotel was on Burgundy Street, at the corner of Ursuline, in the Quarter's northeast section. It was old, three-storied, painted an off-white with dark green shutters and trim and heavy black cast-iron latticework decorating the upper galleries. The sidewalk in front had buckled, there were cracks in the plaster facing, and the sign with the scowling pirate's visage bolted next to the entrance had faded and chipped so that the pirate seemed to be decomposing. But for all that, the place was clean and comfortable and the service seemed adequate. Lara would have approved of it. She liked places with atmosphere and a sense of antiquity, however shabby, and the Pirate's Head reeked of both. She was the one who had picked it out, he remembered, back in April of last year, when they were still married and still planning out vacations together and still pretending to be a happy couple. She was also the one who had written the check for the substantial deposit; if it hadn't been for that deposit, nonrefundable because of the Mardi Gras crush, he might not even be here now.

He went inside. Small dark old-fashioned lobby; small

dark old-fashioned furniture; oil paintings of buccaneers and sailing ships; a pair of muskets and a Jolly Roger over the fireplace mantel. Quaint. It would make an interesting photographic study, and maybe he would bring his camera down later on and take some shots. Maybe. Right now he had his thirst to attend to.

He stopped at the desk long enough to pick up his key; then he went out through the rear doors into the courtyard. It was not much of a courtyard: half a dozen tables grouped under one magnolia and one live oak, some junglelike ground cover, a limestone fountain that looked like a crumbling piece of art deco, a tiny patio with some chaise longues and wrought-iron chairs, and a three-stool bar connected to the hotel lounge. But there was a quaintness about it, too, with its mossy cobblestones and the creeper vines that curled around iron-standard gas lamps and that art-deco fountain. And it was relatively quiet. You could hear the music and the Carnival noise coming from the lower part of the Quarter, but it was muted, tolerable, like a radio turned down low and heard from across a room.

There was only one other person in the courtyard—a slender dark-haired woman in her early twenties, wearing a Spanish poncho over a pair of Levi's, sitting at one of the tables with a glass of wine in front of her. He didn't pay much attention to her at first. He went to the bar and scraped back a stool and sat down. Put his cigarettes and matches on the bartop. While he was doing that, an elderly black man with snow-white hair, dressed in a pirate's jerkin over which was a wide brass-buckled leather belt, came out and asked him what he'd have. He sounded grumpy, and he had cause to be. Having to wear a pirate's costume was enough to make any man of his age grumpy.

"Vodka and ice with a twist."

"Gordon's all right?"

"Yes," he said. "Fine."

The bartender made the drink, put it down on a napkin, and disappeared again. He lit a cigarette, took a small sip of the vodka, savoring it, and felt better almost immediately. Booze was no damn good for you in the long run, but in the short run it helped you over the rough spots. He didn't want to think what it would be like if he were caught up in the Mardi Gras fever without it.

When he lifted his glass the second time he glanced over at the dark-haired woman, because it was better than looking into the semigloom of the inside lounge. She sat loosely in her chair, not moving, her eyes straight ahead. He wondered if she was stoned, like so many others on this Carnival weekend. And it occurred to him that at least some of the pilgrims must have the same feelings he did, that maybe they used alcohol or drugs to insulate themselves from the lunacy and the fear and the loneliness, just as he was doing. Lots of lonely, frightened people in this world, he thought. Lots of broken dreams and collapsed lives. And some of them come to Mardi Gras to look for the same elusive things he was searching for.

For no reason he remembered something a friend of his in San Francisco, Paul Daniels, had said to him once. They had gone down to Mexico for a few days of game fishing, and on the way back they had stopped off at Ensenada and taken in a bullfight, the first one he'd ever seen. He had been appalled at the slaughter, and he'd said so to Paul after it was over. And Paul had said, "Hell, Steve, there are winners and there are losers in all walks of life. Bulls are losers. Why worry about what happens to a bunch of bulls . . ."

He realized he was still looking at the woman. Then he realized he'd seen her before. Yesterday, just after the airport taxi had deposited him here at the Pirate's Head. She had been sitting on the front stoop of one of the ramshackle houses across Burgundy, wearing a floppy straw hat and a yellow sun dress. He'd noticed her because of the hat and because her dress had been hiked up around her thighs. She had also had a big fringed purse made out of brown carpeting material; that same purse was on the cobblestones beside her now.

She seemed to grow aware of his eyes on her and turned her head and looked at him. Caught in the act, he thought, and smiled automatically. She smiled back in a vague sort of way. But she didn't turn her head away again; she kept on looking at him.

He found this encouraging. "Hello," he said.

"Hello. I saw you yesterday, when you got here."

"I saw you too. I was just thinking the same thing."

"You came alone," she said. She had a faint, pleasing southern drawl. "Are you here alone?"

"Yes."

"For Mardi Gras?"

"Yes. Look, it's kind of awkward, talking across open space like this. Would you mind if I joined you?"

"I'm going to be leaving in a few minutes."

"Just for a few minutes, then?"

"If you want to."

He picked up drink, cigarettes, matches, and took them to her table and sat down. She was tall, he saw, and pretty in a way that was ethereal and sensuous, as if she were made up of equal parts of innocence and wantonness. The dark hair, worn long and parted in the middle, had bluish highlights where it caught random rays of sunshine. Her mouth was wide, free of lipstick; the underlip had a swollen look.

Impulse made him say, "Are you a model?"

"No. Why do you ask that?"

"You'd make a wonderful photographic subject. I'm a photographer, you see; I tend to look at people that way."

"What kind of photographer?"

"Oh, portraits, weddings—that sort of thing."

"You're from the West Coast somewhere," she said.

"San Francisco. How did you know?"

"Your accent. I'm good with accents."

"Yes, you are. My name is Steven Giroux, by the way."

"I'm Juleen."

"Juleen. That's a pretty name."

"Yes. Everybody always says that."

"Are you staying at the Pirate's Head, Juleen?"

"No. I live here."

"In the French Quarter, you mean?"

"In New Orleans. The Irish Channel."

"Where's that?"

"South of here. It's a district."

"Oh, I see."

"What's San Francisco like? It's full of queers, isn't it?"

"Homosexuals? Well, it does have a lot of gays, yes—"

"I don't like queers," she said. "You're not a queer, are you?"

The way she asked that, solemn, with her mouth pinched down at the corners, struck him funny and he laughed. "No," he said, "I'm not a queer."

"Are you married?"

He stopped laughing. "I used to be."

"What happened?"

"My wife and I split up. Six months ago."

"Why?"

"That's kind of a personal question, isn't it?"

"You don't have to answer it if you don't want to."

He didn't answer it at first. He took a couple of drags on his cigarette, butted it in the table ashtray, and had some more of his vodka. Then, on impulse again, he said, "She had other men. A whole string of them, I guess. I all but caught her with one."

"And you didn't go for that?"

It seemed an odd thing to say, until he remembered that she was young—not much more than twenty-two, probably. Kids today thought differently than when he'd been young; they had fewer hang-ups, and a much healthier attitude toward sex. His generation was bound by a lot of old-fashioned conventions. He understood that intellectually; it was the emotional bondage that he hadn't quite been able to overcome.

"No," he said, "I didn't go for that."

"You should have had an open marriage."

"I suppose so. On her part, I guess it was." He finished his drink, thought about ordering another, and decided to wait. "How about you, Juleen? Do you have an open marriage?"

"I'm not married," she said.

"Boyfriend?"

"No. I live alone."

"What do you do? For a living, I mean."

"That's not important, is it?"

And it flashed on him, belatedly, that she might be a hooker. The possibility was depressing. He felt attracted to her, as young as she was, and he found her frankness appealing, and he was working up to asking her out somewhere that evening—dinner, maybe. But if she was a hooker—

"It's not important," he said. "I'm just curious. And I did tell you about my profession."

Juleen shrugged. "I'm a potter."

"You make pottery?"

"That's what a potter does."

"For stores? Or do you sell as a street artist?"

"Both."

"Well," he said, and he felt a faint sense of relief. "I'd like to see some of your work sometime."

"Maybe you can."

"I'd like that."

"Are you going to watch the krewe tonight?" she asked.

"I hadn't thought about it. Why?"

"It's the Krewe of Nor—the children's krewe. It starts at seven o'clock."

"Well, I might go. How about you?"

"I don't know yet. Maybe."

"We could go together," he said tentatively. "We could even have dinner—"

"I can't," she said.

"Can't what? Can't go with me to the parade or can't have dinner?"

"Can't have dinner. I might go to the krewe later on."

Strikeout, he thought. As if his ego wasn't battered enough already. But he said, making one last try, "Parades aren't any fun alone. Neither is the rest of the Carnival."

"Why isn't it? Carnival is Carnival."

"I wish I could go along with that."

"Why can't you? Is this your first Carnival?"

"My first Mardi Gras, yes."

"Don't you like it?"

"I'm trying to, but . . ."

"But what?"

"Well, it scares me a little," he said.

She gave him a probing look. "I don't understand that."

"I don't either. It's just that there's a kind of craziness to it all, like something out of control . . . Look, don't mind me. I'm still trying to get over the breakup of my marriage. And a fire that destroyed part of my shop and most of my equipment a couple of months ago. I just need some time to get my act together, that's all."

"Is that why you don't want to be alone?"

"More or less, yes."

Juleen was silent for a time. Then she said, "I can't have dinner with you, but I can meet you around eight-thirty if you want."

Reprieve, he thought. "I do want. But only if you want, too—not if it's because you feel sorry for me."

"I don't feel sorry for you."

"Good. Where shall we meet?"

"Do you know the Cafe des Refugies?"

"No."

"It's on Decatur, between Dumaine and St. Philip. The krewe passes by there. Find a place in front and I'll meet you." Pause. "Do you like jazz?"

"Yes, very much. I'm something of a buff."

"What's a buff?"

He smiled. "A fan. Jazz is a hobby of mine."

"I know a little club we can go to afterward, where there aren't many tourists. The jazz they play there will fuck your mind."

The casual use of four-letter words by women still shocked him a little. He said only, "Sounds great."

"I'd better go now," Juleen said. She gathered up her carpetbag purse and stood. He found himself looking at the tight V of her groin, emphasized by the skinlike fit of the Levi's and visible below the poncho's bottom piping. A faint heat moved through his own groin. He hadn't been celibate since the breakup with Lara, but neither had he been promiscuous. Not by choice; by circumstance. "Eight-thirty, in front of the Cafe des Refugies."

"I'll be there," he said.

She gave him the same faint smile as before, turned, and went toward the doors to the hotel lobby.

He watched the motion of her hips until she had gone inside. He wondered what her breasts were like, and if he would get to find out, and then dismissed the thought. Sex was part of it, sure, but companionship was the main thing.

Even if she didn't want to go to bed with him, Juleen seemed bright and attractive and pleasant to be with, and that in itself would be enough. Meeting her like this, being with her tonight, was far better than having to go out and make an uncertain round of the Quarter's bars, jazz clubs, and topless parlors. Maybe these seven days in New Orleans would turn out okay, after all. Maybe his luck, at rock bottom throughout the physical and emotional disasters of the past six months, was finally starting to change for the better.

THREE

HE had one more drink in the courtyard, told himself he neither wanted nor needed the third of his allotted three, and went upstairs to his room. It was small and dark, like the rest of the Pirate's Head, with a double bed and a few pieces of cumbersome furniture, one of which was a color television set, and two oblong windows so narrow they were like a pair of cannon embrasures. No balcony or gallery outside. The room was on the third floor and the windows overlooked the courtyard; only the outer rooms on both upper floors, facing Burgundy Street, had gallery privileges, and only the inner rooms on the second floor, facing the courtyard, had latticework balconies.

The maid had been in to make the bed and straighten up the room. The drapes were drawn over the windows. He kicked off his shoes and lay down on the bed in the semi-darkness. Even though he'd only had two short vodkas, he could feel them; he wasn't high, but he was drowsy. He had not got much rest last night, either: the excitement of the trip and the time change and too many vodkas squeezed in at Brennan's on Royal Street. He closed his eyes and thought about Juleen. Then his brain began to wind down in slow stages, and after a while it shut off altogether and he slept.

And some while after that, the nightmare came.

He was running in a forest, dark and sere, and someone was chasing him, hard, thudding footsteps close behind, and he didn't know who it was or why he was being pursued. He felt terror, a wild sense of panic, and it made him run faster, branches tearing at his face and clothing, the sound of his breathing so loud and ragged that it seemed to create stuttering echoes in the blackness around him. And he kept running, running, and finally there was light ahead, and when he neared it he saw that it came from fire, a building on fire, and the fire terrified him even more. He ran away from it, around a tree, and there was a woman standing on the other side, dressed all in blue, and he saw that it was Lara. He shouted her name, "Lara!" and ran to her, but when he reached her, when he put his hand on her arm, he realized it wasn't Lara at all, it was a capering skeleton grinning death at him, and he screamed and veered away from it too, but the leering skull toppled off the skeleton's shoulders and came bouncing after him, its teeth nipping at his trouser legs like a demented dog's. The footsteps continued to pursue him, behind the bouncing skull, and he ran screaming until he couldn't run any more, until he stumbled, fell, rolled down a long grassy slope. And when he stopped rolling and came up on his back, he was lying in a room with bright firelight reflected off the walls, flickering, hurting his eyes, and there were faces peering down at him, strange, sad, tragic faces framed in white. One of the faces said, "It's no use, gentlemen, no use," and he said, "Don't you understand, they're after me," and the face said, "It's no use, no use, he's mad," and then all the faces began to laugh, and then they began to scream, and then they turned into grinning skulls with blood dripping out of their eye sockets, and then they crumbled away into shrieking dust—

And he was awake, sitting up on the bed, shaking.

Always the same nightmare—disjointed, senseless, full of raw terror and yet underlain with a ghoulish humor; exact in every detail. He even woke up at the same instant each time. He had had the first one six weeks after the separation, and it kept recurring at irregular intervals ever since. Sometimes it would be a week or ten days between them; sometimes he had the dream two or three nights in a row. It had been six days since the last one. How many days would it be until the next?

He hadn't needed a psychologist to explain the nightmare to him. The painful discoveries about Lara, the divorce and custody suits, the fire, the emotional upheaval, the feelings of dissociation and loss of control of his life— they were what the dream was all about. His subconscious warning him to watch out. Reminding him that no matter how in touch with reality he believed himself to be, the person hadn't been born yet who did not have a breaking point.

And maybe the intimations of madness he kept perceiving were a warning of the same kind. Reflections of his own mind. Reflections in a mirror of warping glass.

But it wouldn't stay warped, he thought. Given enough time, the wounds would heal, the pain would diminish, the nightmares would go away. That was his measuring stick: the nightmare. When there were weeks instead of days between recurrences, he would know he was on his way back to normal. And when it stopped coming altogether, he would know that he had found himself again.

He got off the bed, still shaky, and went into the bathroom. The mirror over the sink showed him an inflamed face, glossy with sweat; red-rimmed eyes and rust-brown curls jutting every which way like uncoiled springs. If I go out like this, he thought, people will think I'm a masker. It was a small joke, unfunny, but he made himself smile at it. Then he brushed his teeth to get rid of the stale vodka taste, splashed on some cologne, wet his hair, and used his electric blower to dry and shape it. The last remnants of the nightmare were gone by then. His mind was clear, and he felt a renewed anticipation for tonight—the parade, Juleen, the jazz club she'd touted to him.

Back in the bedroom, he had a look at his watch. Almost four. He couldn't stay cooped up in here until seven o'clock. For one thing, he was hungry; he hadn't eaten anything since breakfast. All right, then. A stroll around the Quarter—but not Bourbon Street, not tonight—and an early dinner and maybe an hour or two at Preservation Hall or Dukes' Place, and then on to Decatur Street and the krewe and Juleen.

He rummaged through the clothes he'd brought with him and settled on a pair of fawn-colored slacks, an open-necked shirt, and the stylish suede jacket Lara had bought him for Christmas a year ago. After he'd changed he looked at himself in the big mirror over the dresser and decided he cut a pretty dashing figure. He could stand to lose five pounds around the middle, but with the jacket buttoned and belted, you couldn't detect the slight thickening. As soon as he got home he'd have to put himself on a diet, nothing but lean beef, cottage cheese, and carrot sticks for a couple of weeks.

He sat in the room's single armchair and looked through his New Orleans guidebook. The Cafe des Refugies, he discovered, had once been a meeting place for smugglers, pirates, and European outlaws during the 1700s and early 1800s. Sounded interesting. Maybe he'd have a drink in there before the parade started—but only one; he didn't want to get tight tonight. As for dinner . . . the Quarter was thick with restaurants, some of the best in the world, they claimed, although they'd have to go quite a ways to beat the ones in San Francisco; he decided that a place called Felix's, on Iberville, sounded pretty good because they specialized in crawfish and oysters on the half shell. Its menu was also within his budget, while those of some of the more famous places, like Antoine's, were not.

Just as he closed the magazine, the telephone rang.

The sudden sound in the quiet made him jump. Now who could that be? He stood and went to where the phone sat on the nightstand next to the bed. Maybe the desk wants something, he thought, and picked up the receiver and said hello.

"Is that you, Giroux?" a soft-spoken male voice asked.

"Yes?"

"You know who this is, don't you?"

"No, I'm afraid I don't."

"Come on, Giroux."

"I'm sorry, I don't know your voice."

"Are you trying to play games with me?"

"No. Who are you?"

"I don't like stupid crap like that."

"Now wait a minute—"

"I want the photograph."

"What? What photograph?"

"I warned you, you bastard, no games!"

The hair on his neck prickled. He didn't speak.

"Are you there, Giroux?"

"I'm here. Listen, whoever you are, you must have the wrong—"

"The photograph, you understand? Put it into an envelope, write the name Chalmette on the front, and take it to the Creole Grocery on Esplanade Avenue. You got that? Creole Grocery, Esplanade Avenue."

"I tell you, I don't know what you're talking about."

"You'd better know," the voice said, and there was an

unmistakable threat in the words. "I want that photograph no later than noon tomorrow."

"Listen, Chalmette—Is that your name? I don't have any photograph for you. I don't know anything about any photograph—"

"Noon tomorrow, Giroux."

And the line clicked and went dead in his ear.

He put the handset down and stood staring at it. A joke, he thought. But how did he know my name? And what's the sense in a joke like that? Besides, it hadn't sounded like a joke; the threat in the voice had been genuine. It must have been some sort of identity mix-up, then. Giroux wasn't an uncommon name, at least not in a city with the French ancestry of New Orleans. But a photograph . . . how many other Girouxs could be registered in New Orleans hotels who also happened to be professional photographers?

He shook his head, trying to shake away the questions, and turned from the nightstand. Forget it, he told himself. Just one of those crazy unexplainable things that happens; just a crazy coincidence.

Crazy . . .

The hair on his scalp prickled again. And the uneasiness was with him when he left the room and went out again into the sights and sounds and smells of Carnival.

FOUR

HE walked the perimeters of the Quarter, staying clear of its hub streets of Bourbon and Royal. It was a fascinating place—or it would have been at another time in his life, in a better state of mind. A place for artists, historians, antiquarians. And photographers. He hadn't taken his Pentax with him this time, either, and he was sorry that he hadn't. The aura of preserved nineteenth century, the juxtaposition of wealth and poverty, elegance and decadence, old and new, was so startling that he felt challenged to capture the essence of it on film.

Buildings that seemed mostly a hundred years old or more and mostly Spanish in design, with a sprinkling of Gallic architecture that predated the French and Indian War. Mansions with lacework trim and lush courtyards lined up shoulder to shoulder with near hovels; fine homes and apartments hidden behind blank walls and decaying facades; little cottages tucked away between taller buildings; historic landmarks like Lafitte's Blacksmith Shop and the Old Absinthe House; big fancy hotels, small fancy hotels, small quaint hotels, small not-so-quaint hotels; bookshops, art galleries, antique stores, junk shops, specialty shops, cafes, bars, jazz clubs, little theaters, old-fashioned corner groceries and ice cream parlors. Narrow streets jammed with cars and trucks and horse-drawn carriages, lined with gas-style streetlamps and ancient iron hitching posts, some topped with black-painted horse's heads. *Banquettes* of cement, or original bricks, or paving stones, or cobblestones, buckled and cracked and broken in places, with weeds and grass growing out of the breaks. Live oaks, magnolias, tall palms spreading shade behind fancy iron gates and spike fences, in half-hidden courtyards. Apartment balconies crowded with potted ferns and tropical-looking flowers. And the people: shabbily dressed black residents sitting on green-painted stoops, a few playing musical instruments, a few singing, a few drinking wine or hard liquor out of pint bottles; tourists in suits and ties and expensive dresses; kids with long hair and mod clothes, the boys wearing beards, the girls not wearing undergarments; maskers, many of them teenagers, dressed as pirates and Indians and fearsome dragons, some setting off strings of firecrackers that popped like champagne corks and were muted by the constant pulsing beat of the Carnival music.

It all reminded him of Venice, where he and Lara had gone five years ago, on a package tour of Europe. The faces were different, the architecture was different, and it was narrow streets instead of narrow canals, but the atmosphere was the same: a place crumbling in on itself, slowly going to seed, and yet maintaining charm, dignity and a kind of ravaged beauty, like a very old woman who had once been the belle of society and who had never lost her feel for hedonism.

By the time he reached Iberville, and went looking for Felix's, he had both forgotten the telephone call and made up his mind to utilize his skill with a camera. Tomorrow, maybe, if things didn't work out with Juleen, or even if they did, he'd make his way around the Quarter again and shoot a couple of rolls of film. Medium-speed film, ASA 125, to render the subtle details of wood and stone and design more sharply. Use a polarizing filter and a perspective-control telephoto lens. He could make another outing on Monday, too. Photography was something he could absorb himself in—and it was a hell of a lot better than moping around the way he had been, letting things get him down and pursuing a kind of festiveness he just was not equipped to handle right now. He didn't have to restrict himself to the Vieux Carré, either; there were plenty of other interesting places in and around New Orleans. The bayou country, for instance. And the fine old homes in the Garden District that had been touted in the guidebook and that you got to by way of the St. Charles Avenue streetcar. He could even make arrangements for a trip to Lake Pontchartrain.

He found Felix's easily enough, but it turned out he couldn't get in. They were full to overflowing and had a three-hour waiting list already, even though it was only five o'clock. Even if he had used his head and called for a reservation, he probably wouldn't have been able to eat before seven. The other popular restaurants in the Quarter would be just as inaccessible, he thought as he came back out to the street. He could try to hunt up a table at one of the smaller cafes or restaurants on the fringes, but he was too hungry to want to do much more walking around. And the not-very-elegant restaurant that was part of the Pirate's Head, the Gold Doubloon where he'd eaten last night, was sure to be as booked by now as everywhere else. His best bet was to go someplace outside the Quarter, over on the other side of Canal Street.

The sidewalks were teeming now. Three men dressed as hillbillies were standing on the corner of Royal Street, alternately singing verses of an obscene song and taking swigs from imitation corn whiskey jugs. On the opposite corner, a fat man in a flowered shirt and the driver of a cab screamed insults at each other. A Chinese whore in a slit skirt was trying to do business with a grinning bald-headed tourist, saying patiently as Giroux passed, "No, honey, it's not slanted; but when you're all through you'll feel like it was." Across Iberville, two black musicians in red-and-white striped coats played "When the Saints Go Marchin' In" on a trombone and an alto sax, while a man in a dragon mask did an impromptu dance and a chubby girl of fifteen or sixteen vomited into a trash receptacle nearby.

Giroux hurried down Royal to Canal, the widest city street in the world, they said, and now almost as crowded with traffic and people as the narrows byways of the Quarter. He had to go three blocks along St. Charles before the crowds thinned out, and another block after that before he found a restaurant that could seat him.

The menu said they had fresh oysters on the half shell, one of his favorite delicacies; he ordered a dozen. He also ordered a bowl of jambalaya and a bottle of ale. The oysters were small but full of juice, the hot sauce had plenty of tabasco, and the ale was ice cold. He had always wondered what jambalaya was, other than a Spanish-Creole dish, and when it came he found out: a kind of stew made of shrimp, crab, oysters, spicy sausage, rice and cowpeas in a thick red sauce. He lingered over it, savoring the taste. He also lingered over a cup of coffee and two refills, smoking a cigarette with each cup.

He was reluctant to go back out into that Carnival mob. Might as well admit it; it had been a day for self-admissions. If it weren't for Juleen, he knew he would go straight back to the Pirate's Head and spend the evening watching television. He wasn't in any mood for a parade, especially one made up of children, or even for the finest gutbucket jazz in the city. But he was in a mood for love-making; that was the best of all ways to make it through the night. Maybe he *would* get lucky with Juleen. He kept telling himself he would to buoy up his spirits.

When his watch said it was 6:15 he paid the check and made his way out. The sooner he got to the Cafe des Refugies, the better it would be. If the Krewe of Nor offered the same attraction as the one last night, Hermes, the crowd would be so thickly packed behind the restraining ropes that you wouldn't be able to move through it. And Juleen had told him that tonight's parade started at seven o'clock.

He stood in front of the restaurant for a moment, tasting the night air, looking at the dazzling array of lights over on Canal and down by the river. A wind had come up and it was cooler than it had been earlier, almost cold; he pulled the collar of the suede jacket up around his ears. Then, girding himself, he started back toward the Quarter.

He was a block from Canal when he saw the man in the dragon mask, standing across St. Charles under a streetlamp.

A sudden feeling of wrongness brought him to a standstill. This was the third time in the past three hours he had seen a man in a dragon mask—on Ursuline Street while he was wandering, on Iberville after coming out of Felix's, and now here on St. Charles. The same man? It looked like the same mask—big basilisk eyes, greenish "skin," snarling fire-painted mouth—and like the same man under it: lean, wiry, dressed in a black turtleneck sweater and dark-colored trousers. Three times in three hours in three different locations was stretching coincidence a little. Was the man following him? That was how it looked. Following him . . .

The masker turned out of the puddle of lamplight, not looking across at him, and moved away toward Canal. In fifteen seconds he was gone around the corner.

Giroux released a breath, ran a hand over his face. And the word *paranoia* came to him and made him wince. Nobody was following him, for God's sake. The phone call earlier had been some kind of joke or mistake, and a man in a dragon mask popping up wherever he happened to be was just a coincidence. There were plenty of dragon maskers around; it wasn't even the same person. Dragon masks were as common at Mardi Gras as pirate's eyepatches and Indian warpaint and clown makeup.

He walked to Canal, refocusing his thoughts on Juleen, and went into the Quarter on Chartres. At Jackson Square, it was bedlam; crush of people, waves of noise—band music, singing, laughter. There were more maskers out tonight: Gypsies, Egyptian princesses, a black man dressed as a cannibal with a bone hooked under his nose, even a woman made up to look like a peacock, her head framed with an iridescent blue and green fan constructed of stem wire and glitter-sprinkled Christmas-tree ornaments. Two dragons, too, one female and one chubby male. When he passed the second one as he turned down Dumaine Street, he laughed at himself, hollowly.

The length of Decatur, from Canal all the way past the French Market and the old U.S. Mint, had been roped off. It was bedlam there, too; on both sides of the street, already straining against the cables, thousands of adults and children shouted and sang Carnival songs and drank beer or Hurricanes from go-cups. Most of the crowd seemed concentrated in the Jackson Square area, but the Cafe des Refugies was only a block and a half from there, and the sidewalk area in front was already heavily congested. It took him a couple of minutes to push his way to the cafe's entrance.

Getting inside was a physical impossibility. Frolickers were packed in so densely that the doors were jammed open and there was an overspill onto the *banquette*. He wedged himself a dozen yards farther along and then back

against the building of which the cafe was a part, the Hotel
de la Marine, under the hotel's second-floor gallery. And
managed to claim a leaning space between an apoplectic fat
man and a conservatively dressed woman with dark red
hair. The crush of bodies in front of him was like a wall; he
could barely see over and through it to the street. How was
Juleen going to find him in this writhing mass? If it got any
worse, she wouldn't be able to get through from either
direction, not even if she used force.

Crowds had never bothered him before, but he had
never been caught in one like this; never been subjected
close up to so much blaring music and babbling voices and
hysterical laughter. For the first time he experienced a feeling of claustrophobia. Sweat broke out on his face, ran hot
and clammy down inside the collar of his shirt. He unbelted
and unbuttoned the suede jacket, used his handkerchief to
mop at his forehead and cheeks.

"Are you all right?"

The words came close to his right ear, cutting through
the cacophony, and they startled him. He jerked his head
around, found himself looking into the upturned face of the
woman with the dark red hair.

"Are you all right?" she asked again. "You look ill."

"No. No, it's just . . . all these people."

"I know. You're not a claustrophobe, are you?"

"Not before tonight, I wasn't."

She gave him what he took to be a reassuring smile.
She looked to be in her early thirties, attractive in a non-
flashy sort of way, the red hair cut short and waved. The
skin of her face was almost translucent, so that even in the
pale light coming through the hotel windows he could see
the fine tracery of veins in her cheeks and temples and
along the column of her neck.

She said, "This must be your first Mardi Gras, too."

"Yes. And my last."

"I feel the same way. Once is enough."

Once is too much, he thought, but he didn't say it.

"They have a ball afterward, you know," she said.

"Who does?"

"The children. After the parade is over."

"Oh. Yes, that's what I understand."

"It must be fun to watch. Only outsiders aren't invited, of course."

"Not to any of the masquerade balls."

"Too bad, isn't it?" She smiled again. "Are you feeling better? You don't look quite as . . . stricken now."

"A little better, yes. Thanks."

"I think the parade's starting. I hear band music."

So did he, from over in the direction of the old mint. People were beginning to crane their heads that way; he did it, too, couldn't see anything, and glanced at the red-haired woman again.

For no reason he said, *"Laissez les bons temps rouler."*

"Pardon?"

"It means 'Let the good times roll.' It's a saying they have here at Carnival time."

"Oh, yes, I read that."

"My French is pretty bad, I guess."

She laughed. "It couldn't be any worse than mine."

The martial music grew louder, and he could see flickering torchlight over the heads of the people to his left. That was supposed to be one of the attractions of the Carnival night parades: flambeaux carriers. The din in his vicinity began to lose some of its raucousness as the krewe neared; from down by the mint he could hear applause and cheers. He wiped his damp face another time, put the handkerchief away in his pocket. Talking to the red-haired woman had made him feel better, had taken the edge off his nervousness. He thought he'd be all right until Juleen came. He glanced at the woman again, but she had moved forward a couple of paces and was up on her toes, peering toward the street.

The procession began to roll by: young torchbearers, marching bands, marching children, impressive Disneyish floats with masked children riding them and tossing out commemorative wooden doubloons and glass beads as the crowd set up the traditional chant of "Throw me something, mister!" Another band, maskers astride satin-draped Shetland ponies. Confetti showered down from the hotel gallery above, and from other galleries along this side of the street, speckling part of the crowd and part of the pavement. The blare of trumpets and the beat of drums had become the dominant sounds. Particularly the drums; the rhythm of them was like a racing heartbeat. And still another band came, and a float ridden by a dozen little girls who made him think of Marcie and gave him a sharp twinge of nostalgia and pain, and more torchbearers, and another float that bore the Child King of Nor—an acronym for "New Orleans Romance"—who wore regal clothing and a crown and carried a scepter, and still more torchbearers, and still more ponies—

And Juleen.

He didn't see where she came from; his attention was on the parade. She was just there beside him, as if she had materialized out of nowhere, her hand on his arm, her mouth up close to his ear saying, "Did you think I wasn't coming?" He recognized her voice, but when he swung his head around he almost didn't recognize her. She was wearing a long flowing red robe with cabalistic signs imprinted on it, and carrying a stick with the carved head of a snake for a knob. On her head was a *tignon*—an old-fashioned, three-pointed white scarf of the type slave women had once worn. Her cheeks were heavily rouged and painted in white symbols that matched those on the robe.

He stared at her; he couldn't help himself. "My God," he said. "What are you supposed to be?"

"I don't understand."

"What are you made up as?"

"I'm a *mamaloi*," she said.

"You mean a voodoo priestess? Marie Laveau?"

"Yes. But not Marie Laveau. The krewe is almost over; then we can go."

She held onto his arm, standing close to him. He could feel the curve of her breast, the jut of her hip, and he could smell the exotic, musky fragrance of her perfume. Or maybe it was sachet; it didn't quite have the scent of perfume. Her nearness was stimulating, and yet that costume she wore bothered him faintly. He didn't know why, unless it was because the thought of voodoo earlier in the day, when he'd chanced by the Voodoo Museum on Bourbon Street, had also bothered him.

He felt eyes on him and realized that the red-haired woman was staring at him, at Juleen. When he glanced in her direction, she averted her gaze, put it back on the parade, but not before he saw disapproval registered in her expression. Of Juleen's costume? Of how young she was compared to him? Well, the hell with what she thought or what she disapproved of. It was none of her damn business what he did or who he was with.

More flambeaux streaked the night—a last group of young bearers, marking the end of the parade. The crowd cheered and applauded as they passed, as it had periodically throughout; then, when the last line of torchbearers reached Jackson Square, the mass of watchers began to break up. As soon as they could move freely, Juleen tugged him toward St. Philip Street, steered a course around the corner. A feeling of relief came to him; even after Juleen's arrival, the illusion of entrapment and suffocation had lingered. His shirt was still plastered to his back with sweat.

"Where are we going?" he asked her as they turned east on Chartres.

"The jazz club I told you about."

"Sure, but where is it?"

"You'll see. You'll like it, don't worry."

"I'm not worried."

She still had hold of his arm, still walked close enough to him so that he could feel the rippling movements of her body. Fantasies formed and unfolded in his mind's eye, vague and exciting; heat stirred in his loins. It occurred to him that he was reacting immaturely for a man of his age, but that didn't chase the fantasies away, or reduce the sexual heat.

They went straight down Chartres and finally turned left near the Le Richelieu Hotel and the 200-year-old barracks that had once housed the first French garrison in New Orleans. There were fewer people abroad here. When they neared Royal Street, Juleen lifted her snake's-head stick and pointed toward a looming three-story structure on the opposite corner. "That's the Lalaurie house over there," she said.

"Lalaurie. Wasn't Delphine Lalaurie the society woman who tortured her slaves back in the early 1800s? The one who was run out of town by a mob that wrecked the house?"

"Yes. Her ghost still haunts the place. So do the tormented souls of her slaves."

"Come on. You don't believe that, do you?"

"I believe the dead have powers, yes."

"Juleen, you know that's—"

He stopped talking, and stopped walking, and his mouth clamped shut. They were at Royal now, and what he saw in front of the Lalaurie house, in the shadows near the courtyard gate, iced the dampness on his back and sent an unreasonable *frisson* through him.

A man was standing there—motionless, staring across at where they were.

A man wearing a black turtleneck sweater and dark trousers and a fearsome dragon mask.

FIVE

THE jazz club was on Dauphine Street, just off Esplanade
Avenue. He could hear the hot pulsing Dixieland beat
when they were still a half-block distant, but it registered
only faintly on his mind. His thoughts were still back at the
corner opposite the Lalaurie house, still on the man in the
dragon mask.

He was sweating again; the cold night wind turned the
wetness clammy against his skin. Inside he was shaking. He
felt menaced and he didn't know why. The man in the mask
hadn't done anything, hadn't tried to approach him or
speak to him. It was just that he was *there*—four times now,
all over the Vieux Carré. Why? Something to do with that
telephone call, the photograph somebody wanted? It
couldn't be coincidence, not four times like that. The
masker *had* to be following him, and he couldn't come to
terms with that. It wasn't so much the man in the dragon
mask he was frightened of; it was all the craziness that kept
pressing in on him; it was himself.

The name of the club was Père Lafon's, and it was dark
and smoky inside, clogged with tables and patrons. Even

45

though it was still within the boundaries of the Quarter, it was far enough away from the center not to attract swarms of tourists; most of the people were conventionally dressed, with a sprinkling of costumes here and there, and had the relaxed look of natives. Up on a dais at the far end, bathed in floor and ceiling spotlights, was a seven-piece combo: five blacks, two whites; alto sax, trombone, trumpet, clarinet, piano, bass, and drums. They were doing "Ory's Creole Trombone" when he and Juleen came in, the man on the 'bone giving it the same kind of sweet velvety sound Giroux had heard on a recording made by Kid Ory back in the twenties. Good, all right—the real stuff. But it glanced off him, shards of sound that didn't penetrate; he couldn't feel the music inside, where you had to feel jazz to appreciate what it was all about.

His nerves kept jangling, jangling.

Juleen left him just inside the door, saying she would get them a table. The combo segued into Duke Ellington's "Birmingham Breakdown," ran it through clean and hot, and then turned the spotlight over to the rail-thin black man on the piano for "Honky Tonk Train Blues," the composition that had made Meade Lux Lewis famous in jazz circles and triggered the national boogie-woogie fad in the mid-thirties. Juleen came back and took his arm again, led him through the closely set tables to one wedged back in a corner, where there was just enough room for the two of them to sit down.

He'd promised himself he would go easy on the booze tonight, but he needed a good stiff jolt to stop that internal shaking. And a waitress in a fringed vest was already there, smiling and asking them what they'd have. He looked at Juleen, and she said, "A glass of red wine," and he said, "Vodka and ice with a twist, make it a double," and the waitress went away behind him.

Juleen leaned forward. There was just enough light

from a candle-fitted table lamp to give her face, with its painted markings, a grotesque, distorted look. She said, "What's the matter? You haven't said anything since we passed the Lalaurie house."

"Did you see the man in the dragon mask?"

"No. Where was he?"

"In front of the Lalaurie gate."

"I wasn't paying any attention. What about him?"

"I keep seeing him tonight. I think he's following me."

"Why would he follow you?"

"I don't know."

"Are you in some kind of trouble?"

"No, of course not."

"Then nobody would want to follow you. Why don't you forget about the man in the mask? Maybe it's not even the same man. Lots of people wear dragon masks for Carnival."

"It's the same man," he said. "And I can't forget him. Not just yet, anyway."

"Maybe a drink will make you feel better."

"I hope so. I don't want to spoil your evening, Juleen."

"You won't spoil it. Here, I'll give you something to chase away dragons and demons."

From a pocket in her red robe she produced a pouch-type chamois purse, opened it, and took something from inside. It looked like a cross made of short pieces of straw and bound with red yarn. But when she put it on the table between them, next to the light from the candle lamp, he saw that it was a human figure four or five inches long, with a round cloth head that had beads for eyes and a mouth drawn in black crayon.

"What the hell is that?"

"It's a *gris-gris.*"

"A what?"

"A *gris-gris.* A voodoo charm."

"Christ, put it away."

"Why? It'll bring you luck."

"I don't want that kind of luck. Put it away."

Juleen returned the figure to the chamois purse. "Are you afraid of voodoo?" she asked him.

"No. I just don't like it."

"Why not?"

"Because it's pagan."

"Is it? Haitian Catholics practice voodoo, you know."

"I still say it's pagan—"

The waitress had come back with their drinks. He picked up his glass as soon as she set it down, said, "Cheers," touched it against Juleen's wine glass, and drank a third of the vodka in a swallow. The fire of it put spots of heat on his cheekbones, spread a soothing balm across his raw nerve ends. Oil on troubled waters, he thought, and drank again, sipping this time. Ah, God, how he'd needed this.

Juleen was watching him. "Better?"

"Yes," he said. "Better."

The combo finished a number he didn't recognize and then swung into Louis Armstrong's "Knockin' A Jug." He swiveled his head to watch them, saw a heavyset black woman make her way up to the dais between the front tables. Blues singer, he thought. Good. He was in the mood. Blues on blues.

When he looked back at Juleen, she was fondling the snake's-head stick. It had been propped against the wall behind her chair, but she had pulled it around and across her body and was stroking the snake knob, her eyes shut, her head bobbing in time to the soaring voice of the trumpet.

"What are you doing?"

She opened her eyes. "Doing?"

"Playing with that stick."

"It's not a stick. It's a Legba staff."

"What's a Legba staff?"

"Papa Legba is master of the barrier," she said. "Between our world and the spirit world. This is the kind of staff he carries."

"Sure it is. With a snake's head on it."

"Not a snake—Damballah, the holy serpent."

He finished what was left in his glass. "Isn't that carrying it a little too far?" he said.

"Carrying what too far?"

"The voodoo. All that crap about Papa Legba and holy serpents."

The muscles in her face seemed to contract, like a pliable substance suddenly hardening. "It's not crap. Why do you call it crap?"

"Don't tell me you really *believe* in voodoo?"

"And what if I do?"

"In this day and age? You're an intelligent woman, Juleen; how can you believe in haunts and hoodoos and holy serpents?"

"I can believe in anything I want to believe in."

"You think this Papa Legba is a real being?"

"Yes."

"Papa Là-bas, too? That's the old voodoo word for Satan, isn't it?"

"Papa Là-bas exists," she said. "He's everywhere."

"Like God, I suppose."

"Yes. Only more powerful in his own way."

Over on the dais, the heavyset black woman was singing the nonsense syllables of the first scat vocal, another Armstrong classic, "Heebie Jeebies." And that was what this damned conversation with Juleen was giving him—the heebie-jeebies all over again. He looked around for the waitress, located her and caught her eye, and gestured her over.

He said to Juleen, "I don't want to talk about voodoo anymore, all right? If you believe in it, fine, that's your business. Let's listen to the music, let's have a few drinks, let's talk about something mundane."

"What's mundane?"

"Commonplace. The kinds of things people talk about on a date, when they're trying to get to know each other. And please don't keep fondling that stick or staff or whatever it is. Okay?"

"Okay. I didn't mean to upset you."

"Never mind. Let's just forget it."

The waitress appeared, took his order for a refill— Juleen's glass was still full—and moved off again. He lit a cigarette. The combo and the black singer were doing "Graveyard Blues" now, sweet-sad and mournful. Terrific. Just what he needed to hear.

Juleen said, "Do you want to talk about what's troubling you?"

"The man in the dragon mask?"

"Yes. And what happened with your ex-old lady."

"My ex-old lady," he said. "My wife, you mean."

"If you don't want to talk about her . . ."

"I don't know, maybe I do. Maybe I need to spit her out again. You really want to hear the story of my life?"

"I don't mind, if you want to tell me."

"All right, you asked for it." He stared at the end of his cigarette for a moment. Then he said, "We were both going to San Francisco State back in the mid-sixties, before all the political activism got out of hand, and we met on campus and dated a few times and went to bed a few times and decided to get married. I thought I was in love with her and she thought she was in love with me and it took us three years or so to figure out we'd both been wrong. But it was a comfortable relationship, or at least I thought so; we got along all right, no fights, no bitterness, and we were good together in bed, and we liked to do the same things, go to the same places. We talked about having a kid, decided to wait until I'd built up my photography business and she'd gotten her real estate license—that was what she'd decided to do with her business administration training. So it was status quo for five years. She got her broker's license and went to work for a big chain outfit, and I opened a shop and got myself established."

He paused. Juleen seemed to be listening attentively, her hands folded together on the table. Looking at her, in that robe with the cabalistic signs all over it and all over her face, he felt a fleeting sense of surrealism. What am I doing? he thought. Sitting here in a jazz club in New Orleans, pouring out my tale of woe to a strange girl who believes in voodoo and magic charms. This isn't my world. My world is square, not all odd and quirky like this— staunch, stolid, conservative. I don't understand her world; how can she understand mine?

"Go on," Juleen said. "Then what happened?"

He shook himself. What the hell, he'd started it and he might as well go on and finish it. "She forgot to take the pill a couple of times, that's what happened—too much job pressure, she said—and bam, she wound up pregnant. We had a little girl, Marcie, she's almost eleven now. Good kid, bright, cute, looks like Lara. That's my ex-old lady's name: Lara. After Marcie was born it was more status quo. We didn't go out much until she was out of diapers; didn't go out much anyway. Dinner once in a while, a show, a weekend in Tahoe or Reno, a yearly trip somewhere, down to Mexico, over to Europe once, places like that. Not a very exciting life, but it—"

The waitress again, bringing his refill. She'd made it a double, too, like the first one; he should have told her a single. But he didn't refuse it. He sat looking into the glass and warning himself that this had better be his last drink of the night. He could still feel the effects of the first double, and this second double would not only stop the rest of the jangling, it would give him an edge. Any more than this and he'd be good and tight. And he'd wake up with a hangover in the morning.

He drank a little, just a sip. The blues singer, he realized, was doing an old Ma Rainey number, the title of which he couldn't remember. He should know it, but he just couldn't remember. Maybe it was the vodka; it acted on him that way sometimes, fuddling his memory.

> *"If you don't b'lieve I'm sinkin', look what a hole I'm in.*
> *Say, if you don't b'lieve I'm sinkin', look what a hole I'm in—"*

He put his eyes on Juleen again, had another sip from his glass. The internal shaking was almost gone now. Almost gone. "Where was I?" he said.

"You were saying your life wasn't very exciting."

"No, it wasn't. But it was a pretty good life just the same. Comfortable, happy. I thought so, anyway. Lara, it turned out, was restless and bored most of the time. She wanted excitement and plenty of it. That's what led her to the other men. There must have been a lot of them; she said there were later on, after I confronted her. A dozen, maybe. Hell, maybe two dozen. I don't know when it started. Sometime after Marcie was born, I guess. She wouldn't tell me that part of it."

He drank, a bigger swallow this time. Juleen said, "How did you find out? She didn't come out and tell you, did she?"

"Not exactly. But she was ready for me to find out, ready to get shut of the marriage, and she just didn't give a damn about hiding it anymore. Or about me anymore, either. So she let me find out. Made it obvious that she was having an affair—stayed out late at night, lied about where she'd been, obvious lies; things like that. Then I had to go down to Los Angeles to photograph a wedding, old college friend who'd moved there and asked me to do the honors. When I came back I found a man's shirt wadded up in the closet, wasn't mine, that's when I confronted her. She admitted it right away. No more lies. I'd seen it coming for weeks; I just wouldn't believe the truth. Well, I believed it then, all right."

He drank—and the glass was empty. He stared at it in disbelief. The waitress had just put it down; he couldn't have drunk it off that fast, could he? Christ. He had an edge on already. But that wasn't so bad. Talking about Lara and her deceit would have been too depressing without a little edge on.

"Say, if you don't b'lieve I'm sinkin', look what a hole I'm in.
If you don't b'lieve I love you, look what a fool I've been."

"So she moved out," he said to Juleen, "and we both filed for divorce. Didn't make any difference; community-property state, California." He was starting to slur his words. Better watch that. Enunciate. E-nun-ciate. "She wanted custody of Marcie, I wanted custody, too, and I was ready to fight her in court, pull out all the dirty laundry, prove she was an unfit mother on moral grounds. My lawyer said I'd better not do it. Said it wouldn't do me any good because I had no proof, men she'd screwed weren't going to come forward and admit it, she wasn't going to admit it, it would only hurt the child. Child was hurt enough as it was. So I backed off, let Lara have her. What else could I do? Court always awards custody to the mother, bitch or not. I get her on weekends, she says every time she'd rather live with me, it tears my heart out. Says mom's got lots of boyfriends, one in particular keeps trying to get her to call him dad. Tears my heart out."

Juleen didn't say anything. He thought her expression was sympathetic, but he couldn't be sure; it was too smoky in the room and there seemed to be a haze between them. Or maybe it was the vodka. Woman on the dais was still singing the blues. What song now? Something by Bessie Smith. "Empty Bed Blues," that was it. Yeah. Oh yeah. Empty bed blues.

Waitress again. He frowned up at her, squinting a little because of the smoke. "Refills?" she said.

No, he thought. "Sure," he said, "why not? How about you, Juleen?"

"I'm fine, thanks."

Damn fool, he thought. Shouldn't have ordered another drink, you're half-swacked already. What's the matter with you? Pretty girl sitting across from you, even if she is a little flaky, chance to score, chance to chase away those empty bed blues, and you sit here and swill vodka. First you're scared, then you're maudlin. What's the *matter* with you, you stupid jerk?

Cracking up, cracking up, got those old cracking up blues—

Juleen said, "You said something this afternoon about a fire. How did that happen?"

So he told her about the fire. He still didn't know how it had happened. Maybe spontaneous combustion or faulty wiring; and he'd had a lot of chemicals around, a lot of flammable film and copy paper. Or maybe vandals. One window had been broken—but the heat might have done that. It hadn't been a thief, though, he was sure of that much, because the metal cash box in his desk hadn't been touched. Fire started in the darkroom, they'd said, and spread out into the studio. God, how he'd felt when he saw what was left of it. Telephone call had come at ten-thirty that night, got him out of bed; neighbor on West Portal— that was where he'd had his studio, West Portal, an upper-class residential area out near the ocean—this neighbor had seen the smoke and called the fire department and they'd got there in time to save most of the building, if not most of the studio. Smoking ruin, that was what he'd walked into. Everything charred, water damaged—lighting equipment, tripods, filters, reflectors, spare lenses, three good cameras including an expensive Bronica single-lens reflex, samples of his work, part of his files . . . all gone, all ruined. It had been like getting kicked in the stomach after Lara had kicked him in the head. His whole world collapsed around him, and he'd been standing there in the rubble: that was how he'd felt that night.

The fresh drink was in front of him; he hadn't even noticed the waitress come and put it down. He drank. Stuff tasted like water now. Bad sign. Easy. Easy.

Juleen asked, "Didn't you have insurance?"

"Sure, but it didn't cover the full cost of things. I had to use what was left of the savings after Lara took her half, replace equipment, relocate. I'm back on my feet now, making a living, or I couldn't afford to be here. But it hasn't been easy."

Easy. Easy easy easy . . . like a blues refrain running around inside his head. Then he was aware that the music had stopped. Combo and the blues singer taking a break. Good jazz, though—damn good. "Damn good jazz," he said to Juleen. "You were right about that."

She nodded. "Have you got another lady yet, back home?"

"Lady? You mean a girlfriend? No, no girlfriend. A few dates here and there, nothing special. I don't want anything special. No more long-term relationships, no more Laras. Casual from now on. Short-term."

"Did you come to New Orleans to look for a woman?"

"No," he said. "Needed a vacation, that's all. Always wanted to come here, listen to jazz where it was born, see what the Mardi Gras was all about. Now I know. *Now* I know."

Then he told her about the uneasiness, the intimations of madness and violence; and about the telephone call this afternoon; and about the man in the dragon mask. Juleen said that he must be imagining things, there wasn't anything crazy about Carnival. It was just wild fun, that was all. And he must be imagining things about the man in the dragon mask, too. What about the telephone call? he said. He hadn't imagined that. It sounded like a joke, she said. People were always playing jokes and tricks during Mardi Gras.

The combo was back, jamming with "Southern Stomp." And his glass was empty. He picked it up and stared at it. "Empty," he said.

"You can order another."

"Better not. Damn stuff hits me hard."

"You're not drunk, are you? You don't sound drunk."

"I'm not drunk," he said. But he was. Three big doubles, six straight shots of vodka in less than an hour. Drunk, all right, and getting drunker just sitting here. And he didn't care. He was better off drunk than sober tonight. No jangling, no fear, no men in dragon masks, no threatening telephone callers after photographs. Just Juleen. Just good hot jazz—feeling it now, down deep, pulsing in his blood. Just good hot vodka, better than any voodoo *gris-gris* at chasing away demons.

He tried to get her to talk about herself, but all she'd say was that she was a potter and she'd been born in Metairie, a suburb west of the city, and lived in New Orleans most of her life. Lived in the Irish Channel for four years, ever since graduating high school. No men in her life right now. "It's too much hassle, having an old man." That was how she put it.

Jelly Roll Morton's "Cannon Ball Blues"—good piano solo, horns ad-libbing, more improvisation in the final cho-

rus and the extended four-bar coda. Good old Jelly Roll.
Purists claimed his piano was wobbly, that his compositions
were arhythmic, that he and his men had had too much or
too little to say. Crude jazz, they called it. For Christ's sake.
He was a *genius,* for Christ's sake.

Waitress looming over them again. Juleen's voice saying, "Yes, I'd like another glass of wine."

"How about you, sir?"

"No," he said. "No more for me."

Blues singer went back up on the dais. Started something sad and trembly that he didn't know.

"We can go as soon as I finish my second wine," Juleen
said.

"Go? Go where?"

"Home."

"You want to go home?"

"I didn't mean it like that," she said. She reached out
and ran her fingertips along the back of his hand. "I meant
with you, not alone."

He blinked at her. "You serious?"

"Yes. If you want to."

"Sure I want to," he said. For Christ's sake, he
thought. Well, for Christ's sake.

Waitress, with Juleen's wine. Blues singer doing another composition, doing the Wardell Gray solo called
"Twisted." He looked at Juleen, felt himself grinning fatu-
ously. Wants me to go home with her. What do you know
about that? Going to score after all. For Christ's sake.

Music rolling over him, wrapping him inside it like a
cocoon, haunting inside his head. Twisted, twisted.

"Changed my mind," he said to the waitress. "Think
I'll have one more after all. Nightcap—just a single this
time. All right, Juleen?"

"If you want to."

Twisted . . .

SIX

HE stumbled coming out through the door, almost fell. Would have fallen if Juleen hadn't had hold of his arm. Damn. Shouldn't have had that last drink. Drunk as a lord now. What if he couldn't get it up? Poor Juleen. Poor him. No, *stupid* him. Drunk as a goddamn lord.

The cold air slapped at his face. He felt dizzy for a moment, but then the dizziness was gone and he was steady on his feet. Yes, sir, officer, of *course* I can walk a straight line. Drunk as a lord but I can walk the line like a judge. He squinted. Lights swirled, papers swirled, clouds swirled in the dark sky. French Quarter, he thought. Oh my way home with Juleen. Heigh-ho! Gonna lay a pretty miss named Juleen, voodoo makeup and all. Who do? You do, Giroux. Heigh-ho, it's off to get laid we go.

"We'd better take a taxi," Juleen said. "It's a long walk to the streetcar."

"Fine," he said. "Fine."

Walking. People on the streets. Cold; damn wind was cold. Not too many people, though, not around here. Dragon mask? Not afraid of him; if he's here, I'll have a talk with him. I'll say Why are you following me around, you son of a bitch? What you want with me? He squinted again, looking at faces. No dragon mask. Gone. Like he was never there.

Building all lighted in front. Hotel. Taxi parked nearby, and into the taxi we go. Heigh-ho! Juleen saying something to the driver. Juleen sitting beside him. He groped for her hand—soft, nice and soft. Breast against his arm and that was soft, too. Gonna get laid. Here we go.

Moving, away through the swirl of light and the swirl of dark. Stuffy in here. He rolled down the window, leaning across Juleen. Better. Cold wind kept his head clear, kept him from getting car sick. Wouldn't do to get sick, not tonight. Big turnoff, getting sick. She wouldn't want to go to bed with him if he got sick.

Say, if you don't b'lieve I'm sinkin', look what a hole I'm in.
Say, if you don't—

A chill slithered through him; the song fragments slithered away. Damned snake's-head stick of hers was staring at him. Legba staff, Damballah—bullshit. But it was staring at him. Snake's head, big carved eyes. Big carved tongue liable to come flicking out any time. Big carved fangs getting ready to bite his arm . . .

He reached out, swatted the thing from Juleen's grasp. Heard it clatter against the door. Damn thing. Damn ugly evil thing.

"What's the matter?" Juleen asked. "Why did you do that?"

"Don't like snakes," he said. "Evil things."

"Yes. But they're beautiful."

"Evil," he said. "It was getting ready to bite my arm."

Twisted, all twisted in the hole I'm in . . .

Cab turning this way, turning that way. Dark streets now, old houses, old streetlamps on the corners.

"Where are we?"

"Almost home. Just two more blocks."

Stopping. Out of the cab, into the cold. Juleen: "Have you got ten dollars?" Squinting into his wallet, he gave her a bill. Up several steps and into the house. Lights on. Room full of furniture, candles everywhere, big ones and little ones, sticking up out of holders like multicolored erections. He giggled. Room full of erections. But how about me? Will there be an erection for old Steve tonight?

"Do you want a joint?" Juleen asked.

"Joint? Marijuana?"

"Yes."

"Don't use it. No."

"It's good dope. From South America."

"Don't use it."

"I'm going to have one."

"Go ahead. What the hell, both adults here."

Acrid sweetish aroma. "Nice," she said.

Down a hallway, into the bedroom. Into a hall of mirrors. On the walls, even on the ceiling—twenty or more mirrors in all shapes and sizes. Twenty of him and twenty of Juleen blowing pot, seen through a dim smoky haze.

"Hey," he said, "what's all this?"

"I like it with mirrors."

"Watch ourselves make love?"

"It's better that way. Hotter."

"Kinky," he said. "I'm not kinky."

"We don't have to make it in here . . ."

"Never mind. Something new—try it once, why not?"

She came up close to him, put her face close to his, ran her tongue over his lips. Sweet acrid smell, sweet acrid taste. But all he could feel was sudden uneasiness. All he could see were the painted voodoo symbols, staring at him like the snake's head on the stick—

"Wash that makeup off," he said.

"Why?"

"Don't like it."

"You mean it turns you off?"

"Yes. Please, Juleen."

She moved away, opened a door and disappeared through it. He got his clothes off. Must have got them off; next thing he knew he was lying on the big double bed, on the patchwork quilt that covered it, naked, looking up at himself in the ceiling mirror. Ought to be embarrassed, he thought. But he wasn't. Just drunk, drunk as a lord. And horny. Gonna get laid. But the room, the mirror, the image of himself kept wanting to spin and spin, spin and spin . . .

Juleen was there, face scrubbed, taking her robe off. No, twenty Juleens—all smiling, all naked. Forty hard little breasts with hard little nipples. Forty slim white legs and flaring buttocks. Twenty shaved pubic areas, clean as a whistle, the vertical folds of her sex as bare as a child's.

Kinky, kinky.

And she was beside him on the bed, hands stroking his body. Stirrings of warmth, of tumescence. He kept his eyes open, he had to or the spinning would overwhelm him, and he saw himself get an erection. Saw her fondling it. Saw himself clamp his mouth over one of her breasts. Saw her crawl on top of him, saying, "I'll do it to you, that way we can both watch." Saw her moving up and down, up and down

and around and around

and he couldn't stop the spinning any more

spinning

and spinning away

and when the spinning stopped by itself for a few seconds, a long or a short time later, she was gone and the room was semidark and he saw the Legba staff instead, the snake's head swaying back and forth and staring into his face, and he cried out and tried to rear away from that leering evil gaze, but as soon as he did that he saw twenty snakes, forty fangs, twenty sticks, all reaching for him out of the darkness

and there was more spinning, more timeless time

and in his hand he felt wood hard and thin, like a stick

and far away, far far away, he heard someone screaming

and his hands were suddenly wet and sticky

and there was more screaming

and then there was nothing except the snakes crawling through his mind, flicking their tongues, baring their fangs, whispering over and over again, "Twisted, twisted, all twisted in the hole I'm in."

PART II
MUMMER'S SUNDAY

The figure was tall and gaunt, and shrouded from head to foot in the habiliments of the grave. The mask which concealed the visage was made so nearly to resemble the countenance of a stiffened corpse that the closest scrutiny must have had difficulty in detecting the cheat. And yet all this might have been endured, if not approved, by the mad revelers around. But the mummer had gone so far as to assume the type of the Red Death. His vesture was dabbled in blood *—and his broad brow, with all the features of the face, was besprinkled with the scarlet horror.*

—EDGAR ALLAN POE
"The Masque of the Red Death"

SEVEN

He awoke to pain and silence.

It was morning, or at least daylight. Sunshine, cold and pale, illuminated the single window alongside the bed; he could see the window, the sunshine, part of a flowering shrub all without moving his head because they were reflected in the canted mirror suspended on chains above the bed. He was lying on his back, the quilt pulled up under his chin, only his face showing. It looked gray, flecked with beard stubble, the eyes puffy and shining redly, like the eyes of a demon he had once seen in a magazine illustration.

But he didn't want to think about demons.

There was no one in the bed with him. The other side of it did not even look rumpled, as though he had slept here alone during the night. He listened. Outside there were birds, the far-off thrumming of an automobile engine being raced, but inside there was only silence.

He struggled to remember. He knew where he was— Juleen's house, Juleen's bed. He had a vague, disjointed memory of leaving Père Lafon's, of walking, of riding in a taxi, of coming here and seeing the mirrors, of Juleen making love to him. But the details were gone, fragmented and blown away in alcoholic fog. He seemed to recall part of a nightmare, too: that damned snake's-head stick, a voice screaming, another voice hissing like a snake inside his head—

He shivered, and the shiver made him move his head, and the movement unleashed a violent stabbing pain. God! He lay still again and let a soft moan come out of his throat. All that vodka at Père Lafon's . . . no wonder he had a hangover. He damned well deserved it, too. What a fool he'd been. A good-looking young woman like Juleen, willing, bringing him home with her to a bedroom full of mirrors, loving him in a position that Lara had never tolerated because she said it was demeaning, and what did he do but get roaring drunk? There was no question about it any more: he was a lush, an alcoholic. He couldn't face any kind of pressure without a drink, no matter how much he lied to himself, cajoled or threatened himself. His only hope was to keep on admitting it and start doing something about it. Join AA, get the advice of his doctor. If he didn't, if he kept on the way he was going, what was left of his life would be a shambles inside a year. And there wouldn't be any pieces left worth picking up.

The silence intruded on him again. Why was it so damned quiet in the house? Where was Juleen?

What time was it?

He eased himself upward, wincing, so that his head rested higher on the pillow, and brought his left arm from beneath the covers. To see if he was still wearing his watch, to find out the time. The watch was on his wrist, but something else was on it too, obliterating the crystal—something that rocked him, made him stare in shocked disbelief.

His forearm and hand were streaked with a crusty, reddish-brown substance.

Blood—dried blood.

He wrenched himself into a sitting position, unmindful of the fresh surge of hangover pain, still staring at the bloodstains. He turned his hand over, examined it on all sides; there was no cut or abrasion of any kind. Then he saw that the bedclothes had fallen away. And then he saw his exposed upper torso.

There was blood smeared on the sheets.

Blood smeared on his chest, his stomach.

Blood smeared over his right hand.

and his hands were suddenly wet and sticky
and somebody was screaming

The hands lifted as if they were separate entities—as if they were snakes, swaying hypnotically in front of his face. He blinked at them, screwed his eyes tight shut and then brought them open again. The mirrors gave him back his image twentyfold, and those of his bloodstained hands upraised in what might have been a pagan benediction—twenty or more of him, forty or more of the hands, and so much blood . . .

He groped his way off the bed, stumbled across to the nearest of two closed doors. Closet. He threw the door shut again, lurched toward the second. His mind wasn't working; it was swirled through with confusion and pain and a lingering afterimage of all those blood-spattered hands.

The second door opened into the bathroom. He was shaking so badly that he had trouble getting the cold-water sink tap turned on. He put his head under the flow, opened his mouth and drank until he couldn't hold any more.

When he straightened, the medicine-cabinet mirror showed him the blood again.

He plunged his hands and arms under the tap. Found a bar of soap and scrubbed until the skin up to his elbows tingled; scrubbed his chest and stomach the same way with a washcloth. The bathroom floor was slick with water when he finished, but there were no traces of the rust red in it. And none in the basin.

He dried himself with a towel, took it with him into the bedroom. His head felt as if it were cracked in two or three places; his thoughts were still muddled. He stood near the bed, looking at the window so he wouldn't have to look at himself in the mirrors, and listened to the thudding hangover rhythm inside his head. Only to that, because there was nothing else to hear; the house was still shrouded in silence.

Juleen, he thought. What happened—

But that was as far as the thought went. His mind stuttered, shifted away into muzziness; would not pursue the questions that roiled just under the surface.

His clothes were scattered across the floor on the far side of the bed, where the window was—a shoe here, his shirt there, underpants hanging comically off the knob of a dresser drawer. He gathered them up, put them on. Mechanical movements: not thinking at all now. One minute he was naked, the next he was fully dressed. And on his way to the room's third door, in the wall opposite the other two.

It stood slightly ajar. He opened it, heard it creak in the stillness. Hallway. He went along its short length, through an archway at the end. Living room. Filled with candles the way the bedroom was filled with mirrors—dozens of them, all shapes and sizes, in holders of brass, pewter, ceramic, wood, arranged on the furniture, on the fireplace mantel, even on the floor. He had a dim recollection of seeing them last night, of thinking they resembled phalluses. But they didn't look phallic now. The room was filled, too, with a hodgepodge of furniture, some old, some new, all of it cheap-looking. On the walls were half a dozen paintings, impressionistic, of things that he couldn't quite recognize—

Except for one: the portrait of a huge serpent rearing up over a group of tiny black worshipers who seemed to be dancing with heads thrown back and arms and legs out-flung. Woven into the background were the words *Danse Calinda* in bright red script, the color of fresh blood.

Voodoo.

He went deeper into the room, looking for a way out. In a tiny vestibule to his right, he saw what appeared to be the front door; a window parallel to it, straight across, showed him more sunlight, a section of elevated porch, a section of untrimmed lawn and a street with a live oak shading the sidewalk. He took two steps that way, paused again as something else caught his eye. It was off to his left, lying on a throw rug near another, swing-type door.

The hackles lifted on his neck. He moved that way instead of to the front door, not by conscious choice, drawn magnetically to the long slender shape that lay on the rug. Two feet from it he stopped and stared down.

Juleen's Legba staff.

And the carved snake's head and part of its rough-wood length were stained with dried blood.

and in his hand he felt wood hard and thin, like a stick
and far away, far far away, he heard someone screaming
and his hands were suddenly wet and sticky

"No," he said aloud.

The pain in his head increased . . . like voodoo drums pounding out an ancient primitive rhythm. Danse Calinda, boudoum, boudoum. He kept staring down at the Legba staff. And the more he stared, the more it seemed to writhe under his scrutiny, as if any second it would reshape itself magically into a real snake and slither away under the furniture. Or launch itself at him, mouth agape, fangs dripping venom . . .

He stepped around the staff, as he would have if it had been a living python, and pushed open the swing door. Kitchen. Antiquated coil-top icebox, gas stove, sink set in a wooden drainboard. Table and three chairs. Seeing all of these things without seeing them, because his attention was focused on the yellowed linoleum floor—

Blood.

Coagulated splotches of it made an irregular trail across the linoleum, as if it had dripped off something—the Legba staff—when someone walked through the kitchen.

He followed the trail of blood with his eyes, saw that it ended at still another door, this one half-open, showing a wall of darkness beyond. His feet carried him along the same route his eyes had taken, deposited him in front of the door. He listened, heard nothing. And reached out an unsteady hand and pushed the door all the way open.

A set of narrow stairs materialized, leading downward from a short landing. He couldn't see where they ended. The smell of dampness, of mustiness and of something else raw and evil that he couldn't identify, drifted up out of the blackness.

Cellar, he thought.

He took a step closer, put his foot on the landing. He still could not penetrate the thick shadows below. With his left hand, he fumbled for a light switch along the wall inside. But when he found one he did not flick it on. The smell that came swelling up at him was stronger, and now he recognized it, now he admitted to himself that he'd known from the first what it was.

Death—the smell of death.

Don't go down there!

He jerked his hand away from the light switch, backed clear of the door. Chills chased each other up and down the saddle of his back. Boudoum, boudoum. Boudoum, boudoum.

Juleen, he thought.

No, he thought, I couldn't have, I couldn't!

Twisted, all twisted in the hole I'm in—

He fled from the house into the bright crisp Sunday morning.

EIGHT

HE knew people were staring at him, watching him from behind their windows and their fences, but he couldn't stop running. Away from that house of mirrors and candles, voodoo and snakes, blood and death. Down this block, across that street, down another block and across another street, head full of pain and distorted imagery, lungs howling for relief.

His flight ended in a small neighborhood park, and then only because his legs and his wind gave out. He sprawled on damp grass at the base of a tree, sat slumped with his eyes squeezed shut. The sounds he made were a mixture of labored wheezes and throat rattles that were not quite sobs.

The panic ebbed out of him in the same slow way that his respiration returned to normal. After a while he sat up, wiped sweat from his eyes. When he brushed the other hand through his hair he felt a jutting wiry tangle. I must look like a wild man, he thought.

He peered around. The park was a block square, dotted with live oaks, benches, a statue of a Confederate soldier. There was nobody else in it except for a couple of black kids nearby, both of them wearing baseball gloves, both staring curiously in his direction. He got to his feet, went shaky legged to a fountain a few yards away and eased the clotted dryness in his mouth and throat with cold water.

There was a bench adjacent to the fountain. He remembered his watch as he went over there. Ten fifty-five. He sat down on the bench and put his head in his hands.

He could think now, and that was almost as bad as the panic had been. Because it forced him to face something appalling—and the possibility that hidden away inside himself all the thirty-eight years of his life, latent, straining to get out, might be a monster every bit as terrible as Stevenson's Mr. Hyde.

He refused to believe it.

He had not been seized by some sort of drunken homicidal impulse. He was not a monster. He had not hurt Juleen. Maybe she was dead, maybe her body was down there in the cellar, maybe she had been beaten to death with her Legba staff, but *he* was not responsible.

The blood on him—

He wasn't responsible. Someone else had come into that house last night; someone else had bludgeoned Juleen and was trying to blame him. Smeared the blood all over him. Either that, or he had gotten up in his stupor during the night, found her, touched her, touched the stick, and then crawled back into bed.

But why couldn't he remember—

Hangover, that was why. Or shock. Or both. Mind blocking out the memory. Maybe he would remember later, when some of the hangover began to fade. Maybe he wouldn't remember, but that would be all right too. The important thing, the thing he must not forget, was that he hadn't hurt Juleen, he hadn't hurt anybody, he was not a monster.

What he had to do now was to get back to familiar surroundings. The French Quarter, his hotel. He lifted his head. The two black youths were still watching him from a short distance away. Slowly he got to his feet, went to where they stood.

They were both about twelve, lean, smart looking, but without the streetwise veneer of toughness he was accustomed to seeing on so many black youths in San Francisco. Just kids, like kids anywhere. Not afraid of him or the way he looked. On the contrary, hiding smiles and snickers behind their baseball gloves. One nudged the other as he approached. They had seen drunks before, black and white and other colors too; they knew all about drunks at Carnival time.

"Where y'at?" one of them said.

Giroux didn't understand at first. It was the same question he had been about to ask: Where am I at? But then he remembered that it was a slang expression—the New Orleans equivalent of "What's happening?"

"Nothing much," he lied. "What park is this?"

"Don't you know?"

"No. I don't live here; I'm a tourist."

"Tchoupitoulas," the taller boy said.

"Where? The Irish Channel?"

"Yeah. How come you were running so hard?"

The shorter boy said, "Somebody after you?"

The words echoed in his mind. *Somebody after you?* But he said, "No, nobody's after me. I got lost, that's all."

"Happens sometimes during Carnival," the taller kid said. He nudged his friend again. "Folks get lost."

The shorter boy giggled.

"How do I get back to the French Quarter?"

"Walk up that way," the shorter one said, pointing. "Take the streetcar."

"The St. Charles Avenue streetcar?"

"That's the only one we got, mister."

He thanked them and moved away in the direction that had been pointed out. Behind him he could hear them laughing. Let them laugh; let them think he was just another Mardi Gras drunk. They were at least partly right: he was another drunk, a damn miserable sot. That way, they wouldn't say anything about him to anybody. Maybe they would just forget they had seen him.

Somebody after you?

No, he thought. No.

And then he thought: Jesus, what about the police?

Suppose somebody had seen him run out of Juleen's house; suppose the somebody had gotten suspicious and gone to investigate and found the blood and the stick, found Juleen or whoever it was down in the cellar. Suppose they'd called the police, and when the police arrived at the house—Fingerprints! Oh God, his fingerprints would be all over the bedroom, the bathroom. And what if they were on the stick itself? He'd never been in the armed services, asthma had kept him out, but he had been printed once, for his California driver's license. Only his thumbprint, but that would be enough . . .

He left the park, hurried in a fast walk toward St. Charles Avenue. He had to get out of New Orleans. As soon as he reached the Pirate's Head, he would call for a reservation on the first plane heading west, pack his clothes, check out, take a taxi straight to the airport—

No.

That was running away, and he had nothing to run away from. He hadn't done anything, no matter how bad things looked, how much circumstantial evidence stacked up against him. If he ran away, it was the same as admitting he'd done something after all, there *was* a monster trapped inside him. And if the police found his fingerprints, they'd have his name and they'd probably alert the airlines. And even if they didn't, even if he took a flight out, they'd know where to find him. How would it look to them if he suddenly left New Orleans? It would make him look guilty, wouldn't it? Unlawful flight to avoid prosecution for the crime of murder . . . They would extradite him from California, bring him back to stand trial, and they wouldn't listen to anything he tried to tell them.

Maybe he should call them right away, explain what had happened. Only he didn't know what *had* happened. What could he say? "Officer, I woke up with blood all over me but I know I didn't hurt Juleen, I'm not a killer." They'd want to know why he ran, why he didn't just pick up the telephone and call them right away. They'd say he had attacked Juleen in a drunken rage and struck her down with the staff, and carried her body down cellar, and *that* was how the blood had got smeared all over him.

He didn't know what to do. He couldn't run, he couldn't go to the police . . . what else was there? Pretend nothing had happened, go about the business of his vacation as if Juleen had never come into his life? Sit in his hotel room and wait for the authorities to knock on the door?

What am I going to do? he thought.

He kept walking. Ahead, finally, a wide avenue appeared—shaded by evenly spaced rows of live oaks, with a grassy divider strip in the middle that harbored two narrow lines of streetcar tracks. He went to stand on one of the cement passenger islands near the uptown tracks, alone there. His mind kept stuttering back and forth between alternatives, hovering on this one, on that one, discarding each of them over and over again, until one of the streetcars came rattling up the tracks toward him.

It was much older than the ones in San Francisco, painted an olive-green color with red trim. It was much cleaner inside, too—antiquated wooden seats, restored and varnished, and windows that you could open and lean out of. Like stepping back in time to the turn of the century. He asked the driver how much the fare was, saw the man grimace at the stale-vodka smell of his breath, and got a curt "Thirty cents" in reply. He fumbled in his trousers, found coins, put them into the change receptacle.

The car was three-quarters full. He made his way to the back, not looking at any of the upturned faces on both sides of him, and found a place to sit. His stomach kicked as the car lurched forward; almost immediately he felt the beginnings of motion sickness. He opened the window beside him, slumped lower in the seat to let the wind blow against his face.

Somebody in front of him said, "You look as if you had quite a night."

He had been staring out the window; he blinked and turned his head. It was a woman in the seat in front of him, half-turned in his direction, looking at him in a neutral way. At first he didn't recognize her. Then he realized it was the woman he had spoken to at the parade last night—the attractive woman with the dark red hair and the translucent skin.

"Small world, isn't it?" she said. "Or maybe I should say small city."

"I guess it is."

"The last I saw of you, you and your . . . young friend were going off into the heart of the French Quarter. What are you doing way out here?"

Before he realized what he was saying, he answered automatically, "She lives out here."

"Oh, I see."

No you don't, he thought. You don't see anything. But he did not put the thought into words. This time he said nothing at all.

"It must have been quite a party," the woman said in a voice to match her neutral expression.

"I don't know what you mean."

"Well, you've got a party aroma this morning."

"Vodka," he said. "I drank too much."

"So I gathered. Doesn't your friend have a car?"

"Car?"

"Or did the two of you have a fight?"

He looked at her sharply. "Why do you say that?"

"I was just wondering why you're riding the streetcar."

"It was the easiest way to get back to the Quarter," he said. He didn't want to talk to her any more . . . and yet he did. Talking kept him from thinking about Juleen, about his lack of alternatives. Kept his mind off the motion of the car, too. "Why are *you* riding the streetcar this morning?"

"It's one of the recommended tourist attractions," she said. "The Garden District, Tulane University, Loyola University, Audubon Park—all very nice."

"Don't you like the Carnival?"

"In small doses. It's a little too boisterous for my taste, I'm afraid."

"Mine too."

"So you indicated. But you seemed to have enjoyed yourself last night."

"Did I? I don't think so."

"Not even when you were with your young friend?"

"We went to listen to some jazz—good jazz. At a place called Père Lafon's."

"I've never heard of it," the woman said.

"It's not a tourist place. I enjoyed that," he said, but it was a lie. He hadn't enjoyed it. The man in the dragon mask had kept him from enjoying anything about last night—

The dragon, he thought.

He'd forgotten about him. But what if the man had still been around when he and Juleen left Père Lafon's? And what if he'd followed them out to Juleen's house? And what

if he'd got inside, and *he* was the one who had attacked
Juleen?

Why?

Why would the man in the dragon mask want to harm
her? To frame *him* for it? Why? Why had the man been
following him? Why would he want to frame Steven Giroux
for murder? Why, why, why? None of it made sense. . . .

"Is something wrong?"

The woman's voice penetrated, brought him out of
himself. He refocused on her. "What did you say?"

"You had a funny look. *Is* something wrong?"

"No," he said. "It's just this hangover."

"Bad stomach?"

"Yes."

"Have you eaten anything yet today?"

"No, but I'm not hungry."

"You should eat, or at least have some coffee." She
paused. "We're almost to Canal Street. I was going to have
lunch. Would you care to join me?"

"I don't think so," he said. "I've got to get back to my
hotel."

"Where are you staying?"

"The Pirate's Head. On Burgundy at Ursuline."

"That's a long walk from Canal Street," she said.
"You'd feel better if you had something to eat first."

The word *no* formed in his mind. But what came out
of his mouth were the words, "I don't even know your
name."

"It's Mona Jensen. And yours?"

"Steven Giroux. Why would you want to have lunch
with me, Miss Jensen?"

She raised an eyebrow. "You're frank, aren't you?"

"Not usually. But I've got a party aroma, you said that
yourself. And I've been out all night with another woman.
Why do you want to have anything to do with me?"

"I suppose because I like your face. I liked it when I met you last night and I still like it today." She lowered her voice an octave. "I'm not a pickup, if that's what you're thinking."

"I wasn't thinking anything."

"Well, I just wanted to get that established. As a matter of fact, I'm rather old-fashioned in most respects—relationships with strange men being one of them. Besides, you already have a girlfriend."

"No," he said.

"Didn't things work out?"

"No," he said again. "They didn't work out."

The car veered around Lafayette Square. Mona glanced to the front—through the windshield he could see part of the jammed expanse of Canal Street ahead—and then looked back at him again.

"Did you make up your mind?" she asked.

"About what?"

"About whether or not you want to have some lunch."

He started to say, for the second time, that he had to get back to his hotel. But why did he have to get back? So he could pack and run away? So he could sit and brood and wait for the police? He didn't know anybody in New Orleans except Juleen and this woman—and Mona's, now, was the only friendly face in a sea of strangers.

"All right," he said. "Yes, I guess I would."

Because he hadn't hurt Juleen, he wasn't twisted inside. Because he needed some semblance of normalcy in his life right now. Because he didn't want to be alone again just yet.

Because he was terrified.

NINE

THE car came to a rattling stop near Canal and everybody began to clamber off. He let Mona precede him, and when they were standing together on the street she said, "There's a nice little cafe on Carondelet, two blocks up. I ate there yesterday—the food is very good."

"Whatever you like."

They crossed the street, joined the sidewalk throng on Canal. From over in the Quarter he could hear band music. The Venus krewe, he supposed, getting ready for their afternoon march, or maybe already marching; he didn't know or care. Venus was the goddess of love, and there was no love in his life anymore.

Mona walked with her hands in the flare pockets of a pearl-gray knee-length coat; the wind and cold put ovals of color in the whiteness of her cheeks. After a time she asked, "Where do you live, Steven? It is all right if I call you Steven?"

"Of course. I live in San Francisco."

"I'm from Milwaukee. What I do is teach—junior high school, English and history. And you?"

"Photographer."

"That sounds interesting."

"I suppose so."

"I take it you're not married?"

"Not any longer."

"Divorce, the universal malaise," she said, but without any noticeable bitterness. "My marriage broke up two years ago."

"Six months."

"I hope the split was amicable."

"No, it wasn't."

"Oh. I'm sorry."

"So am I," he said.

The cafe was called the Something Court; he didn't pay much attention as they entered. There were a counter and tables inside, more tables in a small palm-studded courtyard in back. The interior was crowded and too warm, too noisy.

He said, "I'd prefer to sit in the courtyard, if you don't mind."

"It might be a little cold."

"The fresh air'll be good for my head."

Only a few of the courtyard tables were occupied. They found a sheltered one near the back, next to a high board fence and one of the palm trees. Menus were already arranged on the table; he picked up the one in front of him, because Mona had picked up hers, and opened it.

The first thing he saw was the beverage list—no hard liquor, but plenty of wine and beer.

He ran his tongue around the inside of his mouth. All the surfaces tasted arid, burned out. And when he swallowed it felt as though there were grains of sand in his throat. An ice-cold beer would taste good—

No, he thought.

But he needed it to soothe away the dryness, soothe his nerves—

Like the vodka last night?

Damn it, no.

What's the matter with you? Can't you see what a trap it is? One vodka leads to another; one beer leads to another. And another. And too many. Whatever happened at Juleen's house wouldn't have happened if you'd been sober. You can't just drink one beer, not any more. Not in the hole you're in.

Mona was saying something to him. He roused himself, shut the menu, pushed it away. "I'm sorry, I didn't hear what you said."

"I said the Creole gumbo is excellent."

"Is that what you're having?"

"I think so."

"Then I'll try it too."

"Are you drinking anything?"

"Coffee," he said. "Just coffee."

A young Cajun waitress came and took their order and went off again. They sat and looked at each other. He felt none of the usual newly acquainted awkwardness and she seemed not to, either. Without trying to, he seemed to have established a rapport with her. Why couldn't he have met her first, instead of Juleen? She was nearer his own age, nearer his own temperament and outlook. What was it she'd said last night at the parade, about one Mardi Gras being enough? And on the streetcar . . . she'd said the Carnival was too boisterous for her taste. Birds of a feather. God, if he could only wipe out last night and the horror of this morning . . .

Mona said, "How long are you staying in New Orleans, Steven?"

"Until Thursday morning."

"Me too. Well, Thursday afternoon. I wanted to return

on Ash Wednesday, but all the American Airlines flights were booked and I prefer American. My travel agent convinced me I ought to stay over in any case, so I could recuperate."

"From what?"

"Oh, from all the gaiety and partying, I suppose. Do you have anything planned for Shrove Tuesday?"

"No," he said, and thought: I might not even be here. I might be back in San Francisco by then. Or I might be in jail.

"There'll be three parades," Mona said. "After the last one, Comus, there's a masquerade ball planned at my hotel. Do you dance?"

"Not very well."

"I thought I might go to the masque. If you're interested . . ."

"I don't know. I'd have to let you know."

"Well, it's an open offer. I'm staying at the Mason House, on Gravier."

"I'll remember that."

"The parades should be interesting," she said. "Particularly Zulu—that's the one where all the blacks dress up in grass skirts and paint their faces and put bones in their noses. Like cannibals, you see."

"Yes," he said.

"Am I talking too much? I don't usually chatter like this."

"No, it's all right."

"It's just that I've been feeling . . . well, lonely. I was supposed to come down with a friend, but at the last minute she had to cancel. Minor surgery to remove a benign cyst from one of her breasts. So it was either come alone or forfeit my hotel deposit."

"That's about how it was for me," he said. "Only it was

my ex-wife and I who planned the trip—eight months ago, not long before we split up."

"Was it that sudden? The decision to end your marriage?"

"Yes."

"Do you want to talk about it?"

He shook his head. "I'd rather not."

"I didn't mean to be personal . . ."

"Don't apologize. It's still painful, is all."

"I understand. But the wounds will heal."

Will they? he thought. He said nothing.

"I know that sounds platitudinous," Mona said, "but it's true in most cases. It was in mine."

"I guess it's easier if you can remain friends."

"Well, Ralph and I didn't exactly remain friends. We saw each other three or four times between the day he moved out and the accident, but we didn't even say hello."

"Accident?"

"Ralph's hobby was collecting guns and he was never careful with them. That was the kind of man he was—reckless. A handgun he was cleaning one night in his apartment accidentally went off and shot him. They said he died right away."

Giroux didn't know what to say. Again he was silent.

"It happened three months after we broke up," Mona said. "So I had two tragedies to cope with—the breakup and his death. It might not have been so bad if I hadn't still loved him, but I did. I'm not the kind of person who can live with a man for ten years unless I love him very much. Or who can stop loving him all at once, no matter what he might have become. Marriage ought to be for life; I always believed that."

"So did I," he said.

"I still believe it."

"But your husband didn't?"

"No," she said. Now there were traces of bitterness in her voice. "He only believed in his work—he was an engineer—and in guns and sporting clubs and long trips alone in the woods. He seemed to lose interest in me as the years went by."

"I know how that must have felt."

"Yes. I tried everything I could think of to keep us together. I suggested a child, but he was dead set against it. I even learned how to shoot so I could take target practice and go hunting with him. It didn't do any good. He just came home one night and said matter-of-factly that he didn't want to live with me any more; then he packed his things and moved out. That was the worst night of my life."

Last night was the worst of mine, he thought. He said, "How did you get through the first few months?"

"A strong will, more than anything else. I never knew how strong I was until then. There were some bad moments, but I managed. I did what I had to do to keep my life together."

She had; why couldn't he? But there seemed to be an essential difference between them: Mona had been born strong and had found her strength when push came to shove; he had been born weak and had lost what strength he had, in stages, when the crisis period arrived. He had always considered himself a durable, tenacious man. Now he knew different. And the knowledge added a sense of shame to the tangle of emotions inside him.

He heard himself say, "Have you thought about marrying again?"

"Oh, yes. But not seriously; there's been no one else."

"Not for me, either."

"But you're not soured on marriage, are you?"

"I'm not sure. Probably not."

"It's still too early for you. You need more time."

He nodded. But did he have more time? How much

time *did* he have before somebody found what was in the cellar of Juleen's house?

The food came. He ate without tasting anything, chasing down each mouthful with hot black coffee. The flip-flopping of his stomach eased somewhat; getting food inside him had been a good idea. Good ideas seemed few and far between these days—and even when he did get one, it came about in spite of him, almost by accident.

The conversation shifted away from marriage, lightened and grew generalized; he was grateful for that. She asked him questions about his photography and he answered them. He showed her his wallet photos of Marcie: toddler to young lady, the most recent taken this past Christmas. She told him she had been born in the dairy country of Wisconsin and had a teaching degree from Marquette and canned fruit in her spare time. She said she liked jazz, so he told her about some of the greats and near greats of New Orleans—Johnny De Droit, Sweet Emma Barrett, Papa Celestin, Johnny Wiggs, Bunk Johnson, Satchmo, King Oliver and Kid Ory and Jelly Roll Morton.

And lunch was over and it was two-thirty, and five minutes after that they were standing on the sidewalk in front of the cafe. Clouds had piled up over the Mississippi; the dark-veined grayness of them promised thundershowers for tonight sometime. It was windier, too—cold.

He offered to walk her back to her hotel, but she said she wanted to do some shopping first. He went with her as far as a gift shop called Mike Sutton's on Canal Street. Near the entrance they stopped and looked at each other again.

Mona said, "I'm glad we had the chance to talk. I enjoyed the lunch, Steven."

"So did I," he said. It was not quite the truth, but neither was it a lie.

"I'd like to see you again. On Tuesday for Mardi Gras, or earlier if you like. You don't have to commit yourself now," she said, misinterpreting his silence. "But if you do want to, call me at the Mason House."

"All right."

She gave him her hand. It was warm—she had had it inside the pocket of her coat—and very small. He hadn't noticed before how small her hands were. This one felt delicate, as if the bones were thin and fragile and he must be careful not to grip it too hard or he might crack them. It was a curious illusion, considering his perception of her as a strong woman; he didn't know why he should have it. He had never been an imaginative man: one of his many faults, as far as Lara was concerned.

He held the hand for three or four seconds. When he let go, Mona smiled at him and said, "Good-bye, Steven," and then turned and disappeared inside the shop.

He stood with the flow of people around him and he felt alone again. Images from the night and the morning crowded into his mind. He had held the terror down during most of the time he'd been with Mona, but now it was back. The aloneness seemed to summon it, conjure it up like a psychic demon. Being alone was part of it; he needed friends, he needed someone to share his bed and his existence, to help him make decisions, to guide him over the rough spots—someone he could lean on. He was not the kind of man who could cope with situations, with his own life, on a basis of self-reliance. When he was alone his weakness poked through like fragments of shattered bone.

He began to walk. He had no place to go except back to the Pirate's Head, and he didn't want to go there because he was afraid of what might be waiting for him. The police, the man in the dragon mask, some other unknown quantity. The Pirate's Head was the one place in New Orleans where anybody could go to find him. Out here in the streets, he was just another citizen, just another anonymous face in the sea of faces that inundated New Orleans for Mardi Gras.

But the streets were not the place for him either. He found that out soon enough. People jostled him; a taxi almost ran him down in a crosswalk, green light his way. Waves of sound you could almost see poured out of the Quarter—as you could almost see heat shimmering on a day when the temperature climbed above a hundred degrees. Drums and horns, those were the dominant sounds. And the drums presided: racing pulse, thudding tempo, boudoum boudoum, boudoum boudoum. There was no such thing as voodoo, voodoo had been dead in New Orleans for fifty years—except for a few like Juleen, isolated worshipers at a crumbling shrine—but the beat went on, the rhythm of voodoo mingled with the rhythm of jazz . . . death and life, life and death . . . and lingered eternally in the bowels of the city, and was resurrected once each year by thousands of voices, hundreds of drums. Boudoum boudoum, boudoum boudoum . . .

He went down North Rampart Street and into the Vieux Carré. A woman stood yelling on a street corner that someone had stolen her purse. A man leaned against the side wall of a building, urinating. A smiling woman, her face made up like a mime, exposed her breasts at intervals to a crowd of men who applauded and cheered each time she did it, who kept urging her to take her sweater off, take the rest of her clothes off, "Let's see what you got inside your drawers, honey, let's see your snatch."

The old cast-iron latticework of the Pirate's Head loomed up ahead of him. I don't have anywhere else to go, he thought. Even if they're waiting for me, where else can I go?

But nobody was waiting for him. Men and women filled the *banquettes*, the nearby stoops, but none of them had a dragon's face. There was nobody in the dark old lobby, and when he went to the desk the clerk told him there were no messages. He still had his key, in the pocket of his jacket; he discovered that when the clerk told him it wasn't in his room slot. He'd forgotten to turn it in on his way out last night.

He went upstairs, opened the door to his room, shut it behind him. Dark in there again; the maid had closed the drapes over the windows. He sat on the bed. Listened to the faint, closed-off rhythm from outside.

Listened to the telephone ring.

He sat there stiffly, with his hands clenched. Don't answer it. Just let it—

Ring.

But he had to know who was calling. Maybe it was only Mona. Maybe she was back at her hotel and she'd decided on impulse to call him, maybe try to make a date for to-night. Sure, that was it. Mona.

Ring.

He reached out, hesitated, and then jerked the receiver out of its cradle just as the bell started to clamor again. "Hello?"

"The photograph, Giroux. Where's that photograph, you son of a bitch?"

TEN

It was the same male voice as yesterday, but no longer soft-spoken; now it crackled with anger and menace. Listening to it, Giroux felt his hand go slick around the receiver, and the taste of metal was in his mouth again.

"Who are you?" he said. His voice had a cracking edge to it; he mended the crack with his own anger. "Who the hell are you?"

"I want that photograph."

"I told you yesterday, I don't know anything about any photograph. You've got the wrong person."

"I've got the right person."

"No. Listen—"

"You listen, Giroux. I'll give you one more chance to play it straight with us. Turn over the photograph and you're out of it free and clear. No more hassle, no more hard feelings."

"I was never *in* anything with you—"

"Get it from wherever you stashed it. Put it in an envelope, write the name Chalmette on the front, take it to the Creole Grocery on Esplanade Avenue. Same instructions as yesterday. Store stays open until nine o'clock tonight. That's how much time you've got."

"How many times do I have to say it? I don't have any goddamned photograph!"

"If you don't deliver, we'll know you're trying to pull some kind of scam. And you'll regret it. No mistake."

"What does that mean? Are you threatening me?"

"Don't deliver and you'll find out."

"For God's sake, will you try to understand that I don't—"

"And remember this, Giroux: you can't run and there's no place you can hide. I'll know what you do and where you go every minute from now on."

"Are you having me followed?"

"I can get to you any time. Any time at all."

"Are *you* the one in the dragon mask?"

"You hear what I'm saying? Maybe you don't believe it. All right—here's a little proof for you. How do you think I know you haven't got the photograph stashed somewhere in your room?"

He couldn't comprehend the question. He said, "What?"

"You stupid asshole, do you think I'd say I could get to you if I didn't mean it?"

"I don't know what you're—"

"Look inside your suitcase," the voice said, and then it was gone.

He slammed the receiver down in frustration. Melodrama, he thought. It had all been like dialogue in a World War II spy film. Except that it was real—life imitating art. And it was more terror.

His headache had worsened, his stomach and his nerves were jumping again. In his mind he saw himself run out of the room, run downstairs, run through the crowded streets until he collapsed the way he had this morning in the park. But it was only a fantasy image; he still had essential control of himself. He went into the bathroom, fumbled a tin of aspirin from his toilet kit, and swallowed four tablets with two glasses of tap water.

When he came out he saw his suitcase neatly closed on the luggage rack, just as he'd left it. *Look inside your suitcase.* Gnawing at his lip, he moved to the case and zippered it open. There was nothing inside; on arrival he had emptied it of clothing, toilet articles, the few other personal belongings he had brought with him. Nothing—

Nothing.

His airline tickets were gone.

They had been tucked inside a clear plastic pouch on the inside lid; he remembered leaving them there when he unpacked. And yet a kind of obsession seized him. He spun away to the dresser, tore open the drawers, rummaged among his underwear and shirts. Then he pawed through his clothes hanging in the closet, his toilet kit, his camera cases, the nightstand drawer; he even got down on hands and knees and looked under the bed.

Gone. Stolen.

He was breathing heavily when he sank onto one of the chairs. How had they gotten in here? Picked the door lock? Used a skeleton key? It didn't matter. They'd been here, that was the point, and they'd searched the room, and when they hadn't found what they were after they had stolen the airline tickets—a warning, a symbolic act. Don't try to leave New Orleans until you come across. We got in once, we can do it again; and the next time it'll be *you* we come after.

Creole Grocery on Esplanade Avenue. Nine o'clock tonight.

Madness.

He had no photograph for anybody; he knew nothing about any sinister damned photograph. No one had approached him in San Francisco, no one had paid him to take a photo and deliver it in New Orleans, no one had entrusted a photograph to him for delivery or safekeeping. The voice on the telephone belonged to a stranger; he had never heard it before yesterday, he was certain of that. The name Chalmette meant nothing to him either, except as the name of an old New Orleans family on whose field the Battle of New Orleans had been fought. Could he have accidentally taken a photo of something or someone back home that was important, maybe even dangerous to people in this area? No, impossible. And even if he had, why would they expect him to bring it with him to New Orleans? Why wouldn't they have come after him in San Francisco? Unless they thought it was a photograph he'd taken here, after his arrival . . . but that didn't make sense, either. He hadn't used his Pentax once since stepping off the plane.

They, he thought. Who were *they?* Gangsters? Spies? A string of movie plots flickered across the screen of his mind: photograph of a deported criminal back in this country illegally, photograph of secret defense plans, photograph of a robbery or murder in progress, photograph of people engaged in sexual activity that could be used as blackmail evidence. Melodrama. Madness. But so were the phone calls, so was the man in the dragon mask, so was what had happened at Juleen's house. And all of that was reality—

Wasn't it?

His whole life had been out of whack the past few months; the strain on his mind was enormous. The nightmares proved that. So did his reaction to New Orleans and the Carnival atmosphere, and his dependence on alcohol. What if it was all some sort of hallucination? The man in the dragon mask, the blood in Juleen's house, the calls— all of it imagined, all of it a waking nightmare? What if his mind had already broken down, thrown his perceptions out of kilter, twisted and distorted events into his own private *Grand Guignol?*

What if all the madness was *his?*

He began to pace the room without realizing what he was doing. No, he thought, and kept thinking it: No, no, no. Coping with reality was one thing; no matter how terrifying the situation became, he could still function. Think, act, react: he had some control over what he did and what happened to him. But there was no coping with madness, because then he would have no control, no assurance of what was real and what wasn't. His mind could lead him in any direction, tell him this was so, or that was so, and that he must do this or that, and pretty soon he would become hopelessly entangled, hopelessly lost.

Madness was simply out of the question.

The phone calls were real; he could replay them as if they had been stored away on memory tapes. He remembered Juleen's house—the mirrors, the blood, the Legba staff, the phallic candles, the *Danse Calinda* painting, the open cellar door, the death smell coming up out of the darkness. And the man in the dragon mask, the way he moved, the way he danced, the way he stood under the streetlamp on St. Charles Avenue and in the shadows of the Lalaurie gate. Yesterday, last night, this morning, this afternoon . . . he had lived through them all, and what he remembered seeing and hearing and smelling and feeling were true memories, they were real.

Mona Jensen was real, too. And that, by God, he could prove.

He went to the phone, dialed an outside line. Then he just stood there, listening to the hum of the empty line. Sweat broke out on his face. What hotel was she staying at? He couldn't remember, he had blanked out the name . . .

Mason House.

For Christ's sake—the Mason House.

He fumbled the telephone directory onto the bed, looked up the number of the Mason House, and dialed it. A man's voice answered. Giroux asked for Miss Mona Jensen, and there was a pause, and then the line began to buzz. Ringing her room, he thought. And ringing. And ringing. Then there was a click, but it wasn't Mona's voice that came on, it was the man's. Saying, "There's no answer, sir. Would you care to leave a message?"

"No," he said, "I guess not. I'll call back later."

He went into the bathroom and drank two more glasses of water. When he came out the room seemed smaller somehow, as if the walls were contracting. Illusion. He crossed to the cannon embrasures, pulled the drapes open. Waning sunlight, sky tainted with cirrocumulus clouds. Nobody in the courtyard below. On the second floor across the way, a man and a woman stood just inside the open window of a room, locked in a tight embrace, kissing. The man's hands slid down over the woman's hips, restless, urgent. Giroux watched. He was not a voyeur, he didn't enjoy spying on people; the scene held his attention because it represented normalcy, two people together, needing each other, chasing away loneliness.

The man began to unbutton the woman's blouse. She broke the kiss and urged him away from the window; the drapes slid closed. End of show. Giroux turned away, looked at the room from a different angle. It still seemed small, contracting, closing him in.

What am I going to do? he thought.

Call the police, he thought. Tell them everything that happened. But how would it look, him calling up out of the blue with a crazy story like that, full of inconsistencies, with no evidence to back up his claims? He'd have to tell the story if they did find his prints and came to talk to him; the truth was far better than lies or silence. But to make the call himself, put himself in their hands, was a step he was incapable of taking right now.

Leave New Orleans, go back home? He could do that even though the return tickets were gone; just report the theft and ask for replacements, or if that took too long, use one of his credit cards to buy a new ticket. But that was still running away—and would it really do any good? The telephone voice, Chalmette, had said he was being watched. Even if he got out of New Orleans, there was nothing to stop anyone from following him back to San Francisco. And there were still the police to consider. If Juleen was dead, if his fingerprints were inside her house, a sudden departure would make him look guilty.

If Juleen was dead.

The television set registered on his consciousness. News broadcasts . . . that was something he should have thought of as soon as he returned. If Juleen had been found, it would be on the news by this time, wouldn't it?

He looked at his watch. Four-sixteen. Too early for TV news, but maybe there was something on the radio. There was one built into the television set; he switched it on and tracked slowly across the dial until he found a twenty-four-hour news station. He listened to a dry-voiced announcer wrap up international developments, plod through national matters, and finally get to the local news. The primary topic was the Carnival. This number of people in town, that number lining the parade routes, another number of events planned for today and tomorrow and Fat Tuesday. So many drunks arrested, so many crimes reported—rape, purse snatching, armed robbery, assault and battery, pocket picking. But no murders, no mention of anyone named Juleen or a house in the Irish Channel.

Had the police been called in yet?

Was Juleen dead?

An idea came to him. Impulsively he went to the

phone, dialed information, wrote down the number he was given for the New Orleans Police Department. Then he dialed the number.

The line made a dozen whirring noises before a harried voice answered, "Police Department, Sergeant Libby."

"Yes," he said, "I . . . I'd like some information."

"What sort of information, sir?"

"About a . . ." The words caught in his throat; he cleared it. "About a crime that might have been committed."

"Might have been committed?"

"Yes. In the . . . in the Irish Channel."

"What sort of crime?"

"I'm not sure. I think . . . a violent crime . . ."

"May I have your name please, sir."

"No, I'd rather not. I'm just trying to get some information . . ."

"I can't give you information on a violent crime until I have your name and the reason why you're calling. Your name, sir?"

"No, I can't tell you that."

"Then tell me why you're interested in a violent crime in the Irish Channel. Do you have some knowledge of such a crime?"

"No, I . . ." He was sweating; the receiver felt greasy against his palm. He couldn't give his name, he couldn't say why he was calling. He couldn't go on talking to a voice named Sergeant Libby. "Never mind," he said, "it's a mistake . . . I made a mistake," and he put the receiver down quickly, before the sergeant could ask him any more questions.

He used a corner of the bedspread to wipe his face, and then lit a cigarette with unsteady hands. Maybe, he thought, nobody had seen him running away this morning, after all. Or if they had, maybe they hadn't become suspicious enough to investigate or to call the police. Maybe it would be days before anyone discovered what was in the cellar— and maybe when the police did come, they wouldn't find any of his prints. He seemed to vaguely recall reading somewhere that it was difficult for forensic experts to obtain clear latent prints at the scene of a crime, that it was the exception rather than the rule for someone to be identified and convicted of a crime on the basis of fingerprints. He should have remembered that earlier, too. Would have it he hadn't been so frightened.

He smoked his cigarette, and immediately lit another. Maybe it'll all work out, he thought. If I can get through this, I can get through anything. Board that plane for SFO on Thursday, as scheduled, and I'll be on my way back to normal.

Stop diddling yourself, he thought.

And then he thought: What am I going to *do?*

He needed someone to talk to, someone to confide in. A lawyer? The only lawyer he knew well was Tom Granger, who had handled his divorce, and Granger was an acquaintance, not a friend, a divorce attorney, not a criminal attorney, and he already knew what Granger would say if he called him. Go to the police, he would say, tell them everything. But it wasn't that easy. If it was that easy, he'd already have done it, wouldn't he?

A friend, then? The only close friend he had was Paul Daniels—architect, fisherman, poker enthusiast, womanizer. But could he tell Paul about this? How do you call up someone two thousand miles away and say, "This is Steve and I'm in New Orleans and there's a chance I murdered a woman last night"?

Still, it would be good to hear a friendly voice, talk to a sympathetic ear. He might even be able to skirt the issue, sneak up on it somehow, instead of just blurting it out. Sure, Paul. He had always been able to talk to Paul.

He went to the telephone again. He dialed Paul's home number, got the long-distance operator, gave her his room number, and waited for a connection. But there wasn't any connection, just fifteen empty rings. It was Sunday and Paul was out somewhere, probably with one of his lady friends, probably getting laid, and there was no one else Giroux could call, he just didn't know anyone else well enough for this.

He began to feel restless, caged. Finally he looked up the number of United Airlines and then called them to report the loss of the tickets. They told him to stop into their downtown office with proper identification so he could fill out certain forms. He said he'd be in right away, because it would give him something to do, a way to get through the next hour or so.

It took him five minutes to change clothes, comb his hair, swallow another couple of aspirin for his headache. The room seemed not much bigger than a closet when he stepped out of it and locked the door behind him.

ELEVEN

HE spent over an hour in the United Airlines office, and it was dusk when he came out again. Congestion in the streets. Lights on the river—the paddlewheel steamers and the boats in the afternoon procession of Allah, King of Algiers. Cold wind, dark sky threatening rain.

As he had done on the walk from the Pirate's Head, he looked around him at the maskers. None, or at least none that he could see, were dragons. But there was no reassurance in that. Chalmette had warned him he was being watched; he believed it. Whoever was watching him didn't have to be wearing a dragon's mask tonight. Or if he was, to let himself be seen. The crowds were so thick it would be impossible to pick out any one person who didn't want to be noticed.

Hurrying a little, he went across Canal and north to Basin Street. This was the area that had once been known as Storyville—the famous red-light district from 1897 to 1917 when gambling houses, saloons, and fourteen fancy "sporting palaces" flourished on a two-block stretch of Basin; when the "Blue Book" directory—an alphabetical

103

list of names, addresses, and race of over seven hundred prostitutes, plus large ads for individual "landladies" and girls, saloons and palaces, whiskey and cigars—was publicly sold in railroad stations, hotels, newsstands, barber shops. World War I, and a public outcry against the corruption of young soldiers, had shut down Storyville for good. Now the Blue Books were premium collectors' items. There were apartment buildings on the once-bawdy turf, and the sporting palaces and prostitutes were dim and fading memories, like the riverboat gamblers and the Creole beauties and the gentlemen who fought duels of honor in the misty dawn.

He had no particular destination in mind. He moved with the flow of people and tried not to think about anything beyond the scraps of New Orleans history his guidebook had provided. The hangover dryness parched his throat, and after a while put the idea of a cold beer into his head. What could one beer hurt? He wasn't going to screw himself up with vodka again; that was a promise he intended to keep. He did not have the slightest desire for vodka. But a beer . . .

He found himself on Gravier. The Mason House was on Gravier, and Mona was at the Mason House. Staying there, anyway. Maybe she had come back from shopping by now. Maybe she would want to have dinner with him, or at least a drink. More than ever, companionship was what he needed tonight—someone to keep his mind off his cares in this "City That Care Forgot."

The Mason House was a newish, high-rise hotel that reminded him of the Hilton in San Francisco: attractive in a functional way, without any particular charm. The big, sprawling, shop-littered lobby was Hiltonesque too. He found a bank of house phones, asked the operator for Mona Jensen's room. The line began to buzz. And kept on buzzing, emptily, until he put the receiver down.

Now what? he thought. He had no conscious answer to

the question, but his legs carried him toward a sign that said *Steamer Lounge;* under it and into a dark room full of mirrors and steamboating memorabilia. The mirrors conjured a mental image of Juleen's bedroom; he avoided looking at his reflection as he passed by them. He sat at the bar and ordered a beer. A small voice inside him said Don't do it, you damned fool, but he wasn't listening. It was only a beer. He could handle a beer or two, couldn't he?

Noise and laughter and people ebbed and flowed around him, but he might not have been there for all that his presence mattered. He was not even an island in this restless little sea; he was just a piece of flotsam on it, drifting in place, going nowhere. But the beer was cold, and it eased the scratchy dryness in his throat. It made him want another, and the second made him want a cigarette, the first smoke he'd craved all day.

After a time his glass was empty and so was the bottle beside it. One more? No, he thought. That's the trap, remember? One leads to two leads to too many. He wasn't out to get drunk tonight, and he'd better not be out to get drunk any other night from now on, either. That was what had landed him in that nightmare with Juleen.

All right. He pushed off the stool, went past the mirrors, still without looking at his reflection, and out into the lobby again. He gave Mona's room one more try on a house phone, but there was still no answer. She had probably gone somewhere by herself for dinner. So the thing for him to do was to follow suit—find a cafe or restaurant, get something to eat. It was almost seven o'clock.

Two more hours until the Creole Grocery closes, he thought.

Two more hours until deadline.

He wasn't hungry; if he tried to eat anything, it would turn to acid in his stomach and come boiling right back out of him. He left the hotel, walked up Gravier a ways. Turned on Basin Street and crossed Canal. Ahead of him, after a couple of blocks, were the high whitewashed brick walls of St. Louis Cemetery No. 1, one of two block-square "cities of the dead" on St. Louis Street—the other, No. 2, was a few blocks away at North Claiborn—and several in the city that the chamber of commerce deemed historically interesting enough to write up in their brochures. Most of New Orleans had been built at sea level and the water table lay within three feet of the surface; graves dug in the ground flooded before coffins could be lowered into them and buried, so a law had been passed in the early 1800s that all bodies had to be interred above ground in vaults or mausoleums or what were quaintly called "ovens." The outer walls of the St. Louis cemeteries were comprised of rows of attached ovens, stacked one above another in a beehive effect. Inside, the two- and three-tiered tombs were laid out in a haphazard maze without plan or design, standing so close together that you had to squeeze between them in order to get to certain ones. All sorts of Creole gentry were buried there, as well as Marie Laveau, the Voodoo Queen . . .

The facts roamed across his mind as he passed. But when they came to Marie Laveau and voodoo, they veered back to Juleen, the Legba staff and the looming snake in her wall painting and the *gris-gris* she had tried to give him in Père Lafon's. He could hear the imaginary drumbeat again, faint and pulsing, like echoes in the valleys of his mind. Boudoum, boudoum. Danse Calinda, boudoum, boudoum.

Voodoo. Cemeteries. Symbols of death and madness everywhere he looked. For a man with no imagination, he told himself, you're doing just fine. But it wasn't funny. Nothing was funny any more. He pulled his jacket collar tight around his neck, hurried past the entrance gate to St. Louis No. 1 without glancing inside. Enough symbolism. Enough cities of the dead.

He kept walking. Came to Beauregard Square, where the Municipal Auditorium blazed with light. That was where each of the krewes held their masquerade balls; Masque of Bacchus tonight. Beauregard Square. Used to be called Congo Square, in the 1800s, because blacks congregated there to make music and dance and practice voodoo rites . . . and enough voodoo, damn it! He went down to North Rampart and continued east, keeping his mind empty. Every block or so he would pause and glance behind him, trying to seem casual about it. No one he saw resembled a dragon.

When he reached Esplanade Avenue he stopped again and stood hunched against the wind for a time. Then he crossed to the south and went down Esplanade, walking slowly, looking at the buildings on both sides of the street. A wooden sign hanging from the gallery roof of a place just off Royal was what he was looking for; it said *Creole Grocery* in faded black letters.

He went past it to Royal, hesitated, and then came back and entered the grocery without thinking about what he was doing. It looked like any neighborhood grocery in any city: close-packed shelves, a counter at the near end, poor lighting. And it smelled like any grocery, too: dust, cheese, spices, cold meat. There was nobody in it except for an old man who looked more Italian than Creole, sitting on a stool behind the counter and watching a program on a tiny portable television.

Giroux went to the counter. The elderly storekeeper looked up from the television, not without reluctance, and peered at him through a pair of bifocals. He said, "Yes?" in a gravelly Italianate voice.

"I'm trying to find a man named Chalmette," Giroux said. "He asked me to leave something here for him—an envelope—but I don't have what he wants."

"Only Chalmettes I know are in the graveyard."

"What?"

"Killed in the Battle of New Orleans." The old man gave him a yellow-dentured grin. *"Una facezia.* Just a little joke."

"You don't know anybody named Chalmette?"

"Not personally."

"Did anyone tell you I'd be coming in?"

"What's your name?"

"Giroux. Steven Giroux."

"Never heard of you."

"Did anyone say anything about an envelope?"

"No. Not to me."

"Maybe to somebody else who works here?"

"Nobody else works here. I own this store and I'm the only employee I got. Been that way twenty-eight years, it'll be that way until I die or the Mafia runs me out."

"Mafia?"

"Rents going up all the time," the old man said. "Shop owners in the heart of the Quarter, they got to pay up to six thousand dollars a month these days. Most buildings the Mafia owns, *capito?* They want to build a gambling center in New Orleans; that's why they're driving up the prices. They'll do it, too, the *maiale.* One of these days."

"But you don't have any dealings with the Mafia?"

"Not me, mister. I hate the Siciliano bastards. They give all Italians a bad name, and they're not even Italians. If you ask me, the government ought to—"

Giroux said, "Thanks, I'm sorry I bothered you," and hurried out onto the *banquette* again.

The man in the dragon mask was leaning against a lamppost across Esplanade Avenue.

Giroux saw him immediately, and he was startled enough to feel a pang of fear. But all night he had expected to see the dragon, all night he had steeled himself for it; it was not much of a surprise. He stayed where he was in front of the grocery, looking across the crowded thoroughfare. It was the same man, all right—the same ugly mask, the same black trousers and black turtleneck sweater. He stared back at Giroux, or seemed to; it was difficult to tell with the mask and the lamplit darkness and the rush of cars between them.

Neither of them moved for twenty or thirty seconds. Then Giroux gathered himself and went down to Royal, and when the light changed at the intersection he cut straight across Esplanade and came up onto the *banquette* near where the dragon stood his ground next to the lamp-post.

"I don't have the photograph you're after," he said. The words came out like bricks, heavy and hard but brittle at the edges. "You can follow me from now until dooms-day, but I don't have any photograph."

The man didn't move, didn't speak. The look of him was somehow implacable, and it was not just the mask that made him seem that way. It was his posture, and his silence, and the evident power in his body and his big, muscle-bunched hands.

Giroux wanted to say something else—plead, shout, make him understand—but he had no more words. They had dried up inside him, old bricks crumbling away to dust. He backed away, turned away, and recrossed Esplanade without waiting for the light to change, dodging between cars. He went up to Bourbon Street, along it into the Quarter without looking back.

He turned into the first bar he came to, shoved through a knot of patrons to the bar and ordered a beer. He wanted vodka but he ordered beer, and when it came he forced himself to drink it slowly. It was like shoring up a weakened levee with sandbags during a storm. Each time a crack appeared, you plugged it the best way you could. And hoped that it was strong enough to hold out, and that the storm did not get any worse.

When he left the bar he expected to see the dragon somewhere nearby. But there was no sign of him. He lit a cigarette, tugged his jacket collar up again, and made his way toward the Pirate's Head.

He was a half-block away, on Ursuline, when he saw the apparition.

There was a crowd of revelers coming down from Burgundy, twenty or thirty of them forming an impromptu parade. One of the group was playing "When the Saints Go Marchin' In" on a trumpet and the rest were singing at the tops of their voices. The apparition was at the rear of the pack, near the corner, arms upraised, swaying in time to the music—dressed all in white, with a white ten-gallon cowboy hat cocked at a jaunty angle.

The impact on him was physical. He stopped and gawked, and the breath clogged in his lungs. When he could make his body respond he started out into the street, not looking anywhere except at the ten-gallon hat. He didn't see the car until the headlights pinned him, the horn blared an angry warning, tires shrieked on the pavement. The car swerved and he jumped back reflexively; metal slashed past him so close that the wind it created spun him half around. A furious face poked through the open driver's window, scalding him with words: "You stupid son of a bitch! You trying to get yourself killed?"

But he wasn't listening. He ran around behind the taxi, ran up onto the *banquette.* The revelers had broken ranks, stopped making their music; they were watching him and the taxi and they dodged aside as if they thought him drunk or deranged when he pushed in among them. The ten-gallon hat was no longer there. He ran to the corner, turned it, looked along the teeming *banquettes* on both sides of Burgundy. Not there, either. Not anywhere. Gone.

As if she had never been.

But she *had* been, he had seen her. Hadn't he? Dressed all in white, wearing the ten-gallon hat. Dancing in an impromptu parade, singing "When the Saints Go Marchin' In." Not an apparition—real, alive.

Juleen.

PART III
COLLOP MONDAY

Then, summoning the wild courage of despair, a throng of the revellers at once threw themselves into the black apartment, and, seizing the mummer, whose tall figure stood erect and motionless within the shadow of the ebony clock, gasped in unutterable horror at finding the grave cerements and corpselike mask, which they handled with so violent a rudeness, untenanted by any tangible form.

—EDGAR ALLAN POE
"The Masque of the Red Death"

TWELVE

Rain.

He stood at the window, dressed in his robe, and stared bleary eyed at the gray sky, at the droplets streaking the narrow glass and beating into the courtyard below. It was a little past 7:00 A.M. and it was the eighth time he had been out of bed in the past two hours. He had not slept much during the night; he kept waiting for the telephone to ring, a knock on the door, the scrape of a key or a pick in the latch. But none of those things had happened. Nothing had happened. Nobody had been waiting for him when he returned last night, nobody had paid him a visit in the anxious two hours between nine and eleven, when he finally went to bed. And there had been nothing on the ten o'clock TV news about Juleen or any sort of violent crime in the Irish Channel.

Was she dead or was she alive?

Had he seen her last night or hadn't he?

The questions kept torturing him, falling against the surfaces of his mind like measured beads of water. He had been sure at the time that it was Juleen, but now he was not

115

sure. Everything about yesterday, the past two days, seemed remote, fragmented, as if they were bits and pieces of the Lara dream that had plagued him again this past night.

He thought again that maybe all of it *was* hallucination, chimera, the product of a bruised mind. No Juleen, no voodoo, no blood, no death, no dragon, no threatening calls, no photograph. Just . . . madness. It was all around him in the city; it could have triggered a string of delusions, couldn't it? Pushed him over the edge, turned him into a walking bundle of psychoses?

Then he thought: No, it happened, I didn't imagine it.

He pivoted from the window, went into the bathroom. The face that stared back at him from the mirror was haggard, tinged with a grayish pallor. He could see the bones under the drawn skin, the outlines of his skull—and across his consciousness flashed the nightmare image of the grinning skulls with blood dripping out of their eye sockets, just before they crumbled away into shrieking dust. He wrenched his head down, thrust it under the cold-water tap, and spun the handle. He kept it there until the iciness of the water made him shiver.

As he shaved he asked himself, not for the first time, if he could find his way back to Juleen's house. But the answer was still the same: No, not likely. He had been too drunk to remember the address she'd given the taxi driver on Saturday night; too panic-stricken to look at the exterior of the house when he ran out of it on Sunday morning, or at any of the neighboring houses, or at any of the street signs. Those minutes of his flight were all blurred, jumbled together in his memory. He didn't even have an idea of how far he'd run, how many blocks or from what direction, before he collapsed in the park on Tchoupitoulas.

Yet finding the house seemed to be the only way he could get to the truth of what had happened—if Juleen was still alive, the blood, what might be down in that cellar. Was there another way to find the house? He couldn't just look up Juleen in the telephone directory; he hadn't bothered to ask her last name and she hadn't volunteered the information . . .

A sudden thought struck him. He had met her *here,* down in the courtyard; and the day before that, when the airport taxi let him off in front, she had been sitting on the stoop across the street. And assuming he had seen her last night, it had been only a half-block from the hotel. It could be she frequented this part of the Quarter regularly. Maybe someone on the Pirate's Head staff knew her, knew where she lived or at least could supply her last name.

The prospect made him hurry to finish shaving, hurry to get dressed. He took the elevator downstairs and went to the desk. The clerk was a heavyset young man with sandy hair and an apple-round face that looked shiny red, as if he had spent time polishing it before coming to work. Giroux asked him if he knew a girl named Juleen. The clerk said he was sorry, no. Giroux described her, said that she had been having a glass of wine in the courtyard on Friday afternoon. The clerk had been too busy to notice, he said, and wasn't familiar with any woman of that description.

A bellboy emerged from one of the elevators, pushing an empty luggage truck. Giroux moved over to him, asked the same questions he had asked the clerk and offered the same description of Juleen. But the result was the same: headshakes and negatives.

He asked the bellboy where his counterpart was— there were two of them on duty at all times; he remembered hearing that just after he checked in—and was told he was upstairs somewhere. Giroux sat in one of the lobby chairs and stared at the muskets and the Jolly Roger over the fireplace and waited for the second bellboy to come down. There was nobody else to talk to at the moment. It was too early for either the restaurant or the lounge to be open, or for their staff to have reported for work. And he would have to wait until four o'clock before the night clerk and bellboys came on.

Fifteen minutes passed before the second bellboy appeared. And three minutes after that, Giroux had another set of headshakes and negatives to cope with.

He went outside. The rain had slackened into a misty drizzle and jigsaw shapes of blue showed here and there in the overcast, like color patches on a gray quilt. There was not much wind; it seemed warmer than it had last night, with a faint mugginess in the air. He looked both ways along Burgundy, down Ursuline, at the crumbling buildings nearby. There were no dragon masks anywhere, no women in ten-gallon hats.

He walked down Ursuline until he came to a cafe. Out front were several machines that dispensed newspapers, and he found enough change in his pocket to buy a copy of the morning *Times-Picayune.* Inside, the cafe was already crowded but he found a stool at the counter and claimed it. Coffee was all he wanted, despite small pangs of hunger; but he made himself order a couple of the squarish sugared doughnuts called *beignets* to go with it. Then he went over the paper carefully, page by page.

No mention of anyone named Juleen. A man had been knifed to death in the suburb of Metairie, but he was identified as a cocaine dealer and police suspected the homicide was drug related. There was nothing else of even remote possibility.

It should have relieved him, but it didn't. The nagging doubt remained: Suppose no one had found the body yet? Suppose it was still down there in the cellar?

He ate his *beignets,* drank his coffee, paid his bill. When he went outside again the rain had stopped altogether and the sun was trying to come out. Refuse from the night's merrymaking littered the gutters; a man in a clown's costume was sleeping propped up in a sheltered doorway, with urine stains all over the front of his baggy trousers. The odors of liquor, candy, garbage were sharp after the rain; he could feel the weight of the doughnuts in his stomach as he walked back to the Pirate's Head.

Collop Monday, he thought. The day before Shrove Tuesday, the day of the Krewe of Proteus, King of the Briny Deep. How was he going to spend it? Go photographing in the Quarter? Wait around the hotel for something to happen, maybe try to call Paul again later on?

No, damn it, he told himself. You're going to do something positive. Play detective, as you started to do a little while ago. Get on the St. Charles streetcar and find the park on Tchoupitoulas and try to locate some familiar landmarks that would lead to Juleen's house. Go to Père Lafon's, if it was open in the daytime, and ask the people who worked there if they knew Juleen. It hadn't seemed on Saturday night that she was known; he couldn't remember anyone hailing her when they entered, anyone talking to her, any sign of recognition on the waitress's face. But he had been occupied with his own thoughts, his own demons, and all he'd really been aware of had been his need for a drink.

There was resolve in him when he reached the hotel. Up to his room so he could exchange his overcoat for his jacket—it kept getting warmer, now that the sun was out—and to catch one more radio newscast, and then on his way. Père Lafon's first, the Irish Channel second. He entered the lobby, started across to the elevators.

"Mr. Giroux."

He stopped and turned. The polished-apple clerk was gesturing to him from behind the desk.

"What is it?" he asked.

"Package for you, sir."

"Package?"

"Yes, sir."

He went to the desk. The clerk had swung around to the shelf under the mail cubbyholes; when he turned back again, Giroux saw that he was holding a parcel wrapped in brown paper. It was smallish—a foot long, half that much in width, and maybe six inches deep—and it looked light, judging from the way the clerk held it easily in one hand.

The clerk put it down on the desk. Giroux's name and room number, and the name of the Pirate's Head, had been block-lettered on the paper with a black felt-tip pen. There were no other markings.

"This came about fifteen minutes ago," the clerk said.

"Who delivered it? There aren't any stamps."

"Oh, it wasn't the mailman. A deliveryman brought it."

"What deliveryman?"

"I didn't really notice. He was wearing a cap—the kind all deliverymen wear. Is it important, sir?"

"I don't know," he said. He stared at the package. The dougnuts were still congealing in his stomach; he felt a faint queasiness. "Did he say who it was from?"

"No, I'm afraid not."

He picked it up. Light, yes; it didn't seem to weigh more than a few ounces. He wet his lips. "All right, thanks. I'll open it in my room."

The clerk gave him an odd look. "Yes, sir. It's your package."

He carried the parcel into one of the elevators, stood staring at it some more as the car ascended. Who would be sending him a package? The man on the phone, Chalmette? But why? Unless—

Jesus, he thought, a *bomb?*

The car jolted to a stop and the doors opened. He didn't move. The hallway was silent; he was surrounded by silence. He lifted the package, gingerly, and put his ear against it and listened. More silence. Then he had a mental image of himself, standing in the elevator, listening to a package, and the whole idea of a bomb struck him abruptly as ridiculous. Why would they want to blow him up? They thought he had something they wanted, the mystery photograph; they'd come after him sooner or later, confront him, maybe even attack him, but they wouldn't send him a bomb.

They. Who were *they?* The Mafia?

Madness . . .

The doors started to close again. He jabbed the Door Open button, stepped out into the hallway and hurried down to his room. Inside, he set the package on the table. Kept looking at it as he shrugged out of his coat.

The block lettering on the paper seemed to have been done by a masculine hand. And the only men who knew he was in New Orleans, staying at this hotel, were Chalmette and the dragon. So it had to be from them. But not a bomb. A bomb would have weight. Dynamite was heavy; any kind of explosive device was bound to have weight, wasn't it?

Stop diddling yourself, he thought. Open the damned thing and find out.

He picked up the package again, shook it gently. Something wobbled inside; he thought he heard the rustle of tissue paper. He brushed the back of one hand across his mouth, and when he set the parcel down this time he began to tear off the brown wrapping paper. Inside it was a cardboard box, like a shoebox, with the lid fastened down with cellophane tape. He broke the tape loose, backed off a half-step so that his body was arched into a crooked question mark, tense, ready to leap away, and then eased the lid up. Nothing happened. He took the lid off, set it aside. Tissue paper. With the tips of his fingers he spread it so that he could see what it encased.

It was a doll—a voodoo *gris-gris*.

Not like the one Juleen had shown him in Père Lafon's; this one was larger, better made. A male doll, molded of soft clay, dressed with bits of black cloth cut to resemble trousers and a shirt. Glued to the bulbous head was a curl of real hair the same color as his own; the eyes were a pair of black beads and the mouth was a slash of red paint. Around the neck was a strip of red yarn, tied like a kerchief . . . or maybe a noose.

He stood motionless for several seconds. The doll looked as ugly, as repulsive as would a severed finger or a dead animal. Finally he reached out with his left hand, picked it up. He didn't want to touch it, but the deadly fascination it held for him was magnetic. And he could see that under it was a sheet of white typing paper folded lengthwise—a note of some kind.

He held the doll up, turned it to glance at the backside. Then, with his right hand, he picked up the sheet of paper.

Something wet began to trickle down over his left wrist. Sweat. He paid no attention to it. When he got the paper open he saw that there was printing on it in the same block letters, with the same felt-tip pen, as on the outer wrapping. The printing read:

THIS WILL HAPPEN TO YOU.
L'APPÉ VINI, LE GRAND ZOMBI
L'APPÉ VINI, POL FÉ MOURI!
                    PAPA LÀ-BAS

More sweat flowed on his left wrist. Too much sweat. He looked at it this time, and what he saw made him recoil so violently that he sprawled backward onto the bed.

The wetness on his wrist was not sweat; it was blood. Bright fresh blood that came trickling out from under the fetish's clothes.

The doll was *bleeding* . . .

THIRTEEN

HE hurled the thing away from him. Droplets of blood spattered the air, the curtains as the doll banged against the window glass and then fell to the carpet. The head broke off; he could see it roll under the table, its black-bead eyes winking in the lamplight. The painted mouth looked as though it were screaming.

He stared at the crimson streaks on his hand and forearm, and it was like reliving the scene yesterday morning in Juleen's bedroom. He wheeled into the bathroom, ran cold water, scrubbed the blood off his skin and off the cuff of his shirt. When he finished he was panting as though he'd run a long distance.

Dolls don't bleed, he thought. It's a trick of some kind. Dolls don't bleed.

He went out and over to the table; his legs felt loose, boneless, like stalks made of rubber. The headless corpus of the fetish was bleeding into the carpet, the blood leaking out through the hole where the head had been. He caught up a piece of the brown wrapping that was still on the table, used it to pick up the doll. Then he rotated them in his hand so that the paper was under the thing and absorbing the

123

outspill. He set them down on the table.

It took him less than thirty seconds to find out how the trick had been worked. The doll was hollow from neck to groin, and inside the hollow, suspended from the shoulders on hooks molded into the clay, was a thin condom tied off at the top. It was the condom that had contained the blood. Poking through the doll's chest and back were four short pins, points filed sharp, flattened heads concealed under the shirt and trousers. When he had picked up the doll the pressure of his hand had pushed the pins further through the clay, so that the sharpened points penetrated the condom and released the blood. It had flowed out of the cavity and onto him through half a dozen tiny holes in the groin, legs, and hips.

Ingenious little trick. Diabolical.

This will happen to you.

A warning. But from who? Chalmette and the dragon? Or Juleen? She was a voodoo worshiper; he had heard and seen enough evidence of that. But she was dead—or was she? And if she wasn't, why would she want to send him a malicious thing like this bleeding doll?

He picked up the doll's head, wrapped it with the corpus and the paper, and stuffed it back inside the box. Then he put the lid on and the box into a wastebasket in the bathroom. He got a towel and soaked it in cold water. There was a lot of blood to clean up—the big stain on the carpet, the spatters on the window curtains and on the glass and elsewhere—and it took him the better part of half an hour. He didn't think while he did it; his mind switched off and he worked like an automaton. Most of the stains came out all right, but not the big one on the carpet. That one looked like a map of California, long and narrow and slightly bent in the middle, and he could not seem to eradicate it. Blurred its borders but that was all. At length he moved the table a few feet so that its rounded base covered most of California, with only a little of the San Diego area peeking out to one side.

He ran more cold water into the bathroom sink, scrubbed the bloody towel in it and left it there to soak. When he came out this time he saw the sheet of white paper lying on the floor near the bed's headboard. It must have fallen out of his hand when he saw the doll bleeding on him. He caught it up and looked at it again.

L'Appé vini, le Grand Zombi
L'Appé vini, pol fé mouri!

What was it—French? Creole? Or some bastardized voodoo dialect? Grand Zombi. Zombies, the walking dead of Haitian legend. Maybe it was a threat to turn him into a white zombie. A giggle slithered out of him. *White Zombie.* Old Bela Lugosi movie, about an evil plantation owner in Haiti; he'd seen it on television not too long ago, on one of those nights when he couldn't sleep. High camp. Funny, except that it wasn't. They were out there, all right. Not zombies, not Papa Là-bas, but bogeymen just the same. Better not laugh. There were all kinds of bogeymen in the world these days.

He folded the paper carefully and put it into his trouser pocket. His shirt sleeve was still wet; he took the shirt off and put another one on. Put his jacket on. Emptied the reddish water out of the sink and ran fresh in on top of the towel.

The telephone rang.

He stood rigidly, listening as it rang again . . . a third time. Then he thought: Uh-uh, not this time, no way. And went to the door and opened it and stepped into the hall. He shut the door against the jingling noise, moved past the elevators and took the stairs down to the lobby.

Outside, the sun was shining and people were out in droves and Carnival sounds rolled across the sky. He walked until he found himself in front of Père Lafon's. It was open and doing a brisk business for a Monday morning. But this was Collop Monday, and he remembered, now, that few places in the Vieux Carré ever closed during Mardi Gras week.

Up on the dais inside, a three-piece combo was doing a version of "Jazz Me Blues." He barely heard the music. He went to the bar, and when he got the bartender's attention he asked about Juleen. The bartender was a jazz buff; he kept snapping his fingers in time to the beat. Never heard of her, mister, he said. Giroux buttonholed a harassed-looking waitress. Sorry, I don't know anyone named Juleen. Another waitress. Sorry. He thought about going from table to table, asking the patrons for information like a beggar after change. Instead he went out into the fresh air and began to walk again.

There were bookstores on Royal Street, new and used both; he had seen them during his earlier wandering. He entered the first one he came to, but they didn't have much of anything on voodoo. Neither did the second. But the third one did—a small section of books, most of them at least thirty years old. He spent ten minutes looking through them before he found an explanation for the two lines on the message that had come with the doll.

They were part of an old Creole song about Marie Laveau, which boasted of how much voodoo power she possessed. Le Grand Zombi had nothing to do with dead men resurrected from the grave; it was the chief god of the voodoo religion, the holy serpent otherwise known as Damballah. The loose translation of the two lines, according to one of the books, was: "He is coming, the Grand Zombi. He is coming and he brings death."

Giroux left the store, went all the way down to Decatur to avoid the crush of people in the heart of the Quarter, and pointed himself toward Canal. Inside was a feeling of detachment—a vague awareness that he was still functioning like an automaton, with his mind half-switched off. As if the shock of the bleeding doll had driven all the emotion out of him, or crowded it back into a corner of himself. Overload of feeling. Short circuit. Not good if it lasted too long; you could withdraw too far. But for a while it was good. Like a shot of Novocain to numb an aching tooth.

On St. Charles Avenue he boarded a jammed streetcar and rode it out to where he dimly remembered getting on yesterday morning. Then he walked southeast until he found the park on Tchoupitoulas. Kids were playing there, some of them black, but none resembled the pair he'd talked to. If they'd been around, he could have asked them which direction he had come running from. He thought it might have been from the south, but the details of his flight continued to be a jumbled smear in his memory.

He went six blocks south, turned left, and came back the six blocks along another street. Nothing looked familiar. The houses were all small, modest, shaded by trees, guarded by fences and shrubbery and dogs, some of them ramshackle, some belonging to blacks and some to whites, with older-model cars in the driveways and parked on the street.

He kept trying to jog his memory. He seemed to recall trees—several trees in the vicinity of Juleen's house. But what kind they were escaped him. There were a lot of live oaks growing along the sidewalks; those in the yards were of fifty different varities. And every yard seemed to have one or two or more. What color was Juleen's house? He couldn't remember. Did it have a fence around it? He seemed to recall going through a gate. Did it have a front porch? Yes: he had seen part of an elevated porch through the window when he first entered the living room. Yet nearly all the houses he passed had fences and porches. What about the neighboring houses? He hadn't noticed them in his panic. Characteristics of the street itself? He hadn't noticed.

He walked up one street, down another, and saw nothing that struck a familiar chord, remembered nothing more about Juleen's house. It was almost four o'clock when he gave it up and sank onto one of the benches in the park. The sun was gone; the sky looked restless again, presaging more rain, and there was a light wind blowing in off the Mississippi. The day had a faded gray look. So did his surroundings, as if all the color was slowly being bleached out of the trees and houses.

The detachment had faded out of his mind, too. He was thinking again, and he felt lost, trapped, desperately alone. The only option that seemed left to him now was to pack up and leave New Orleans as soon as possible. Tonight, if he could get a flight. Tomorrow morning at the latest. If he stayed, Christ knew what might happen. Blood on his hands a third time, maybe—his own blood. And yet leaving was running away; ultimately he would regret it. Even if the police didn't come after him, even if the photograph hunters left him alone in San Francisco, he would never know what had really happened to him here. And the mystery, along with his own cowardice, would haunt him for the rest of his days.

He couldn't make a decision. He still needed someone to confide in, someone to help him decide what was right. He just did not have the equipment to deal with a major crisis, to be a loser in this world he had never made. Guidance, direction, reassurance—those were all vital to him. He was the ultimate social animal. Alone in the jungle, he stood damned little chance of survival because he was not one of the fittest. It was painful to have to admit these truths, but then the truth was often painful.

He left the park, started back toward St. Charles. On Magazine Street, a thoroughfare bulging with antique shops and junk stores, he found a bar and grill that had a private phone booth. Inside the booth, with two dollars in change, he put through a long-distance call to Paul Daniels's office in San Francisco.

But Paul wasn't there. His secretary said that he had gone to San Diego on Saturday to "meet with a client," which was a euphemism for a tryst with a woman, and wasn't expected back until Wednesday evening. No, she didn't have a San Diego number for him. But there was the possibility he might check in, if Giroux wanted to leave a number where he could be reached.

Giroux gave her the number of the Pirate's Head and told her to have Paul get in touch with him as soon as possible. But he didn't hold much hope that that would happen. When Paul was away somewhere with a woman he seldom gave much thought to business or friends.

Nothing going right, he thought as he left the bar and grill. Everything piling up against him, walling him off. Now he had nobody to talk to. Now he was completely alone—

Mona, he thought.

Could he talk to her? Could he tell her what had been happening to him? Would she understand, or would she think he was a dangerous lunatic and betray him to the police? It was Mona or no one. And he could make up his mind when he saw her. Whether he confided in her or not, at least she was a friendly face, someone to offer him solace for a few hours.

On the way to St. Charles he bought a copy of the afternoon paper, the *States-Item.* He read it on the streetcar ride uptown. Still no clue to whether Juleen was alive or dead.

And if she was alive, what about the smell that had come to him out of her cellar yesterday morning? He had not been wrong about that; he remembered it more clearly than anything else. It had been the unmistakable odor of blood and death.

If Juleen was alive, who was dead in her cellar?

FOURTEEN

Two mimes with white-painted faces were putting on a show in front of the Mason House. A noisy crowd, most of them kids and teenagers, had gathered to watch; Giroux could hear them shouting and laughing some distance away. One of the mimes carried a belt sack of candy and other favors, and he dipped into it as Giroux pushed his way through, tossed a handful in his direction. A piece of hard candy glanced off the side of his head; a fat teenager chasing after another piece elbowed him sharply, perhaps deliberately, in the ribs. He gritted his teeth, ran up the hotel steps. Carnival fun. Mimes and children—and violence.

He was on his way to the house phones when he saw Mona. She was just emerging from one of the elevators, alone, wearing a wine-colored pantsuit but no coat, and carrying a big gaping shoulder purse. He changed direction and approached her, and when she saw him her face blossomed into a smile. It had warmth in it, that smile; it said she was glad to see him. But when he stopped in front of her and she had a good look at him, a kind of solemnity came into her eyes. He did not need a mirror to know that the strain was naked on him.

"Steven, hello. What brings you here?"

"You," he said. "I thought I'd see if you were in."

"That's a nice surprise. I've been hoping you'd call."

"Well, I did call, last night. But you were out."

"I went to dinner and a show. As a matter of fact, I phoned you, too, when I got back. And again a little while ago. We seem to have kept missing each other, until now."

"Are you going somewhere?"

"Not really. I was just about to have a cocktail."

"I'll join you, if it's all right."

"Of course. I'm glad I didn't come down five minutes ago. We might have missed each other again."

"So am I."

They didn't go into the Steamer Lounge, where he'd been last night; instead Mona led him around an ell to a lobby bar partitioned off with potted palms and azalea plants. The furniture was nineteenth-century French in style—marble-topped tables, marquise settees and chairs. It reminded him a little of the lobby bar in the St. Francis Hotel in San Francisco.

They ordered drinks—a beer for him, a brandy old-fashioned for Mona—and then sat in companionable silence for a time, getting to know each other a little better with their eyes. It was the first time he had looked beyond the superficial arrangement of her features, and what he saw reassured him. There was strength in her; he could see it in the way she held herself, in the steady dark-hazel eyes. He imagined that it was almost an effluvium, like the subtlest of perfumes. She was not the kind of person who would go to pieces in a crisis; she would meet it head on, attack it, resolve it one way or another. That was what he wanted to believe, at least.

He couldn't tell what she was thinking of him. She kept

her own emotions clothed, private. She sat with her hands folded on the table in front of her, favoring him with the small warm smile. He had a vague impression of a cat: she could probably sit like that for long minutes, if not hours —calm, patient, relaxed, in perfect command of herself. She seemed to be his exact opposite, and that made her exactly the type of person he needed right now.

From his shirt pocket he took his cigarettes and matches. The motion of his hands seemed to break the mood of silence; as he lit the last cigarette in the pack, she said, "What's troubling you, Steven?" in a quiet voice that carried traces of concern.

"Pretty obvious, huh?"

"Yes. Pretty obvious. Yesterday and today both."

"It's a long story—complicated. And it doesn't make much sense."

"Does it have to do with the breakup of your marriage?"

"No. Not really."

"Do you want to talk about it?"

"I don't know if I should."

"I'm a good listener," she said.

"You've never heard anything like this."

"You make it sound mysterious."

"Macabre would be a better word."

A faint frown marred the translucent skin of her forehead. "Are you in some kind of trouble? Is that it?"

"I seem to be. But I don't know why."

"With the police?"

"Maybe. Others, too."

"Others?"

"I don't know who they are. Or what they want from me."

The frown deepened for a moment, then abruptly smoothed away. Mona unfolded her hands and leaned toward him, but before she could say anything their drinks arrived. Neither of them spoke until after they had lifted their glasses—Mona taking a small sip of the old-fashioned, he swallowing a third of his beer.

She said then, "Steven, are you going to tell me what you're involved in?"

"I'm trying to decide. It might frighten you."

"I've been frightened before. Have you . . . done something wrong?"

"You mean committed a crime? I don't think so."

"How can you not be sure?"

"Because it's all crazy." He drank more beer. "Crazy," he said again.

"Does it have to do with that girl you were with on Saturday night?"

"Yes. Partly."

"Something that happened while you were intoxicated?"

"Partly."

"Steven . . ."

"It makes *me* look crazy," he said, and then paused. "I'm afraid that's what you'll think."

"You're not crazy."

"You haven't heard the story yet."

"Look, Steven, you need someone to talk to about this, that's obvious." No impatience in her voice; no uneasiness. She wasn't afraid of him or of anything he might tell her. At least not now. "I'm here and I'm willing to listen. Maybe I can help. I will if I can."

"Why? We're practically strangers."

"Yes. But I could ask you the same question. Why would you think of confiding in me? You must have thought of it or you wouldn't be here like this, talking the way you have been."

"I don't know anyone else in New Orleans," he said.

"Is that the only reason?"

"I . . . no, I guess not. I felt you were the kind of person who might understand. I felt . . ." He broke off, shaking his head. Words wouldn't come to him; he couldn't explain what he'd felt because he really did not know himself.

Mona said, "It's a rapport. Two people meet and find that they can relate, they're sympathetic to each other. I like you, Steven. And I want to know you better, help you if you're in trouble."

He finished his beer, sat silent again listening to the murmur of conversation around them. A middle-aged couple took the table immediately to their left; the woman, a heavily made-up bottle blonde in a flashy silver gown, positioned her chair within a few feet of Mona's—close enough to hear anything above a whisper. She gave Mona the cold, disdainful look of the faded and plain for the young and attractive. The eavesdropper type. You could almost see her ears twitch.

"Okay," he said at length. "But not here. It's too crowded here. Somewhere where we can be alone."

Mona nodded.

"Your room?" he said.

She hesitated this time, and the sudden thought came to him that she might be misinterpreting his suggestion. He started to touch her hand, to reassure her, but then he realized that she might misinterpret that too. He put both palms flat on the table; they were sweating and he could feel them sticky against the cold marble.

"I'm not making a pass at you," he said *sotto voce*, "if that's what you're thinking. I only meant—"

Her reaction surprised him: the smile again, more solicitous than anything else, and she reached out and touched his hand, briefly, with her fingertips. "That wasn't what I was thinking," she said. "I'm not worried about that.

I was thinking that my room is quite small and not very comfortable."

The bottle blonde was looking at them; he could see her disapproving face at the edge of his vision. He turned his head and glared at her. She glared back at him, prim and hard eyed; her face, seen straight on, was like a dried apricot caked with talcum powder. He looked back at Mona again.

"We could go somewhere else," he said.

"No. There's more privacy upstairs than anywhere else."

He motioned to the waitress, got the bill, paid it. The blonde was still staring at them, holding a martini between thumb and forefinger, poised just below her overpainted lips. When Mona stood up her hip bumped sharply against the blonde's chair, jarred her hand and sloshed gin down the front of her silver gown.

"Oh I'm so sorry," Mona said. "How clumsy of me."

The woman bared her teeth and made spluttering noises. The man with her seemed to be struggling between indignation and amusement.

Mona took Giroux's arm and they went out of the lounge. He said, "Did you do that on purpose? Spill her drink?"

"She had it coming. Did you see the way she was looking at us?"

"I saw."

"I hate women like that. Insufferable bitches, every one of them."

Like Lara, he thought. The bitch among bitches. Another fifteen or twenty years and Lara would be just like the blonde, sitting in hotel lounges, overdressed to the nines, glaring at younger people, all sanctimony and disapproval at the same sort of things she'd once done herself. Now that he thought about it, she'd exhibited tendencies in that direction throughout their marriage. Poor Marcie, having to grow up in that kind of shadow. But Marcie was adaptable —unlike him, a survivalist; she'd be okay. And Lara would get hers someday, too, with any luck.

One of the lobby shops near the elevators was a combination newsstand and tobacconist, and as they passed it he remembered that he was out of cigarettes. He was going to need nicotine to help him get through his summary of the past two days; he'd better get some. He said as much to Mona, detoured into the shop, and met her again at the elevators. He was already tearing the fresh pack open when the car stopped at the ninth floor.

Mona's room was as small as she'd led him to believe —a rectangle just large enough to hold a bed, a dresser, a nightstand, a TV set, a small writing desk, and a single armchair. Two people could not have fit comfortably inside the bathroom at the same time. The drapes were drawn; Mona set her purse on the dresser, crossed to unveil the window. Dark, twilit sky. City lights off to one side. The view straight ahead was of another tall narrow building not far away, half of its windows showing light, half of them dark, so that it looked like a giant squared-off phallus decorated with a mosaic of black and yellow squares.

He looked away, looked at Mona. Giant phallus, he thought. Jesus.

She said, "Sit down, Steven. Take the chair; I'll sit on the bed."

He took the chair. Put a cigarette between his lips and lit it. Sucked in smoke, blew it out. Mona sat facing him, waiting, and again he was reminded of a cat. He had always liked cats because he admired their self-sufficiency, their imperturbability. That was Mona: imperturbable. She wouldn't get excited when she heard what he had to say. She wouldn't think him a dangerous lunatic, she wouldn't throw him out and right away get on the phone to the police. He was sure of that now.

He told her.

It took him twenty minutes, and by the time he was finished he had smoked four cigarettes, stripped off his jacket and opened his shirt, and was sodden with sweat. Mona said nothing the entire time, barely moved. He could see vestigial reaction on her face—surprise, puzzlement, anger; but no fear. For the most part, her expression remained the same: a kind of neutrality etched with concern. Imperturbable, yes. And strong. Strong.

When he said, "That's everything, as far as I know it," she stood and went slowly to the window. Looked out for a few seconds, then turned and came back to stand in front of him. Her eyes were grim.

"Poor Steven," she said gently.

"It's crazy, isn't it? Just like I told you."

"Yes. It's crazy."

"But *I'm* not crazy," he said. "No matter how wild it sounds. It's the truth, Mona, I swear it. I don't know what happened in Juleen's house but I didn't hurt her or anyone else. And I don't know anything about that photograph." He stood up, so that his face was closer to hers. "Do you believe me?"

"Of course I do."

"You're not just saying that?"

"I believe you, Steven," she said.

FIFTEEN

INSIDE him there were stirrings of relief. He felt almost purged. Her acceptance was like a whole truckload of sandbags at his beleaguered emotional levee—shoring up his courage, adding her strength to what was left of his. He no longer had to face the storm alone, and that made it a little less terrifying to deal with. She'd help him decide what to do. With her to depend on, he'd get out of this, weather it, find his way back into a world he understood and that bore him no personal malice.

Mona took his arm, tugged him down into the chair again. She said, "Do you still have the note that came with the doll?"

"I think so. My jacket pocket."

The jacket was lying on the bed. Mona picked it up, found the note, read the message. "The handwriting isn't at all familiar?" she asked.

"No."

"It looks like a man's printing."

"I thought so too."

"But you can't always tell. It might be a woman's."

"Juleen?"

"You said she was mixed up in voodoo, that she tried to give you another fetish on Friday night. The bleeding doll could be some of her work."

"If she's alive."

"She must be alive. You said you saw her."

"I thought I saw her. But I could be wrong about that. I was upset at the time and I only had a glimpse before she disappeared. It could have been some other woman in a ten-gallon hat, someone who resembled Juleen."

"Then why did she disappear so suddenly?"

Rhetorical question. He shook his head and lit another cigarette. "If it was Juleen I saw," he said, "then who was dead in her cellar yesterday?"

"Are you certain about . . . what you smelled?"

"Positive. Someone was dead down there."

"Maybe it was someone she killed herself."

"Why would Juleen kill anyone?"

"Why does anyone kill anyone else? There are reasons. It would explain the blood you found on your hands and arms."

"How would it?"

"She must have smeared it on you while you were unconscious. Or someone else did, if she was the victim."

"To make it look like I'd done it?"

"Yes."

"But then why wouldn't the police have been called right away? If they had been, they'd have found me there in bed and arrested me. No, it doesn't make sense that way either."

She sat facing him again. Her eyes were intense, alight with determination, like a fireglow glinting through greenish-brown glass. "Well, there has to be some explanation. And some connection between Juleen and the man, Chalmette, who keeps calling you about the photograph."

"Why do you say that?"

"I can't believe you could get mixed up in two separate horrors in three days. Can you?"

"I guess not," he admitted.

"Suppose," Mona said slowly, "suppose Chalmette thinks you got the photograph he wants from Juleen?"

That possibility hadn't occurred to him before. He sat up straighter, squinting through the smoke from his cigarette. "But she didn't give me a photograph. Why would he think she had?"

"It could be she was supposed to give it to you. Or threatened to for some reason." Mona paused. "She didn't give you anything else while you were with her, did she?"

Only her body, he thought. "No."

"Did she say anything about photographs or photography?"

"No."

"Not even a casual mention?"

"No. I told her I was a photographer when we first met, but that's the only time the subject came up."

"Could she have slipped something into your pocket or your wallet at any time?"

He shook his head. "I'd have found it by now if she had. Or they would—Chalmette or the dragon."

"They could be the same person, you know," Mona said.

"Yes, I thought of that. It's possible. I never heard the dragon's voice; he never spoke to me."

"Did Chalmette give you any clue what the photograph might be?"

"You mean what it depicts? No."

Mona was silent for a time. He watched her think; his own mind was empty, incapable of anything beyond stimulus-response. At length she said, "I keep thinking about the voodoo. What if the photograph has something to do with voodoo?"

"Why would a voodoo photograph be so important?"

"Blood sacrifices," Mona said meditatively. "That's one of the staples of voodoo worship."

"I don't see . . ."

"Goats or lambs or chickens; that's what they usually kill in their ceremonies. But in the old days, if you can believe what you read down here, some cults offered human instead of animal sacrifices. 'Goats without horns,' they were called."

"My God," he said. "A photograph of a human sacrifice?"

"Something like that, anyway. Otherwise, how does voodoo enter into it? Why did you get the bleeding doll and the message? They could *all* be voodoo worshipers—Juleen and Chalmette and anyone else who's involved."

He felt cold, as if his skin had been brushed with ice. "But they don't have cults like that anymore," he said. "Primitive voodoo rites haven't been practiced in fifty years or more."

"Haven't they? What about Charles Manson? Or those Zebra killings you had in San Francisco?"

"They didn't have anything to do with voodoo—"

"No, but it's the same principle. Devil cults, religious cults—there are secret organizations like that all over. You never hear about them until they do something really sick, like murdering Hollywood celebrities, and the police and the news media get on to them. A voodoo death cult *could* exist in New Orleans. Why couldn't one?"

"All right, maybe one could. But what would they want with me?"

Mona was silent.

"A goat without horns," he said, "is that it?"

"It's possible."

"No it isn't. No. If that was it, they'd have killed me by now. Sacrificed me or whatever." The words seemed to drift in the air, twisting and curling like the smoke from his cigarette; he imagined them shrieking, as the crumbling heads in his nightmare shrieked, only this time it was the shrieking of manical laughter. Two adults sitting here talking about voodoo sacrifices and goats without horns. Asylum humor: inmates swapping jokes in their padded cells. Or take it one step further: the Grim Reaper winking behind his goddamn scythe.

Mona was still silent, watching him.

"Besides," he said, "where does the photograph fit in? I don't have any photograph; I don't know anything about any photograph. And who's dead in Juleen's cellar? Another goat without horns? And why put the blood all over my hands? What's the point in that, if I'm going to have my throat cut in the name of Papa Là-bas or the Grand Zombi or whatever the hell deity they worship?"

"Steven, I don't have any definite answers." Calm. Reasonable. But it wasn't *her* they were talking about. "It could all be part of some filthy ritual. Or there could be something else involved, some unknown factor—something you've overlooked."

"I haven't overlooked anything."

"You can't be certain of that."

He felt the need of movement; the chair had become a confinement. He stood and tried to pace. But the room was too small; it was only eight paces to the window, eight paces back again. Animal in a cage, he thought. He stopped after two turns, leaned his hip against the dresser, and added the smoke from one more cigarette to the dryness in his mouth, the burning in his lungs.

"It's not a voodoo death cult," he said.

"Because you don't want it to be?"

"Because it isn't."

"Then what else is there?"

"Something else, that's all."

"Something that isn't as terrible?"

He started to protest again, but the words seemed to bind up in his throat. When he swallowed them, different words, bitter, came up in their place and spilled out of him. "You're right," he said. "I don't want it to be a voodoo cult. I don't want it to be anything deadly. I just want it all to go away and leave me alone."

"That won't happen, Steven."

"I know," he said. He met her gaze. "You must think I'm a weakling."

"I think you've been badly used. What you've been through would unnerve anyone."

"Maybe. But the truth is, I don't function well in a crisis. I never have."

"But I do," she said. "You won't have to face it alone any longer."

"I'm grateful for that. Only what can I do, even with your help? I can't run home to San Francisco, I'm afraid to go to the police; I'm even afraid to go back to my hotel—Christ knows what I might find there this time. I tried playing detective and that didn't work either. What can I *do?*"

She came over to him, close, and took hold of his arms. There was power in her grip; the bite of her fingers was like metal. "We'll find a way to get you out of this," she said.

"What way? How?"

"There's an explanation for all that's happened; we'll find that first. Then we'll know what to do."

She was standing so close to him that he could feel her breath, silky, against his face; smell the faint aroma of the brandy old-fashioned she had had downstairs. He could smell her perfume, too—subtle, smoky sweet. Her eyes were steady on his, probing. Bright, hot, all green in this light: emeraldfire. Tugging at him, urging him, saying, Come on in, it's warm and safe in here . . .

"Mona," he heard himself say, and her hands were no longer clutching him, he had his arms folded tight around her and she was a yielding weight against his body, soft and metal-hard at the same time.

Her hair was silky, too—dusky red silk. And clean, shiny. He had always had a passion for clean shiny hair; it was the thing about Lara that had attracted him to her in those long-ago college days. He lifted one hand, brushed it through the silkiness. And saw as he did so that the hand was unsteady.

"You're shaking," Mona said against his chest.

"Yeah," he said. "Nerves."

She leaned her head back to look at him again. Her lips were wet; he could see them glistening. Silver on red, and the emeraldfire above.

"You've got to relax, Steven."

"I can't relax."

"You have to. You're so tense you can't think."

"Maybe a couple of drinks . . ."

"No. There's another way."

He knew what she meant instantly, and she confirmed it by kissing him. Her mouth belied the strength in her; it was soft, soft, and there was hunger in it, and it brought hunger into him too. He tasted her tongue, felt her hands stroking his back. The rhythm of his breathing began to change, to grow quick and irregular.

He broke the kiss. "Mona," he said thickly, "you don't have to do this—"

"I know," she said. "But you need it. And I want to."

She took his hand and led him the short distance to the bed.

SIXTEEN

NOTHING happened in the first few minutes.

He lay with her under the covers, unable to get warm. Unable to respond to her nakedness, or to the gentle maneuverings of her hands, or to the softness of her lips on his closed eyes, his throat, his own lips. Her breasts, like her mouth, were soft—the only soft things about her; the rest of her body, wrapped over his, rippled with strength. He clutched at one breast, kissed it, stroked the flats and curves of her with urgent fingers. Trying for an erection. Willing it. Trying too hard.

"It's all right," Mona whispered. "It'll happen, I'll help you. It's all right."

He had never been impotent before. In all the years with Lara, he had not had a single failure in bed. Always ready, that was him. Lara used to tease him about it in the early years of their marriage. Mr. Up-and-Coming, she'd called him. Or Stiff Steve. It had always embarrassed him, her outspokenness on the subject of sex. She'd teased him about his embarrassment, too, told him he was a prude at heart. Big joke between them. But at the end, when prude was the mildest thing she'd call him, it had been anything but a joke. She said he'd never really satisfied her in bed; said he'd been too eager all the time and finished too fast and never thought enough about her needs; said she'd only had half a dozen orgasms the whole time they were married and all the rest she'd faked. Bitter, vicious words. Lies, he'd thought at the time, meant to sting and hurt. But were they lies? Were they?

"It's all right, Steven. Just go slow, try to relax. It'll happen soon."

Yes, they *were* lies. He'd constantly tried to please Lara sexually; he'd never entered into lovemaking with only his own gratification in mind. He'd loved her once, damn it. He'd loved the bitch. Always tried to please her, make it as good as he knew how. He was not a poor lover. The woman just after Thanksgiving, the one he'd met at the party in the Marina—what was her name? Paulette? According to her, he was a damn fine lover. Best she'd had in a long time, she'd said. Three times that night, and once in the morning after they woke up. Four times in less than twelve hours.

"That's it, darling. That's good, that's nice."

And Sonje, don't forget Sonje Voorhees. Dutch girl, thick accent, toothy smile. Big hips, big boobs. One of the caterers at the Sea Cliff wedding last month. Orgasms by the bucketful, judging from what she'd said and how she'd reacted. Like an acrobat, that Sonje. Contortionist. Her favorite position was to get on top. Like Juleen. No, don't think about Juleen. Sonje. On top. Big breasts swaying. Saying, Give it to me, give it to me, in her thick Dutch accent . . .

"There. Oh yes. Now you're ready."

And he was. No more memories, he told himself—Now there was Mona, and Mona was real, and the hunger in his loins was a heavy throbbing ache.

He made love to her.

No, that wasn't right, he thought a long while later, when they were sated and lying in the first moments of rest. He had not made love *to* Mona, or even *with* her; she had made love to him. She had been the aggressor throughout, the leader, the guide, and he had followed and obeyed. And it had been good. Much better than with Paulette or Sonje, because there was a bond between Mona and him, a depth of feeling that went beyond the sexual. Almost as good as it had been with Lara in the early days. No holding back. Giving and receiving. Full measure of everything.

After a time Mona rolled onto her side and began to stroke his cheek. It was dark in the room—she had drawn the drapes and shut off the lights—and he couldn't see her face, but there was a tenderness in her voice when she said, "Do you feel better now, darling?"

"Yes," she said. "Much better."

"Relaxed?"

"Yes."

"Good. It *was* lovely, wasn't it?"

"Mmm," he said.

"It's been a very long time for me. Since before Ralph decided to leave me—weeks before. I'd almost forgotten how lovely it could be."

"You haven't been with anybody in over two years?"

"No one."

"That's a long time to go without sex."

"For a man it is. For a woman it's different. Or it is for me, anyhow. I have to care about someone before I'd think of going to bed with him. There was just no one I cared about until I met you."

"I'm flattered. And even more grateful."

"Don't be. Do you want a cigarette? I don't mind if you do. Ralph used to smoke afterwards. He said that was when cigarettes tasted best."

"He was right. But I don't want one just now. I've been

smoking too much lately. Drinking too much, too."

"I'm not surprised."

"Not just because of what's happened here. The past six months. The marriage breakup, the fire, losing custody of my daughter. All of it."

Mona said, "Fire?"

"Didn't I tell you about that yesterday?"

"No. A fire in your home?"

"My studio. Two months ago. I still don't know how it started. Vandals, maybe, or faulty wiring. The fire marshal couldn't tell what it was. Did several thousand dollars worth of damage. Insurance covered part of it, but not all; it took most of what was left of my savings after the settlement to get back in business."

Mona was silent for a space. Then she asked, "What kind of woman is your ex-wife? What's she like?"

"Well, she used to be a decent human being, when she was younger. Kind, good-hearted, fun to be with. Then she got ambitious, and restless, and hungry for things I don't pretend to understand. We all change, but the changes in Lara . . . they weren't good. I don't know the woman she is today—I don't want to know her. If she didn't have custody of Marcie, I'd stay as far away from her as I could."

"Do you think she hates you?"

"Probably. I think she must have during the last year or so we were married. A lot of venom came out of her when we had the final blowup."

"Is she the vindictive type?"

"You mean where I'm concerned?"

"Yes."

"I wouldn't be surprised. I'm convinced part of the reason she wanted custody of Marcie was so that I couldn't have her. She knew I'd always been closer to the girl than she had, and I think she resented it."

Mona was silent again. "What if she went further than

that?" she asked after several seconds.

"How do you mean?"

"What if that fire in your studio wasn't caused by accident or by vandals? What if Lara was behind it?"

It jolted him. Sat him up, made him prop himself against the headboard and stare at the pale oval of Mona's face in the darkness. "My God," he said.

"I'm not saying she did do it. But from what you've told me, she seems capable of it. Don't you think?"

"I don't know." He didn't want to believe it. Lara? She was a lot of things, that bitch, but overtly malicious? Creeping around in the alleyway behind his studio in the middle of the night, opening the back door—she'd given him back her key, but she could have had a duplicate made—opening up and slipping inside and setting the fire and then sneaking out again . . . He couldn't visualize it. It was too foreign; that was why the possibility had not occurred to him. And yet, she *had* changed for the worse, and he no longer knew her; she could have become that cruel and vindictive. She could have. "I don't know," he said again.

"Did she know you'd decided to come to New Orleans?"

"What?" He was still trying to imagine Lara as a skulking firebug.

"You said yesterday that you'd planned the trip together several months ago," Mona said. "But did she know you'd made up your mind to come by yourself?"

"Well, I sure as hell didn't tell her."

"She could have found out, though, couldn't she?"

"I suppose so. I did tell Marcie. Why? What are you getting at?"

But as soon as he asked the question, he realized what it was she was suggesting. There was a jolt in that, too. He reached out to the nightstand, fumbled around until he found where he'd put his cigarettes. When he struck the last match in the folder, the sudden flare showed him Mona propped up on one arm, looking at him gravely; shadows played in the hollows of her face, made dark splotches of her nipples. He sucked in smoke, shook the match out.

"Suppose she's behind all this too," Mona said.

He said, "No."

"It's another possibility, Steven."

"No, it isn't." He watched the glowing end of his cigarette, watched it retract the darkness redly when he inhaled, like seeing parts of a bedroom appear under ultraviolet light. Parts of Mona, too, still studying him.

"Why isn't it?"

"She'd never go that far. Besides, she doesn't know anybody in New Orleans; neither of us ever did. And she doesn't know anything about voodoo either."

"Are you positive of that? You said you didn't know her any longer."

"Why would she do it? Just to get back at me? I don't buy that; it's crazy."

"She could have got mixed up in something, some sort of intrigue connected with Chalmette. Or Juleen."

He didn't say anything. He could feel himself starting to tense up again. The cigarette smoke burned in his lungs, made his throat feel scratchy.

Mona said, "Was she interested in your work?"

Non sequitur. "I don't know what you mean."

"Did she enjoy photography? Did she ever help you in your studio?"

"Sometimes."

"Then she knows how to use a camera."

"So what?"

"And how to develop film? Does she know how to do that, too?"

"Mona, for Christ's sake—"

"What if *she* took the photograph Chalmette wants?

What if she's the person they're after? Her name is Giroux, isn't it? She hasn't taken her maiden name back?"

"No. But damn it, that's just as crazy . . ."

"Some sort of misunderstanding," Mona said. "They don't know her personally; all they know is that someone named Giroux from San Francisco has a photograph they want. When they checked they found that a San Francisco photographer named Giroux was coming to New Orleans. Or was already here. And they assumed it was their Giroux."

God. "Where does the voodoo come in, then?"

"The possibility I mentioned before—a voodoo death cult."

"Lara wouldn't be mixed up with a goddamn voodoo cult!"

"How do you *know?*"

"I was married to her, wasn't I? She's never had any interest in religion or the occult or anything like that."

"Well, she might not be a member of the cult. But she could be involved with one of its members. If the cult was large enough, it might have secret branches all over the country—one in San Francisco."

Wild, he thought. Voodoo cults, goats without horns, vindictive arson, intrigue and mistaken identity . . . skipping all over the place, going nowhere. Mona had too much imagination, that was the thing. He didn't have enough, and she had too much, and there was no sense in any of it. No sense in what had happened, no sense in his theories or in hers. His hand shook again when he mashed out his cigarette; the glass ashtray rattled, spilled ashes and filter ends over the nightstand.

"Steven?"

"No more speculations about Lara, all right? Or about voodoo death cults. I've had enough for one night."

"How else are we going to find out the truth?"

"What good are guesses? We need facts."

Pause. Then she said, "Yes, you're right," and stirred beside him, moved closer; reached out to caress his chest. "You're all tense again."

"What did you expect? All that stuff about Lara— Christ, I've got enough to cope with without imagining her as some kind of evil voodoo priestess."

"I'm sorry, darling. I should have realized."

She kept on caressing him. Her lips brushed his face, his neck, the hair on his chest. After a space she said, "Do you want to make love another time?"

"No, I don't think so."

"All right. Maybe we should sleep awhile."

Her ministrations were beginning to ease him again. His mind was still full of distortions, but they seemed to be fading, breaking up, like some sort of cinematic special effect. Lassitude flowed into him, the product of a fatigue that was almost wholly mental. Tired. So damned *tired.*

"Can you sleep now, darling?"

"Yes," he said. And listened to her murmur things to him, and felt her hands and mouth kneading his skin, and felt his eyelids grow heavy. His consciousness began to drift, rocking, as if it were in a boat on a heavy sea. Mona's voice faded away into silence. And he slept.

And some time later the nightmare came.

Running in the forest, someone chasing him. Wild terror. The building on fire—and Lara behind the tree, peekaboo, I see you. But she wasn't blue this time, she was all in red, she was drenched in blood, and there were cabalistic symbols on her body that undulated and opened like gaping mouths to smile hideously, revealing red-smeared fangs. And her head fell off and chased after him, snapping at his heels; he could hear the fangs clicking together like the little metal balls of Captain Queeg. But Captain Queeg had been crazy and he wasn't and he ran and ran, and stumbled and fell down the slope, and the faces impended above him, and now all of them wore terrible dragon masks. Juleen's voice said, "It's no use, gentlemen, no use," and he said, "Don't you understand, they're after me," and Chalmette's voice said, "It's no use, no use, he's mad," and the dragons began to laugh, to scream, to breathe fire. Then they turned into voodoo dolls with blood dripping out of their eye sockets, and then they crumbled away into shrieking dust—

He cried out, "No!" and jerked upright, and as always he was awake.

Darkness. Three or four seconds of disorientation, until he remembered where he was. Mona's room. Mona's bed. He lay still for a moment, to let the wildness go out of him and his pulse rate slow down. Then he rubbed at the oily perspiration on his face, reached out for the warmth and strength of Mona beside him.

She wasn't there.

His hand touched empty sheet, cool against his fingers. He blinked into the darkness, looking blindly toward the bathroom. But there was no strip of light showing there, no light anywhere in the room.

"Mona?"

Silence.

And the sheet beside him was cool; she hadn't been lying there for some time.

Little tendrils of unease began to wind through him. He threw back the blankets, swung his legs off the bed. Fumbled over the nightstand until he found the lamp and the switch for it. The darkness fell away, seemed to wad itself into the corners of the room. He looked around him, squinting in the pale light.

"Mona?"

The word seemed to suspend itself in the air, as if the room had become a vacuum; he imagined he could hear its aftersound for seconds in the heavy silence. He caught himself looking at his hands, as though part of him expected to find fresh stains there. But his mind cowered away from the implications of that, refused to dwell on it. There was nothing on his hands, nothing on his arms except gooseflesh. Cool in there. Cool like the sheet on Mona's side of the bed.

"Mona?" he said a third time, and in the stillness that followed he thought: She's not here, why keep yelling for her? Then he thought: But then where is she? His watch was on the nightstand, next to the lamp; he picked it up. Twelve-fifteen. After midnight. Where would she go at this time of night?

He stood up, shivering a little, and padded to the bathroom. The door was open; he could see without putting on the lights that the narrow enclosure was empty. He pivoted to face the room again. His clothes were where he'd pitched them, lying across the one chair. But he remembered Mona having folded her clothes on top of the dresser, and they weren't there now. Her purse was there, though, positioned in front of the mirror so that it looked like two purses side by side.

Where would she go without her purse?

The uneasiness kept uncoiling; he struggled against it. It's okay, he thought, there's nothing wrong. She just went out for a few minutes. She'll be back pretty soon, with an explanation. There's nothing wrong.

Cold in there. But he didn't want to get back into bed. He caught up his shirt and underpants, put them on. Then his eye fell on the package of cigarettes, speckled with ashes spilled from the tray, and immediately he wanted a smoke. He got a cigarette out of the pack, but when he went to light it he saw that he was out of matches. Damn. He surveyed the room another time. Mona's purse. Maybe she had some matches in there. She didn't smoke, but you never knew what a woman might carry in her purse.

Why didn't she take it with her? he thought again. Where did she go?

He crossed to the dresser. The purse—or shoulder bag or whatever they called them—was large and well used, made out of leather. It had a zippered top, but the zipper was open and he could see comb, compact, pocket mirror, the usual female impedimentas. He opened it wider, did some tentative rummaging inside. Notebook, pen, eyebrow pencil, a booklet of stamps, three blank postcards depicting New Orleans landmarks. No matches. Another pen, felt-tip this time. Some loose change. A United Airlines ticket folder. A paperback guidebook to New Orleans. But no—

He quit rummaging and stared at the ticket folder, remembering something Mona had told him at lunch on Sunday: "I wanted to return home on Ash Wednesday, but all the American Airlines flights were booked and I prefer American." And the folder had red-ink markings on it that said 24D. Assigned seat number. In the smoking section, and Mona didn't smoke.

He caught up the folder, saw the printed letters *SFO* on the baggage-claim stubs stapled to the front, and ripped the tickets from inside. They were for a round trip from San Francisco to New Orleans. And the name on them was S. Giroux.

They were his, the ones that had been stolen from his suitcase at the Pirate's Head.

SEVENTEEN

HE stood for what seemed a long time, looking at the tickets. The shock he'd felt at first evaporated, and the aftermath was one of numbing desolation. As though the last of his emotions had burned out in one brief flash, like the filaments of a light bulb giving way, and now he was dark inside.

He laid the tickets down on the dresser. Put on the rest of his clothes, put on his jacket, picked up the tickets again and slid them into his jacket pocket. Went into the hallway and summoned an elevator and rode downstairs. Went outside and away from the hotel, shivering.

An icy wind off the river swirled refuse in the gutters; the night air had a damp feel, and the sky was swollen with clouds again. The cold gave him back an awareness of himself, pushed thoughts like whimpers through the emptiness within.

Mona too. All of it a lie—the theories, the sex, the comfort. The hope. Why? Trying to win his confidence? So he'd give her the photograph he didn't have? Some other reason? Mona too. No one to trust anymore. Just him,

159

alone. Trapped in a world that was no longer real, that had become twisted and was ruled by illogic. Madman's world. Everything came down to that. No matter which way he turned, he saw madness leering at him like a specter from the shadows.

He walked. He did not know where he was, after awhile, but it made no difference because he had nowhere to go. The streets grew darker, emptier. A man in a raincoat gave him a long passing look, furtive, as if appraising him as a potential victim. But nothing happened. Muggers and footpads had no interest in him. He was prey of a different sort.

He stopped on a street corner. Something massive loomed off to his left, thrust up surrealistically against the turbulent sky. Superdome. Home of the football Saints, home of an occasional Super Bowl, home of fun and games. He looked away. A street sign jutted nearby: South Prieur. Long way from the Pirate's Head. Long way from anywhere. But he couldn't walk the streets all night. Too tired, so damned tired. Back to the hotel, then. If something else, somebody else, was waiting for him there, no matter. They couldn't do anything more to him . . . except kill him, and that at least would put an end to it.

He went along South Prieur until, at Canal Street, it became North Prieur. Not many people out this late, this far from the Quarter; but there were cars rushing by, buses —too much noise, too many lights.

When he reached St. Louis the light was against him and he stopped to wait for it to change. Footsteps approached behind him, echoing. And just as the signal flashed green, a voice he knew—the voice of Chalmette— said, "Your time's up, Giroux. I want that photograph."

He just stood there. The light was green, the traffic moved, but he could not make himself move—couldn't go forward, couldn't go sideways, couldn't turn around. He was not afraid; he felt nothing except the hollow numbness. And yet at the same time he was terrified. Twitches of emotion still alive in him after all. Little screaming whispers. The hair prickled on his scalp; he imagined it standing up, bushy, like the fur of a frightened cat.

"You hear me? The photograph."

He opened his mouth and words dribbled out, thick and moist, like spittle. "I don't have any photograph."

"Tonight. Right now."

"I don't have any photograph."

"Or you're a dead man. A pile of shit in the street."

"I don't have any photograph."

"Take me to where you've got it. Now."

"I don't have any photograph."

But he was talking to the night, to the empty street; no one was listening. He made himself move. He turned around slowly, being deliberate about it, oh very deliberate. The man, Chalmette or whoever he was, stood two feet from him—heavyset, muscular, wearing a sheepskin vest and Levi's; wearing a mask. He expected to see the mask, but it was not a dragon's malevolent visage that glared at him. It was a devil's. A voodoo devil's: hideous, painted in streaks of white and red, a Negroid caricature. But Chalmette was not black; the one hand that hung at his side shone pale white in the misty street lights. The other hand was in the pocket of his vest.

"Take me to the photograph, Giroux."

Take me to the photograph, Giroux. Take me to your leader, Chalmette. There was laughter inside him, frothing —a witch's brew. If he stood here much longer, he would lose control of himself and the laughter would spill out into cries and he would attack Chalmette. And that wouldn't do. Chalmette was bigger than he was, stronger, more dangerous. Chalmette—

—took his hand out of the vest pocket.

There was a knife in it.

He gaped at the weapon. Hunter's knife, with a fat double-edged blade; light glinted off the whetted surface. A little giggling sound popped out of his mouth—one bubble from the witch's brew. On North Prieur, a car hissed by. Somewhere a long way off, horns were playing "North Rampart Street Parade."

"The photograph," Chalmette said. "Now."

He started to shake his head, caught himself and held it so rigid he could feel the strain in his neck muscles. Chalmette still showed him the knife, moving it from side to side, slicing the air with it. It was only when a taxi came down Prieur and signaled for a turn on St. Louis that he put it away again inside the vest pocket.

Giroux looked at the taxi. He thought of jumping out into the street, yelling for help from the driver, but his body would not respond. He was still trying to make himself act when the taxi completed its turn and went by. Its taillights laid a smear of crimson on the darkness; the engine sound began to diminish.

Then he moved. Too late, but he could not keep on standing there; he could not. In the same jerky, robotlike way he had dressed and left Mona's room, he started away from Chalmette—lateral steps that took him into St. Louis. Chalmette held his position until Giroux had gone a dozen paces. And then, warily, he began to follow.

Walking half turned was awkward, like the scuttling of a crab. He made himself face front, made himself walk at a measured pace. He wanted to run, but his legs felt as heavy as stumps of clay; if he ran it would be like running in a dream, all mired in place and going nowhere, and Chalmette would catch him and use that knife on him. Cut his throat, maybe. Jesus. Cut his *throat* . . .

Intersection. He crossed it, started down another block. Across the street to his left were industrial lots and buildings, a line of railroad-spur tracks and darkened box-cars. Straight ahead, two blocks away, was the elevated highway above North Claiborn Avenue. He looked over his shoulder. Chalmette was still the same distance behind him —devil mask gleaming in the darkness, streaks of white like fresh white blood.

A light mist began to fall, cold and spidery against his face. The black street glistened. In the distance the lights of the Municipal Auditorium at Beauregard Square shimmered against the cloud-heavy sky. There was nobody on the sidewalk here, no cars visible anywhere at the moment. The world might have shrunk and mutated into a dark place, sealed off, where he walked and Chalmette walked and fearsome things crawled and snuffled in the shadows.

Another intersection. Where am I going? he thought. Chalmette seemed to think he was being led to the photograph, but there was no photograph. The police? Maybe he could lead Chalmette to the . . . no. He didn't know where the police station was, and Chalmette wouldn't let him get that far even if he did—

Car coming.

He heard the hiss of its tires on the pavement, saw its headlights reflected, blurrily, in a nearby window glass. He looked behind him. The car was just crossing the last inter-section, moving slow, almost drifting. Police patrol? Chal-mette seemed oblivious to it. He did not look back; he walked with his head down, both hands in his vest pockets.

Giroux's pulse picked up tempo; he could hear it thud-ding in his ears: boudoum boudoum, boudoum boudoum. The car passed Chalmette. The sidespill from the head-lamps outlined him briefly before they slid past and probed toward Giroux. He squinted against the brightness, looking for markings—flasher light, official insignia. But there were no markings; not the police, just an ordinary car. And it was fifty feet from him now, gliding, making whispering noises on the damp pavement.

Forty feet.

Thirty-five—

And he lurched sideways, into the street; whirled and ran at the car, arms upraised and semaphoring frantically. Did all of that without planning it, without thinking about it, just did it and shouted "Help me, help!" as he ran. The car slowed to a stop, angled away from him. The lights were blinding; all he could see behind them was the looming shape of the car. He dodged out of the glare, ran toward the driver's door. Beyond, on the sidewalk, Chalmette was at a standstill, staring.

The car door opened and the driver came up through it.

It was the man in the dragon mask.

A cry came out of Giroux that was almost a scream; he checked his momentum so abruptly that his foot slipped and he skidded sideways onto his hands and knees, scraping skin, jarring bone. But he was up again at once, scrambling, backing off, running away from them this time with the *boudoum boudoum* in his ears and another cry in his throat.

He ran out of the street, onto the sidewalk, and then back into the street across the next intersection and under the elevated highway. They were both after him, on foot and with the car; he knew that without looking, he could hear the pounding steps and the rumble of the car's engine. High whitish walls bulked up ahead of him. He veered into their shadow, saw what looked to be a gate ahead. Saw the street alongside turn glassy black, gleaming with reflections of light, as the car bore down on him.

When he reached the gate—wire mesh, surmounted by strands of barbed wire—he clawed handholds and climbed it like a monkey in a cage. He was almost to the top before he realized what lay on the other side.

Crosses, hundreds of them. Tiered vaults. Winged angels, grieving marble figures. All jumbled together like a collection of bones, shining black-white in the misty dark.

Old St. Louis No. 2.

Boneyard. Cemetery. City of the dead.

The car had stopped a few feet away, Chalmette was pounding up, there was nowhere else to go. He caught the top strand of wire, felt a barb slice into his palm, felt the stickiness of blood, and hoisted himself up to where he could throw a leg over the top. Another of the barbs snagged his trouser material on the other leg. He hung there astride the gate, kicking wildly. Chalmette was there by then; so was the dragon. Both of them lunged upward, trying to reach his leg so they could pull him back.

He wrenched free of the barb, tearing cloth, tearing flesh, and half fell down the gate on the inside. When he picked himself up he was staring at the devil mask and the dragon mask, inches away through the mesh. Their fingers were hooked through, curled and clutching, like talons. He wheeled around, stumbled to where a narrow pathway seemed to lead into the maze of tombs and vaults. Behind him they began climbing the gate; he could hear the scrape of their shoes against the mesh, the metallic grating sound of the gate wobbling in its frame.

Hide. Hide!

The path went this way, that way, ultimately nowhere at all. The monuments to the dead towered around him—marble, granite, whitewashed brick. Flowers jutted everywhere from mounted flowerpots, some fresh, giving off a cloying odor, some withered, and some made of glass and beads and twisted wire, everlasting. He found another pathway, cut off it and squeezed behind a three-tiered tomb topped by an iron cross. He leaned against it, panting silently, listening.

They were over the gate now, inside the cemetery. He could hear them prowling around. Hide, he thought again. But not here; too open here, little plot of stubbled grass, not enough protection. He pushed away from the tomb, groped between several others, ducked around one made of rough stone. They were bunched more tightly here, an older section, bottom ovens sunk into the earth and their inscriptions obliterated. He crouched down, wedged his body against a slab of cold marble. In front of him, another lone slab, canted off-center, bore an epitaph in bold black letters; he was close enough to read what it said, even in the darkness.

For the virtuous there is a happier and better world.

The witch's brew bubbled again; he clamped his teeth shut, tightened his throat muscles, to keep any more of it from leaking out. Pain throbbed in his cut hand, in his leg; blood trickled down into his sock. The silence around him was acute, charged with crackling tension, broken only by scrapes and small thumps some ways off. Let them search. They could search all night. But they wouldn't find him. Oh no, not here in the dark, hidden the way he was.

But the panic stayed with him, gnawing just under the surface. He'd thought he was beyond fear, beyond panic, but he hadn't been. He had not even been close. Before tonight, the threat to him had been an abstract, something that *might* happen; even the blood in Juleen's house, the smell of death from the cellar, represented something that *might* have taken place. But now it was real, immediate; now it was happening. Knife, car, chase, search—deadly menace, the promise fulfilled.

The beat of his heart would not slow down. More pain crept through his chest, tightening, expanding; he had difficulty getting enough air into his lungs. He wondered if he was having a heart attack. God, what an irony that would be. He might have a seizure and die before they could kill him. And if he died, the city would not even have to remove his corpse. They could just fold him up and stuff him into one of the ovens right here in Old St. Louis No. 2. Steven Giroux, RIP. For the virtuous there is a happier and better world.

The mist thickened, blew icy against his face. He shivered and kept on shivering. The wind picked up and made vague whistling sounds among the monuments. That was all he could hear now; no more searching noises. Maybe they'd gone into another part of the cemetery. Maybe they'd gone away—

Footfall, close by.

Another.

He went rigid. No, he thought. No, he was too well hidden. They couldn't find him *here.*

The steps came closer, scraping along the ground.

On the far side of the marble slab, a rustling.

And a black figure, black dragon, loomed into view like one of the winged statues come to life.

No, God, please—

Something in the dragon's down-stretched hand. And the devil right behind him.

"No," he said aloud, and almost lost control of his bladder, and grunted with the effort to hold it. Crouched there, petrified, trying not to pee on himself, saying No, *no,* as they moved toward him, as the dragon leaned down and jammed a wet thing against his face, as a dizzying medicinal smell mingled with the damp moldy stench of the cemetery, as the night and the terror closed around him and swallowed him alive.

PART IV
FAT TUESDAY

And now was acknowledged the presence of the Red Death. He had come like a thief in the night. And one by one dropped the revellers in the blood-bedewed halls of their revel, and died each in the despairing posture of his fall.
—EDGAR ALLAN POE
"The Masque of the Red Death"

EIGHTEEN

BOUDOUM.

Boudoum, boudoum.

He opened his eyes. Lighted room, walls with roses on them, an old brass ceiling fixture . . . but it was all moving, blurring and blending together like images in a kaleidoscope. Sickness boiled up in him; he squeezed his eyes shut again. But the spinning and the blending kept on behind the closed lids, in crazy-quilt patterns of light and shadow. He rolled over on something yielding—a bed, its springs creaking—and caught hold of the edge and clung there as if it were a precipice, vomiting into the chasm below.

Boudoum.

Boudoum, boudoum.

The spinning stopped, the sickness went away as soon as his stomach was empty. He rolled onto his back again, lay weakly with his arms splayed out at his sides. There was pain in both, pain in his right hand in both legs: stinging, localized. The pain in his head was much worse—a kind of malignant slicing over the ears and across the forehead, as if someone were cutting through his skull with a handsaw.

Boudoum.

Boudoum, boudoum.

He eased his eyes open again. This time the room stayed stationary, stayed in focus. The roses on the walls had once been red; now they were faded a rusty brownish color, like dried blood, and petalless in places where the old paper had peeled away from the wallboard. The ceiling fixture was tarnished, rococo, made to look like a cluster of grapes; the three elliptical bulbs in it were dark. A lamp on a linoleum-topped table gave the room its light. He could see the lamp and table when he turned his head, and two spindly chairs, and a window with a torn shade half-rolled up, and a painting of a bayou swamp somber with cypress trees and whiskers of Spanish moss.

He had never seen any of it before.

He put his palms flat on the bed, wincing, and managed to lift himself into a sitting position. The room wavered, righted itself, held steady. He saw his hands: flecked and crosshatched with puncture marks, with bloody scratches. The right knee of his trousers was torn. So were both pantlegs, and so was the front of his shirt; more scratches and abrasions showed through the tears. He was no longer wearing his jacket.

When he got his feet down on the floor he wrapped both arms around himself and sat that way, tilted forward, while his stomach kicked and burbled. The faint medicinal odor came to him: chloroform. And he remembered the cemetery, the looming figures—but only for a moment. Then his mind seemed to curl in on itself, to snip off the memory as if with a pair of mental scissors.

Boudoum.

Boudoum, boudoum.

His insides were beginning to settle down. He raised his head, found himself looking at the window. Through the glass below the shade, he could see darkness and the scudding movement of clouds. But that was all. The pane was dry, and that told him it was not raining. He dragged his left arm up. He was still wearing his wristwatch; the crystal was badly scratched but he could see where the hands were pointing. Five fifty-six. Morning? It must be; it didn't get dark at six in the evening now. Dark, not raining, 6:00 A.M.—those were the only things he knew.

He shoved off the bed, seemed to have no equilibrium at first, and tottered sideways into the withering roses on the wall. He caught his balance before he fell, used the wall to steady himself; then he made his way along it to the room's only door, opposite the foot of the bed. He took hold of the knob, rattled it.

Locked.

He put his ear against the door panel and listened. But there was nothing to hear. Nothing except—

Boudoum.

Boudoum, boudoum.

The sound intruded for the first time, and he realized it was an external tempo, not the throbbing pulse in his head. A steady rhythm coming from a distance, inside or outside the building—he could not tell which. A familiar beat, primitive, elemental, heavy with passion.

Drums.

Voodoo drums.

'He ran away from the door to where the window was. He let the shade flap all the way up and pressed his face against the cold glass. At first he couldn't see anything except massed shapes and vague outlines; but then, as his pupils dilated, there was a rift in the running stream of clouds, and a quarter moon appeared briefly like a lopsided mouth. The shapes and outlines took on form and substance, became a recognizable scene.

It was not what he expected to see. It was not buildings, streets, city sights; it was not New Orleans. It was a three-dimensional, life-size blowup of the painting that hung on the wall: broken-armed cypress trees, whiskers of Spanish moss, palmetto clusters, the placid water of a bayou nearby. Stretching away from the bayou was an ir-regular rectangle of grass, and in the center of that were tangles of wind-gathered brush and discarded junk rusting in piles. The branches of a live oak were visible at the near end of the grassy area, half hidden by the angle of a weath-ered outer wall. Directly below the window was a slanted porch roof, loose shingled and buckled in disrepair: the room he was in was on the second floor of some kind of house.

Bayou house, bayou swamp. Isolated: there were no lights anywhere. They had taken him out of the cemetery —cut the barbed wire, lifted him over the gate; that must be how he'd got all the cuts and scratches—and afterward brought him down into the bayou country. To torture him? But he couldn't give them a photograph he didn't have, and when they finally realized that, when they finished with him, then what?

Boudoum.

Boudoum, boudoum.

What were they doing out there? Some sort of cere-mony or orgy, maybe . . . Marie Laveau, moonlight rituals near Bayou St. John, danse Calinda, l'appé vini, le Grand Zombi. Mona talking to him about voodoo death cults, and Mona was one of them. Was that what they intended to do with him? Kill him . . . sacrifice him . . . goat without horns?

There was a temptation in him to lie down on the bed, sink back into the desolation he had felt after leaving Mona's room. Let it happen, no matter what it was. Let them torture him, sacrifice him, slit his throat and drink his blood—let it be over and done with because it was hopeless anyway, he would never get free of this nightmare. But it was only a temptation. He wouldn't do it because he couldn't, the fear would not let him. Fear ruled him now; fear dictated everything. And fear said he had to try to save himself.

He caught onto the window sash, heaved upward. It would not budge. Then he saw that there was a catch lock at the bottom, rusty and frozen from disuse; but it would not budge, either. He glanced around the room another time, saw nothing useful, and fumbled through his pockets. Nothing.

There was a small table beside the bed, on the far side where he had vomited. He went there and tugged open the drawer. Clutter inside: a deck of cards, a broken pencil, two packages of contraceptives, a half-dozen black candles, four packets of matches. And a hypodermic syringe, a length of rubber tubing, an old blackened spoon with its handle bent in half like a baby's spoon.

Syringe, spoon, tubing—drugs? He took the spoon back to the window, tried to pry the catch loose with it. The handle bent even more; the lock stayed frozen. He scraped at the rust, managed to chip flecks of it free. The rasp of metal on metal seemed loud in his ears, and it made him afraid someone was close enough to hear the noise. How many of them were here? Just Chalmette and the dragon? Or others too—Juleen, Mona, ones he didn't know? They might all be where the drums were, however many were around. And the drums had to be some distance away, inside or outside the house; he'd be able to tell which when he got the window open. If he got the window open. But they might have left somebody nearby to watch over him, somebody who might come in at any time . . .

He kept scraping quietly at the catch, listening for footsteps, trying not to listen to the drums. More rust flaked off, but when he gripped the lock it still refused to yield. Outside, the blackness began to lose some of its density; it would be dawn in less than an hour. And he had to be out of here by then, a long way from here. Voodoo ceremonies ended at dawn; whatever bayou orgy they were holding would also be finished by then. Then they would come swarming through the house, ready for him again.

Scraping, scraping—and another five minutes and most of the rust was gone. He tried the latch one more time. It still wouldn't open, but he thought he could feel it give a fraction when he put pressure on it. He jabbed at it with the spoon, frantically now. Light was just beginning to filter into the morning sky; the twisted shapes of the cypress swamp reared up in sharp silhouette, like images captured in a still photograph. And the drums seemed to have changed tempo, to be gathering momentum toward some sort of frenzied climax.

He put the spoon down, took hold of the catch again, this time with both hands, and mustered all the strength he had, and wrenched. The lock moved, creaked, but would not break loose. He twisted again. And again, grunting, breath spewing out between his teeth. And again—

There was a sudden snapping and it broke free of its seal, turned in the slot: open.

The effort had weakened him. It took him another minute to tug the sash up far enough, squeaking and grumbling in its frame, so that he could put his head and shoulders through the opening. Cold wind, tinged with the smell of swamp water, swept against his face. He sucked at it greedily, letting it brace him, as he peered down over the slope of the porch roof.

The drums were outside, he could tell that now; somewhere out back of the house, where more live oaks and other vegetation bulked up in the darkness. He thought he could hear chanting too, a single voice, but too far away for it or the words to be distinguishable. There was no one visible on the grass below, or on the wind-rippled bayou, or anywhere else within the range of his vision. And no other sounds except for insects and frogs and the faint far-off droning of an airplane—seaplane or some other light craft.

He eased a leg over the sill, straddled the dry-rotted wood. The joining of the roof and the front wall was three feet below the window; he slid out and down until his foot rested flat against the shingled surface. It gave, creaking, when he put weight on it. The shingles looked old and crumbly, and he was afraid that when he laid his full hundred-and-eighty pounds on them he would crash through, tumble onto the porch below. Afraid, always afraid.

When he got the one foot anchored he swung the other over the sill, using his hands and forearms to brace himself, grimacing at the pain in his cut palm. The shingles held him, but under protest—more groaning sounds that were muffled by the wind. He leaned back the length of his arms and peered along the wall. There was another window on the far side, same size and distance from the roof, and he could get to it easily enough. But its glass was dark, with a shade pulled down inside and curtains drawn over that; for all he knew it was locked as tight as this one had been. And even if he could get through it, it would still leave him somewhere inside the house, with no knowledge of how to get out again. No, he had to go down the slant of the roof and then swing off to the ground at its lowest point. From here, the drop looked to be seven or eight feet—not far if he paid attention to where and how he landed.

He put his back to the window, eased down along the wall until his buttocks rested on the shingles. He kept both feet planted flat, knees drawn up, and spread his hands out at his sides; then he began to scoot downward, slowly, using his hands and feet as guides and as brakes. It was the same method he had used to come down off the roof of his father's garage, in the little town of Sebastopol where he'd grown up. He'd done it dozens of times, even though he was not supposed to go up on the garage, and the only time he'd fallen had not been his fault. It had been the fault of a friend named Jimmy and it had cost him a sprained ankle. Childhood memory; it flickered across his mind, old and grainy and faded, like a sepia halftone. And then was gone, lost in the urgency and the constant pounding beat of the drums.

He had no difficulty getting halfway down, at an angle toward the lower left-hand corner. The roof kept on groaning, making little snapping firecracker sounds; pebbles dislodged by his passage rattled down the slant and over the edge. He was making too much noise but there was nothing he could do about it, or about the scrape of the shingles over the inflamed cuts in his hands. But no one appeared in the yard, no lights went on in the windows above him. Nothing changed in the surrounding tableau except that a little more gray seeped into the sky, softening the black, bringing tree and other shapes into clearer relief.

The lower half of the roof was more treacherous. Its downslant was sharper, and when he was into it he felt himself starting to slide. He dug his heels into the shingles, leaning forward at the waist. Momentum veered him farther left. For a sickening instant he thought he was going to skid right off into midair, like a skier off the edge of a downhill run. He twisted onto his left hip, clawing at the shingles for a handhold—

His legs whipped out over the bottom edge, near the corner; the upper half of him flopped over, belly down. But he managed to get enough of a grip on the side edge to brake his momentum, keep his torso on the roof. He clung there, dangling, trying to peer back and down through a thin gauze of sweat at the ground underneath him. He couldn't do it, hanging the way he was. And he couldn't pull himself up, either; the strength was already running out of his arms. He could hear himself grunting with the strain.

If there was anything below him, anything sharp or bulky . . .

He allowed his upper body to slide a few more inches, until the roof edge dug into the area below his breastbone. Then, sucking in breath, he let go of the side edge.

He remembered to go limp as he dropped, so that the shock of impact was cushioned when he struck ground. And that was all he struck—soft earth, yielding. He toppled sideways, rolled over, felt wet grass brushed cold against his face and arms, and came up onto his knees facing the house, ready to lurch to his feet.

He was still alone.

The porch—a side porch, screened—was dark inside. The two windows he could see adjacent to the porch were also dark. Behind him, the swamp stirred with morning life. But nothing stirred in the house.

The drums, he realized, had changed tempo again, still building toward a crescendo. There was a pause in the chanting. He moved into the shadowed angle where the porch met the side wall of the house proper; stood wiping dampness off his face, blood off the opened cut on his palm. The chanting began again, louder, slurred a little, sibilant. And now, as it came drifting eerily through the fading darkness, he could identify the voice. The recognition made his skin crawl.

The voice, hissing like a snake, was Juleen's.

NINETEEN

HE moved out of the shadows, along the side wall toward the back. He couldn't stay here near the house; he had to get away, and in order to do that he had to know where they were so he wouldn't stumble into them. But it was more than that, too, more than the need for escape. The drums and Juleen's chanting voice were morbidly compelling, almost hypnotic. He wanted to see what they were doing, at the same time he dreaded seeing it. He had been terrified of the unknown too long now. He wanted to look into the face of his terror.

When he reached the back corner he inched his head around it, stared out across the rear yard. A few live oaks, a shed of some kind in ramshackle condition, and part of a garage with boards broken out of its visible wall. Beyond the garage was more bayou swamp, dominated by grotesque cypress and thick webs of Spanish moss. Light wavered in there—firelight. That was where the drums and the chanting came from; that was where they were.

He crept out from the house, looking up at it as he went. All dark back here, too. Staying in pockets of darkness, he made his way to one of the oaks and then to the shed. Close up, it smelled like an abatoir; his stomach convulsed and he had to struggle to keep from gagging. He saw the reason for the stench when he came around the front of the shed. A dozen or more alligator hides were draped over poles, curing; bones and butchered remains, some of it rotting and acrawl with insects, were strewn on the far side. Whoever lived here was an alligator hunter—alligator poacher, what the Cajuns called a *caimanero,* because it was illegal in Louisiana to butcher wild gators for their hides.

He made an effort to pinch off his nasal passages, to breathe through his mouth as he started for the garage. He had to be less than a hundred yards from where they were: the drums were loud, fevered, and he could hear the chanting clearly enough to make out the words. Juleen seemed to be saying the same ones over and over, an unmistakable voodoo litany.

> "HE-RON MANDÉ
> HE-RON MANDÉ
> TIQUI LI PAPA
> HE-RON MANDÉ
> TIQUI LI PAPA
> HE-RON MANDÉ
> HE-RON MANDÉ
> DO SE DAN DO-GO
> HE-RON MANDÉ . . ."

At the garage he stopped to look at the other side of the house. All dark. There was a rutted gravel driveway in front of the garage; on it was a battered pickup truck, twenty years old or more, and behind that was a car that looked like the one the dragon had chased him with on St. Louis Street. There was no front license plate on the truck, but a luminous bumper sticker gleamed in the graying light. It said: *I FOUND IT!*

Found what, for God's sake? he thought.

Boudoumboudoumboudoum . . .

He moved along the garage wall to the back, looked around the corner. The swamp began a dozen yards away, and the firelight was coming from another fifty yards or so within. But he could not see the source of it yet; it was filtered through the dense swamp growth. Don't go in there, he thought. But the drums and the chanting were like the pipes of Pan, all twisted and evil. He had to see. He had to know.

He stepped into the open, crouched low. A path had been worn in the grass; it led diagonally into the swamp, between a pair of decaying logs that had fallen against each other—or been laid against each other—to resemble a crude cross. Clouds of mosquitoes swarmed to meet him as he passed under the cross; he pawed at them at first, then gave up the effort and let them feed at will. He pushed through the underbrush, skirting clusters of palmetto mired in the boggy earth, following the path. In the half-light, the broken trees were like rotting skeletons, the Spanish moss like giant tattered cobwebs.

The drums filled his head now, savage and demanding. Juleen had stopped her chant, but only for a few seconds. As he moved, she started in again—a different litany, more chilling that the first because it contained phrases that he recognized.

"KAN SÔLÉID TE KASHE,
LI TÉ SORTI BAYOU,
POU, APPRENED LE VOUDOU,
OH, TINGOUAR, YÉ HÉN HÉN,
OH, TINGOUAR, YÉ ÉH ÉH
L'APPÉ VINI, LE GRAND ZOMBI,
L'APPÉ VINI, POL FÉ MOURI!"

Shapes materialized ahead of him, screened by the trees and moss, outlined blackly by the firelight. He moved off the path, carrying mosquitoes with him, into the shadow of a splintered cypress. And from there he could look straight through a break in the swamp growth.

There were three of them—Juleen and Chalmette and the dragon—in a small grassy clearing. Despite the cold, they were buck-naked; their bodies painted in white and red streaks, like savages, the men still masked. The fire was in the center of the clearing, blazing inside a ring of stones, and the three of them formed the points of a triangle around it. The men were sitting cross-legged, hunched forward, each beating on a skin-covered cask with what looked to be a bleached animal bone. In Chalmette's free hand was a long slender pipe . . . opium pipe? hashish pipe? Juleen was standing, arms and legs spread, eyes closed and head thrown back. There were black ribbons with silver bells on them tied around her ankles and wrists. And oil on her breasts and stomach and shaved abdomen: it glistened in the firelight, gave her a bronze sheen. Behind her was a crude altar, made of wood and painted black, draped in a scarlet cloth decorated in the same cabalistic markings she had worn on her body Saturday night. On top of the cloth were half a dozen lighted black candles, a stained wooden bowl, and two cages; the larger of the cages, wire fronted, had a chicken in it. And on the grass near the fire were the headless carcasses of two other chickens, one of whose wings still flapped with death spasms.

Giroux could feel his skin crawling again, rippling with a prickly chill. This was not an ordinary voodoo religious rite; this was pure atavism, a sacrilege, a reenactment of something unspeakable from the dark wastes of time. It made him feel confused, unclean. It brought the panic welling up, scuffing across his nerve ends.

Juleen finished her litany and stood with arms

upraised; she seemed to be quivering, and the look she wore was the look of the possessed. But he could not hear the bells on her wrists and ankles for the crashing thunder of the drums.

Chalmette swayed to his feet and took the pipe to her, placed it between her lips, waited while she sucked smoke from it. Then he brought it around to the dragon and performed the same ritual with him. When he sat down again, Juleen began another chant—a five-line verse, repeated over and over. This time the two men joined in.

"Eh! Eh! Bomba hen hen!
Canga bafie te
Danga moune de te
Canga do ki li!
Canga li!"

The words came faster, matching the rhythm of the drums. Their bodies writhed wildly where they sat or stood. The chanting and the drumbeat all blended together into a single mad note, echoing in the semigloom of the swamp, drowning out all other sound, driving away all reason and sanity. Juleen twitched and jerked her way to the smaller cage on the altar, opened it, pulled something out. Snake. Big, evil-looking spotted snake. And she danced with it, wrapped it around her, rubbed it over her breasts and between her legs. Held its head up close to her own, put her tongue out to touch the flicking tongue of the snake.

He wanted to shut his eyes, back away, run—but he did none of those things. The hellish ritualism of it held him in thrall.

The dance with the snake went on for minutes, with the drums and the chant at the same fever pitch. Then Juleen returned the thing to its cage, opened the wire-fronted cage and withdrew the remaining chicken from inside by its neck. Giroux knew it was squawking because he could see its open beak, but he could not hear it. She raised it high over her head, held it that way for a second, and then picked up something from alongside the cage. Firelight gleamed on steel: a long, thin-bladed knife.

She poised the chicken over the wooden bowl and cut off its head with a single slashing stroke.

She held the decapitated chicken until most of its blood had drained into the altar bowl. Then she raised it high again, let the last of the blood dribble down over her breasts; finally hurled the corpse from her. It danced around in a circle, as if looking for its head, and toppled quivering with the other dead hens. Juleen picked up the bowl, drank from it. Took it to the dragon, watched him raise the mask just enough to drink. Took it to Chalmette. When the bowl was empty she returned it to the altar, turned and began to rub the blood into her breasts as if it were a lotion, until her hands were stained and dripping and her body shook as though with palsy.

There was a sudden percussive crescendo, and the chant ended, and Juleen shouted, *"Aie! Aie! Voodoo maignan!"*

The drums stopped.

The two men scrambled to their feet, rushed to her, caught hold of her. The three of them danced round and round, embracing one another, making no sounds except for the slithering of their bare feet in the grass and the melodic tinkling of Juleen's little silver bells. The swamp itself was hushed, breathless, almost a vacuum. They danced for a minute, two minutes, and then they sank down in a tangle of arms and legs, and it became a blood-spattered orgy: one of the men mounted her, the other man—

Giroux could not watch it any longer. The fear, mixed with revulsion, drove him away from the tree and back over the boggy ground to the path. He had to force himself not to run. Moss caressed his face, cold; he stepped on something that broke and made a faint cracking noise in the stillness. Be careful, for God's sake—they'll know you're here! He watched the ground, watched where he put his feet, and groped his way through the mosquitoes and the swamp growth until he emerged, shivering, on the grass behind the garage.

Gray dawn light had swallowed most of the darkness. The house loomed up on his left, sagging, weathered the unhealthy color of a fungoid growth after a rain. The shed seemed to list in his direction; its abbatoir stench, carried on the cold breath of the wind, assailed him. He stumbled alongside the garage, head down. He couldn't seem to think. Thoughts kept forming and then breaking off, splintering, like fragile things made of glass.

Instinctively he stopped next to the battered pickup in the driveway. The driver's window was down; he put his head through the opening. No key in the ignition. He half ran to the car ahead, saw that it was blue and had four doors and that all the windows were rolled up. He tugged at both doors on the near side. Locked. He put his face against the front-door glass, squinting. No key here, either. Empty. No goddamn *key* . . .

He spun away from the car, stood with his head swiveling loose on his neck. The driveway hooked through a tumbledown, gateless fence a hundred yards from the garage, joined a graveled road beyond that stretched away along the bayou. There were no other houses visible in that direction, no sign of another human being; the road dwindled into the greens and browns of the swamp rising above it, wall-like, tremulous and whispery in the wind. The other way, in front of the house, he saw a short, narrow boat canal that had been dug at right angles to the bayou. A rickety dock, shaded by a lean-to, flanked the near length of the canal, and turned upside down on the dock was the kind of dugout canoe the Cajuns called a pirogue.

He started over there. The bayou was a placid clay color, like a sheet of polished and pebbled brown glass—easy rowing, even for somebody who knew little enough about maneuvering boats. But to his left, the bayou narrowed and wound into swampland so thick that trees growing on the opposite banks intertwined with vines and moss overhead, to create a kind of tunnel; and to his right it cut sharply off from the road, some distance away, and seemed to curl back into the fen. He stopped, uncertain. A vision unfolded in his mind: alligators with yellow eyes, dark green snouts, gleaming rows of teeth; cottonmouth moccasins gliding through the currentless water; alien territory, dark, empty, menacing. What if he got in there and couldn't find his way out again? The Louisiana bayous were no place for strangers, no place for city dwellers. No place for *him* . . .

The road. Follow the road, he thought, find another house, get help.

He turned again, went back toward the driveway.

And froze in mid-stride, with his head craned forward.

The three of them were coming out of the swamp. Naked, painted, streaked with chicken blood, the two men still wearing their masks—looking right at him, running.

TWENTY

HE ran too, without hesitation, coming out of his frozen stance the way he had been taught to come out of the blocks at the starter's gun when he'd run the 440 and the 880 on his school track team. Before he had gone ten yards he was moving at maximum speed, at an angle across the grass toward the driveway.

They pounded after him, cutting between the truck and the car.

He reached the drive sixty yards from the fence. His shoes made crunching noises that he barely heard—an undersound in the roaring that filled his head. He did not want to look back—you lost speed when you looked back —but he did it anyway. They were less than forty yards away, the dragon in the lead. The look of them made the witch's brew of last night froth up again. Chasing him like savages in the wilderness, all naked and bloody, a pair of witch doctors and their throwback queen. Farce. More asylum humor. Somewhere a cosmic audience was watching all this, convulsed in their seats, howling with demonical laughter. That was the only clear thought in his brain, and it simmered there, bubbling in the witch's brew, like a piece of meat in a cauldron.

Out beyond the fence, onto the bayou road. His lungs were starting to protest; cigarettes and inactivity had robbed him of the wind he used to have. The muscles in his legs wanted to cramp. He blinked, trying to see through the gray light at what lay ahead. But nothing lay ahead except the graveled ribbon, the bayou, the twisted shapes of the swamp pressed in on both sides.

He looked behind him again. They had fallen farther back, much farther back . . . they were barefoot, that was why, and they couldn't run barefoot on the gravel, and they were trying to keep pace through the tall debris-strewn grass that flanked the road. It looked like they were dancing —arms thrown out, legs kicking, breasts bouncing, genitals flapping up and down. He thought he could hear the cosmic laughter now. The gods up there, whoever they were, were rolling in the aisles; oh, it was funny, all right, hilarious. Why don't you leave me alone, you bastards? I never did anything to you. And he did not know if he ment the gods or the three of them back there, dancing and flapping and bouncing in pursuit.

The bayou made its turning ahead on his left. A short distance beyond, the road went the other way and the swamp reared up into a rich woven green barrier in front of him. He could feel himself winding down, sputtering; his breath came in ragged little explosions. When he started into the curve in the road he staggered, almost fell. Looked across his shoulder again as soon as he regained his stride.

They were no longer chasing him.

They had turned back, were running the other way.

A feeling of nascent hope came into him. He knew that they had not given up, that they were going back for the car or the truck; but it would take them minutes to run all the way into the house, find keys, come out and start a cold engine. Seven or eight minutes, at least. He could stay out in the open that long. If he didn't come on a house or a car, something, then he could get off the road and hide in the swamp. It grew dense along here, trees tall and spindly and so close together, so interwoven with creepers and brush, broken branches and down-logs, that it looked impassable. They wouldn't know where he'd gone into it. They wouldn't be able to search it. They could cruise up and down the road all day, looking for him, but they'd have to give it up sooner or later. And when they did he would get free.

The cramping in his right leg had grown worse; it was either slacken his pace or risk the leg giving out on him. He slowed into a trot. Ahead, the road jogged again, back to the left. The swamp growth was tight on both sides of it, overlapping in places to block out the sky. The smell of it was oppressive on the cold air: dampness, earthy decay; tannin and cypress mingled with the faint, elusive fragrance of blossoms. Birds screeched and frogs croaked, hidden among the foliage. Animals, or maybe snakes, rustled in the dark-green shadows.

He reached the jog in the road, went into it. Halfway through he saw what lay beyond. The bayou looped back on his left to parallel the road again for some distance, so close that there was nothing but a narrow grassy strip separating the two. On his right the vegetation thinned abruptly into a rumpled, boggy meadow strewn with wildflowers and dried brush. The meadow stretched out for fifty or sixty yards before the swamp reclaimed the terrain.

There were still no signs anywhere of human habitation; still no boats on the bayou or automobiles on the road.

He would have to move off the road pretty soon now. At least half the seven or eight minutes he had given himself had passed. Get beyond this open stretch, then into the swamp next to the meadow. The tightness in his leg had eased; the pressure in his lungs had also eased, and he had some of his wind back. He stepped up his pace again, head down, legs driving on the loose gravel.

Two-thirds of the way past the meadow, he heard the car come boiling along behind him.

He pulled his head around. One of the neighbors, someone to help him . . . but the engine was being revved up, and he could hear, too, the rushing noise of tires sliding on gravel. They *couldn't* have got inside the house, got the keys, started the car, come this far along the road, all in less than five minutes. And yet he knew it was them. Knew it even before he saw the car, the blue car, hurtle through the jog, fishtailing, throwing up a spray of earth and pebbles in its wake.

A wildness took hold of him. He jerked his head to the front, looked left, right, straight ahead. But he was trapped, he had no line of escape. Jump into the bayou and they'd be in after him in a few seconds, and there were alligators and snakes, and he was not much of a swimmer. Stay on the road and they could run him down if they felt like it. The meadow was no good because he could never get into the swamp before they got to him—but the meadow was all he had. He swerved in that direction, with his head full of the engine noise.

Wind tangles of brush rose ahead of him, made him veer parallel to the road in order to get around them. Brakes squealed, tires skidded a few yards away; the engine noise diminished to a rumble. And his foot jammed down crooked against something hidden in the grass, threw him off stride and then into a long lurching fall that put him on all fours. He scrambled up, half turned, and saw them running at him from the car—just the two men, still naked, still masked and bloody. One of them, the dragon, had a knife. Savages. Pagans. And he tried to run backward, stumbling, and went down again over a rotting limb that cracked like old bones when he landed atop it.

Then they were on him.

The hard edge of a foot slammed against his temple—glancing blow, sharp stinging pain—and he tried to grab the flailing leg, and another foot kicked him in the stomach. All the air went out of his lungs; he heard himself make retching noises. He couldn't see. There was sweat in his eyes, something else that might have been blood. He swung his arms, thrashed his legs, tried to scuttle away. But they swarmed over him, pummeling his head, his back, his ribs. Blackness welled up behind his eyes and he thought he was going to suffocate, thought he was about to die. Then his lungs inflated convulsively, amid lances of pain, and he heard someone screaming, and knew it was himself. They kept on kicking him and hitting him until he stopped struggling, until the screams became whimpers and his consciousness seemed to career around inside his head. He did not even know when it was that they stopped; one moment he was down in the grass with them beating on him, and the next they had him up, sandwiched between them, and were dragging him back to the road.

He had no strength left, no control over his body. His legs scraped under him like sticks. When they got to the car one of them opened the rear door and they shoved him inside, face down across the seat. Hands bent his legs in, slid one knee over ridged rubber matting. The door slammed. He heard them in the front seat, a long way off, saying words to each other that sounded slowed down, distorted, like a recording played at half-speed. The engine roared, and that, too, was distorted, and the car moved, and the motion made him want to be sick. The car moved, his stomach moved, but nothing came up or out except little belches that tasted like blood.

There was an empty time, a black space where dragons

and devils danced around a fire that had no flames and gave off no heat. Then there was a jolt, and awareness again: the car had stopped. He heard one of the voices, and this time it was normally pitched, intelligible. Chalmette's voice. It said, "All right. We'll put him in the house."

Another voice: "Where?"

"Storage pantry. No window in there."

Doors opening, hands on him again—rough hands pulling him out, standing him up. Images wheeled in front of his eyes: garage, pickup truck, gray house, green grass, gray sky, green swamp. Cold wind against his face, and the smell from the shed, the smell of death. He made an attempt to pull free, but it was feeble and reflexive, like the last empty struggle of an alligator trapped, stunned, ready for butchering. The hands gripped him harder, dragged him along to the house.

Through a door, into musty darkness. He seemed to be blind; shapes appeared in his vision but he could not tell what they were. Another voice said, "Good, you got him." It sounded like Juleen's voice and it came from close by, but he could not see her either.

"Yeah." Chalmette. "He stayed on the road."

"Did anyone see?"

"No. Nobody out and around this time of morning."

"What now?"

"We'll put him in the pantry until we're ready."

The word *ready* echoed dimly in his mind as they hauled him across wooden floors, through tunnels of darkness. Ready. Ready, ready, ready. Ready for what? Goat without horns. Voodoo. Kill me too? Cut off my head like the chickens'? He tried to put the thoughts into words, but he had no voice. He couldn't see and he couldn't speak. He could only hear, and feel—pain, layers of it piled up like a de Sade parfait.

They stopped. A key made a scraping sound; door

hinges creaked. Then the hands shifted from his arms to his back, pushed him and sent him stumbling through a wall of black. He ran into something yielding, went over and down with it; a sharp edge dug into his ribs; there was the banging clatter of cans or jars spilling out of a box and rolling across the floor. He rolled over himself, grunting, and lay there hurt. Listened to the door slam shut, the key scrape again in the lock, the diminuendo of footsteps and the last can or jar come to rest against a wall.

Listened to silence.

TWENTY-ONE

HE lay motionless for a long while, until his eyes adjusted to the gloom. Vague outlines appeared, unidentifiable; opposite him and down low where he lay, a strip of pale light marked the bottom of the door. His mind began to adjust, too. Thoughts crawled up through the layers of pain, formed a cohesiveness that was wrapped in self-pity.

They were going to kill him and he didn't know why. Maybe they would never tell him; maybe he would die without knowing—and that would be almost as terrible as dying itself. Only two or three more minutes out there and he would have got away from them, he'd have been safely hidden in the swamp. How could they have started their car and come after him in less than five minutes? There just hadn't been enough time . . .

But then he saw how there could have been enough time: a spare key hidden somewhere on the outside of the blue car, in one of those magnetized containers, so that they hadn't had to go all the way into the house. Sure. Gods had set that up too, just like they'd set up everything else. They had never given him a chance. A bumbling puppet,

197

that was all he was. A jester in a cosmic masque.

The darkness was making him claustrophobic. He could feel it pressing down on him, as if it had weight and substance. He rolled over again, onto hands and knees, and pushed his body off the floor; stood wobbly with his legs spread, orienting himself by the strip of light under the door. The area around his kidneys felt inflamed; so did his ribcage, the left side worse than the right. When he tried to take a deep breath, pain stabbed upward into his armpit and made him gasp. Broken ribs? Didn't make any difference, he thought bitterly. They were going to kill him anyway, sooner or later. He was sure of it now.

He groped his way to the door and fumbled blind along the wall next to it. No light switch. But they had to have a light in here somewhere. Pantries had to have lights in them, how could you find anything in the goddamn dark? He moved away from the door again, waving his hands in the air in front of him, searching for a pull cord or chain. Didn't find one of those either. A dull, impotent rage began to work inside him. Why wasn't there a light? Why couldn't they let him have a little light? He was going to die pretty soon, it wasn't asking much to chase away the dark for a while, he couldn't stand to wait in the dark—

One of his questing hands brushed against a wall, slapped at the same time across something that felt like a hanging piece of string. He clutched at the string with desperation, caught hold of it, jerked downward. Weak yellowish illumination crowded the darkness back into heavy folds, like blackout curtains being opened. Low-wattage bulb, and not on the ceiling; on the wall to the left of the door. What the hell kind of place was that to put a pantry light? On the wall, for Christ's sake. On the *wall.*

The pantry was an oblong box, a dozen feet deep and eight feet wide, with crooked homemade shelves along three walls. Exposed ceiling beams extended down to within a foot of his head, and cobwebs guarded the shadows between them. Part of the floor space was taken up with boxes of canned goods; it was one of those that he'd fallen over and broken open. The only way in or out was through the door.

He sat exhaustedly on a stack of two cartons; there was nothing else to do. In the pale light, he saw the patterns of black on his hands. Cuts, scrapes—blood. Third time, now. The blood Sunday morning in Juleen's house, the blood yesterday from the voodoo doll. Only not the same as those two times because it was *his* blood, just as he'd been afraid it would be.

Juleen, he thought.

He'd seen her, heard her, she was here . . . not dead after all, not harmed on Saturday night. Then whose body had been down there in her cellar? Whose death had he smelled? Voodoo rites . . . goat without horns . . . Mona. What about Mona? Why hadn't she been out in that clearing earlier, smoking dope and dancing naked and making it a foursome for the orgy?

His head ached; he could not think about it any more. He had no answers to any of the questions. There were no answers. Cosmic masque, that was the nonanswer to everything. All set up, all written out—and everybody had a script except him.

Minutes ticked away. It was cold in the pantry; his muscles and joints stiffened, and he began to shiver. He got up and limped back and forth. The rage welled up, mingled with the fear, and seemed to erupt inside him: he ripped jars and bottles off the shelves, shattered them against the walls. But the outburst did not last long. The fury left him all at once, and he sank onto the boxes again. Sank into desolation again. What was the use? It was all hopeless. Let them come for him, let them get it over with. That was all he asked. Make it soon, and make it quick.

He was sitting there like that, slumped on the boxes and slumped inside himself, when the footsteps echoed outside the door. He looked up, heard the key rattle in the lock. Good, he thought dully, it's about time. The door opened, and the two of them appeared, Chalmette and the dragon, both dressed in Levi's and pullovers, the dragon with Chalmette's fat-bladed hunting knife in one hand. They stood looking in at him, or past him at the wreckage on the floor.

The dragon said, "What did you do in here, man?"

"Bastards," Giroux said. The word tasted good in his mouth and he said it again. "Bastards."

"I could stick you, you know that? I could cut you up like those 'gators out back."

"Ease off," Chalmette told him.

"He didn't have to break things up like that, did he?"

"Never mind that. It's only a few bottles and jars."

"Who's going to clean it up?"

"Juleen'll clean it up. What's the matter with you?"

"I'm stoned, man. And it's my pantry."

Chalmette made a beckoning gesture. "Okay, Giroux. Out of there."

"So you can beat me some more? So you can kill me?"

"Out of there."

He got painfully to his feet, limped out into a dim, narrow hallway. Neither of the two men touched him as he went past. Chalmette said, "Just keep walking," and he obeyed, and when he came to the end of the hall Chalmette said, "Left," and he turned left through a doorway. That put him in an old-fashioned parlor: old mismatched furniture, blackened fireplace, grime on the walls and dust balls and candle wax on the floor. Over the mantlepiece was a painting similar to the one in Juleen's house—giant snake rearing above kneeling worshipers, with the words *Danse Calinda* in scarlet across the bottom.

A straight-backed chair had been positioned in front of the hearth; the dragon told him to sit in it. He did that, and the two of them came over in front of him. He didn't look at them. He looked at his hands, saw that they were shaking, and locked them together between his thighs. Then he looked at the cracks in the bare floor at his feet.

Chalmette said, "Where's the photograph?"

"I don't have any photograph."

One of them slapped him across the face. Not hard; just hard enough to snap his head, to sting. He still did not look up. The boards in the floor were warped and stained; here and there he could see nailheads poking up.

"The photograph, Giroux."

"I don't know anything about a photograph."

Another slap.

"Where's the photograph?"

"I don't know."

Slap.

"The photograph."

"Why don't you ask Juleen where it is?"

Slap.

"The photograph."

"Or Mona. Ask Mona."

Slap.

"What did you do with it?"

"I don't have your damned photograph."

Slap.

It went on and on like that. He kept staring at the nailheads in the floor, counting as many as he could see. One, two, three, four . . . Then the dragon said, "Let me cut him a little," and a nailhead of panic poked up inside him and made him lunge off the chair. They caught him, shoved him back down. Slapped him.

"Where's the photograph?"

"I don't have any photograph."

Slap.

Sometime later the dragon laughed and said he was enjoying this. He said he wanted another joint, he was enjoying it so much, but Chalmette told him no, not yet. "But it's Mardi Gras, man," the dragon said, and Chalmette said, "The photograph, remember? We've got to have the photograph." And the dragon said, "Sure, the photograph," and laughed again, and slapped him.

"Where's that photograph, man?"

"I don't know."

Slap.

On and on, on and on. Thirty-eight nailheads in the floor. Or was it thirty-nine? Or was it fifty-two?

"The photograph. Where is it?"

"I swear to you, I don't know."

Slap.

He waited for the question to be asked again. One of the nailheads was shiny on one half and stained with black wax on the other, so that it looked like a half-full moon. There was a kind of fuzziness inside his head, growing and creeping and turning gray at the edges. Saliva dribbled from one corner of his mouth. But he had no hands to wipe it away; his hands were still clasped between his thighs.

"Goddamn it," the dragon said, "where's that photograph?"

"I don't have your photograph."

Slap—harder this time.

Chalmette said, "That's enough. We're not getting anywhere. He's not going to talk."

"Maybe if I cut him a little . . ."

"He's cut up already. Look at him."

"Yeah. How about a joint, man, what do you say?"

"Not now. We've got things to do."

"But I'm starting to come down."

"Good. You can fly later; we can both fly."

"The real shit?"

"Why not? Juleen's holding, isn't she?"

"Fly me to the moon," the dragon said, and giggled.

"But not until later. Giroux comes first."

"Giroux and the photograph. Yeah, right."

They moved away from him, left him bent forward on the chair, like something broken in the middle. He could hear them talking to each other, but not what they were saying. And he wouldn't look at them; he refused to look at them.

The dragon and Chalmette quit talking, and one of them went away somewhere; he could hear a heavy tread going up a flight of stairs. The other one came back to him. Chalmette's voice said, "Get up, Giroux." But he couldn't get up. He could not make his body respond. Hands grabbed him again, hauled him to his feet and held him upright. A few seconds later he heard the heavy tread come back down the stairs, come into the parlor.

"How about these, man?"

"They'll do."

Another hand thrust something at him, up close to his face. Clothing—a faded workshirt and a pair of patched Levi's. He stared at them stupidly.

"Put 'em on," Chalmette told him.

"What?"

"Off with those rags of yours. Put these on."

"Why?"

"Just do it."

He did it. They didn't help him; they just stood watching as he fumbled his torn shirt off, stripped out of his tattered slacks. He had to sit on the chair to get the trousers off. His legs were a maze of scratches and ribbons of dried blood; he stopped looking at them, too. Covered them with the loose-fitting Levi's.

"I can't button the shirt," he said.

"Never mind that."

"Can't pull up the zipper either."

"Don't worry, man," the dragon said. "If your meat falls out, we'll just cut it off for you. No fuss, no muss."

Chalmette laughed. They both laughed. Then they gave him a wet towel and told him to wipe the blood off his hands and face. Then they took hold of him, one on either side, the way they had earlier, and pulled him out of the parlor, out of the house.

Sunlight danced off the brown water of the bayou, reflected like needles against his eyes and narrowed them to slits. The blue car was parked in the driveway, but the pickup was gone. When they got him to the car they leaned him against it, and Chalmette took a length of cord from one pocket and tied his hands behind his back. A thick red bandanna came out of another pocket; Chalmette wound it into a narrow strip, looped the strip over Giroux's eyes, knotted it tightly at the back of his head.

"Why are you tying me up like this?"

No answer. One of them reached out and opened the rear door; the other one's shoes scuffed through the gravel as he went around to the driver's side. Fingers splayed against the back of his head, pushed it down, pushed him inside and across the seat. He curled himself on his side, drawing his knees up. The rear door slammed. He heard them settling into the front seat, and then both front doors banged shut and the engine coughed, began to rumble.

"You just lie still back there," Chalmette said to him. "Don't raise up and don't try to slide the blindfold off. You understand?"

"Where are you taking me? What are you going to do?"

Neither of them answered him this time, either.

The car jerked into a turn and the tires made crunching noises as they rolled down the drive.

TWENTY-TWO

THE roads they traveled at first were unpaved, badly rutted in places. The jounce and sway of the car pitched him all over the seat. He curled tighter, fetally, until his chin touched one pulled-up knee, and tried to occupy his mind by listening for sounds. But there was little to hear—car, the cry of a bird, a jet plane flying overhead, the passage of three other vehicles. Chalmette and the dragon had nothing to say to each other or to him.

After a time they turned onto a paved road. More cars here; he could hear them whistling past. Trucks, too—big ones. He smelled petroleum, remembered vaguely that there were oil wells and pipelines and refineries all over the bayou country. A sentence from his reading ran across his mind: *The first oil well in the Louisiana bayous was drilled by Texaco in 1935.*

It was the dragon who finally broke the silence. "I think I'll have a joint. You want one, too?"

"Not while I'm driving. Not with him in back."

"I'm getting the fidgets, man."

"Then light up. Just keep it out of sight."

The acrid sweetish smell of marijuana drifted through the car.

"Things'll be heating up in town," the dragon said. "We missed Rex and Zulu this morning, you know?"

"The hell with Rex and Zulu."

"Zulu's the one I like. All those niggers dressed up like cannibals. Remember last year? That big bastard from—"

"Shut up about last year."

"Mardi Gras, man," the dragon said dreamily. "Don't you just fucking love it?"

They made another turn somewhere—onto a freeway or divided road this time, because their speed increased. The rush of the wind outside, the smoother, steadier motion of the car, combined with fatigue to put him into a torpor; it was neither sleep nor wakefulness, but a blending of the two, so that he seemed suspended in time and adrift within himself. Now and then sounds penetrated—a blaring horn, the thunder of a heavy truck passing or being passed, the disembodied voices from the front seat—but they seemed to glance off his consciousness, as surreal as the rise and fall of sounds in a dream.

A sudden sharp braking nearly rolled him off the seat. The dragon's voice said, "What the hell?" and then Chalmette's answer: "Stupid mother cut right in front of me. Almost hit him. Why don't these old farts learn how to drive?"

He opened his eyes under the blindfold; he felt cramped, damp with gritty sweat. They were moving slowly now. Horns honked, and not far away he heard the blast of a ship's whistle. In the front seat Chalmette said, "Look at this. Damn bridge is always jammed on Mardi Gras."

Bridge, he thought. He heard the ship's whistle again, and then the faint far-off music of a steam calliope. Mississippi River; New Orleans. Taking him back to Juleen's house?

They rode at a crawl for several minutes before the pace picked up again. The dragon's voice said, "How you doing back there, Giroux?" but he didn't answer. There was nothing to say. He eased himself onto his back, splaying his legs out to relieve some of the knotting in his muscles.

The calliope music grew louder for a time, faded and was replaced by the pulsing beat of jazz. New Orleans, yes. One of them rolled a window down; the throb of horns and drums seemed to surge into the car. They were on a city street: stop and go, stop and go, and people yelling somewhere, and the noise of traffic. They passed a bunch of revelers singing off-key—"If Ever I Cease to Love," the traditional song of Mardi Gras.

"If ever I cease to love,
If I ever I cease to love,
May I be stuffed
With sausage meat,
If ever I cease to love."

They made a turn and the singing voices diminished and were lost in other voices, other rhythms. They turned again. Quieter now, at least close by; but the Carnival noises pulsed in the background, and in his ears they were as thick with pagan delirium as the voodoo drums in the swamp this morning.

And then the car stopped and he heard the emergency brake being pulled on; but the engine did not shut off. One of them leaned over the seat back, tugged at the cord around his wrists. The dragon's voice said, "End of the line, Giroux."

The fear flickered in him—but that was all, just a flicker. Then it died and he was calm. An empty barren calm, like a derelict ship in the aftermath of a storm.

The dragon could not untie the cord from his wrists. He felt the point of a knife, and a moment later his hands were free. Chalmette told him to sit up but not to touch the blindfold. He sat up, rubbing at both wrists. His skin was cold.

"Listen up," Chalmette said to him. "When I tell you, open the door and get out. Take three steps, stand still, count to sixty. Then you can take off the blindfold. If you haven't got your brains up your ass, you'll go straight to wherever you stashed the photograph and wait for us to contact you. Don't try to leave town. And don't try calling in the cops; we'll know about it if you do, and you'll be a dead man. Sooner or later, Giroux—a dead man."

He could not seem to grasp the meaning of the words. "Are you letting me go?" he said, and it came out like the croaking of a frog.

"You've got until midnight. Understand?"

He managed to nod.

Something was pressed into his hands—smooth, round, ball-like, only it seemed to be made of wax. "That's a reminder, in case you forget," Chalmette said. "Now open the door and get out."

He opened the door, fumbled his way through it. Behind him he thought he heard the dragon giggling; then the Carnival sounds seemed to swell up in his ears. He took two steps, stumbled, regained his balance and took another step. Stopped. The air was cool, almost warm, but there were chills on his neck. He began to count to himself, slowly.

The car drove off; he heard it go. But he kept counting anyway, at the same slow pace, until he reached sixty. When he pulled the bandanna from his eyes, the impact of light and movement and bulking shapes was almost physical. He blinked several times, pawed at his eyes, slitted them. His surroundings settled into focus: railroad tracks, big building across a roadway with the word *JAX* in huge red letters along the edge of its roof. He moved his head in quadrants. Mississippi River, Greater New Orleans Bridge in the distance. Familiar section built up quayside—

Moonwalk.

He was at the foot of Jackson Square.

Two or three people in the vicinity were staring at him. He realized that, and looked down at himself, and saw the shirt they had given him hanging open, the fly of the Levi's unzipped, a ball of black wax in one hand and the red bandanna in the other, his chest and arms crosshatched with scratches. God. He stuffed the bandanna in one pocket, managed to zip up the fly. Then he limped away from the staring eyes, past the Jax Brewery building. Went across Decatur Street, dodging traffic and people and one of the horse-drawn carriages that lined the *banquette*. Went into the Square and found a bench to sink down on.

He looked at the ball of black wax. That was all it was; crudely fashioned, about the size of a baseball, with no markings of any kind. Not much weight, either. A reminder, Chalmette had said. More voodoo?

He was still looking at it when he sensed somebody standing near him. He glanced up. It was an old black woman, rail-thin, hair like tufts of white wool. Her mouth was pursed and her eyes showed disapproval; she pointed a gnarled cane in his direction.

"What you got there?"

"This?" He held up the wax ball. "I don't know."

"Where'd you get it?"

"Somebody just gave it to me."

"Bad," the woman said. "You'd best get shed of it."

"What is it?"

"Conjure ball."

"Voodoo?"

"No such thing as voodoo anymore," the woman said.

"But that's what that is. Evil *gris-gris;* I've seen 'em before. Break it open."

"Why?"

"Break it open. You'll see."

He broke it open. The wax was pliable; he had no trouble pulling it apart. Inside, at the core, was a wad of something that looked like hair, skin, nail clippings.

"They come from you?" the woman asked. "Hair and such?"

He looked closer at the wad. The lock of hair was curly, the same color as his. "I think so."

"Bad," the woman said. "Throw it away."

"Why? What does it mean?"

"Death, that's what it means. Conjure ball means death. Somebody doesn't like you, mister. No friend would give you a conjure ball, not even for a joke."

He said, "No, it wasn't a friend," and got to his feet. There was a trash receptacle not far away; he went to it and threw the wax ball inside. The woman watched him while he did that, nodded to herself, and then moved off on her cane.

He buttoned the shirt, went out of the Square onto the Chartres promenade. Bands, maskers, the jammed open-air Pontalba Bar. He hesitated, looking toward the bar. He needed a drink, several drinks. What time was it? Automatically he looked at his watch, saw that the hands indicated three-twenty, and thought: No, it's too early, it's not five o'clock yet. Then he realized how insane that was, the idea of regimenting his drinking after all he had been through. His mind was still dazed, out of sync. And maybe that was a good thing because it kept him from losing control.

He started toward the bar. And then came to a standstill and fumbled at the pockets of the Levi's. His wallet wasn't there. They had stolen it, or he had lost it, or it was still in the pocket of his own trousers back at the bayou

house. He had no money, no identification. He had nothing
any more.

Except the Pirate's Head. He could go there, get a
drink there—

The police, he thought. I could go straight to them
instead. They'll believe me now, they'll give me protection.
Won't they?

*Don't try calling the cops; we'll know about it if you do, and
you'll be a dead man. Sooner or later, Giroux—a dead man.*

He shook himself. He couldn't think yet, he couldn't
make decisions; he needed time. And a drink. God yes, a
drink. The Pirate's Head, then. Nowhere else to go right
now. And nowhere to hide.

He got through the crowd, went up Pirate's Alley to
Bourbon Street. Banners floated everywhere, silk sheets
and crepe-paper bunting draped balconies and half-
obscured building fronts—all in purple and green and
gold, the crown colors of Rex, King of Carnival. Firecrackers made gunshot noises around him. Most of the people
he saw were masked and costumed—men dressed as sandwiches, bales of cotton, hillbillies, gorillas, steamboat gamblers; women as playing cards, Marie Antoinette and
Cleopatra, flappers, Creole queens. Illusion everywhere;
buffoonery. And all of it draped in its own bunting of wild
merriment. The jazz beat flooded over him, never ebbing.
Passersby kept singing the foolish verses of the Mardi Gras
theme song he had heard earlier, the song an actress
named Lydia Thompson had sung for a visiting Russian
Grand Duke, Alexis Romanov, over a hundred years ago.

> *"If ever I cease to love,*
> *If ever I cease to love,*
> *May cows lay eggs,*
> *May hens give milk,*
> *If ever I cease to love.*

"If ever I cease to love,
If ever I cease to love,
May the queen in Buckingham Palace die,
May we all get drunk tonight,
If ever I cease to love."

He walked faster, shoving his way through the milling crowds. He kept telling himself it was only a few more blocks, he could have a drink, he could have ten drinks, he could wrap himself in the quiet of his room and lick his wounds. Only a few more blocks . . .

The smells washed over him: popcorn, beer, sweat, vomit, cotton candy, rum. He also knocked over a masked vendor, jostled an enormous black man in a red velvet-and-ermine costume and spilled his beer. Indians and Dutch maids and Peter Pan in rhinestones danced in the street. Strangers held hands and formed human ropes that seemed to coil around him, the way the cord had been coiled around his wrists and the bandanna coiled over his eyes.

He got up Ursuline somehow and saw ahead, through swirls of purple and green and gold, the crumbling architecture of the Pirate's Head. A procession of horses was prancing by, some drawing carriages full of costumed merrymakers, some carrying riders in spangled gold outfits; the animals' tails were dyed and plumed in purple, and the smell of their manure was ripe in the air. Trumpets blared. A mynah bird in a tinfoil-wrapped cage, carried by a scrawny Mephistopheles, began shrieking, "Birds can't talk! Birds can't talk!" Someone on the hotel gallery scattered confetti that fluttered down, glinting, like tricolored snow.

He found a way through the writhing mass on the sidewalk, into the lobby. Stood in the air-conditioned coolness, panting a little, dripping sweat. A masked couple came out of one of the elevators, gave him curious glances and detoured around him. The desk was draped in the Rex colors; the bellboy, at his post, wore a pirate's mask and so did the clerk. They looked at him as he approached, but without any particular interest, as if nothing they saw on Mardi Gras could surprise them.

"Key, please," he said. "Twenty-two." His voice sounded hollow, corroded. Birds can't talk, he thought. Dead pigeons can't talk.

The clerk gave him his key. And three pieces of paper. "Messages, sir."

He looked at them. They were from Mona, all three of them. She had called and wanted him to call back.

"I don't want these," he said, and crumpled the papers in his hand. "Throw them away."

He put the wad down on the desk, moved away without waiting for a response. He started for the lounge, thought better of it when the door opened and a woman came out and he had a glimpse of dozens of maskers inside. He changed direction, got into an empty elevator, rode it up to the third floor.

It was stifling in his room. He switched on the air conditioner, turned its controls to High Cool. Then he went to the phone, called room service, and told them to send up a fifth of vodka and a bucket of ice as soon as possible. The man said it would take twenty minutes or so, and he said for God's sake can't you make it faster, and the man said they would try but they were very busy right now —everybody was thirsty and everybody was hungry on Mardi Gras.

He slammed the receiver down and went into the bathroom. Avoiding his image in the mirror, he stripped out of the shirt and Levi's and put his battered body under the shower. He let the spray massage him for a long while, changing the temperature from hot to cold, hot to cold.

The cramped pain in his muscles eased; the bruised areas around his ribcage and over his kidneys lost some of their soreness. Cleansed of grime and dried blood, the cut in his palm had a raw inflamed look, but the other cuts and abrasions seemed superficial.

When he was out of the tub he located his traveler's bottle of Merthiolate, swabbed it on his palm, wincing, and then bandaged the cut. The mirror was opaque with steam; he wiped a circle clear with the towel, confronted himself. He did not look as bad as he had expected. The only marks on his beard-dark face were a scratch on one cheek and a cut on the temple where he'd been kicked. Only two of the bruises on his body were badly discolored, and both of those were smallish, under his ribs and along his back.

He wrapped the towel around himself, went out to sit on the bed. But he could not sit still. He was up again almost immediately, pacing on his sore legs. Where the hell was room service with the vodka? He called down again, but he couldn't get through; the line was busy.

He stood holding the phone. Call the police, he thought again. Tell them about the kidnapping. Tell them the whole story. They'll believe you, they'll find Chalmette and the dragon, they'll put a stop to all this. Theats or no threats—call the cops.

But he couldn't do it, not just yet. Not until he had a drink. Christ, how he needed a drink!

He also needed a cigarette. The sudden craving for tobacco sent him to the dresser, where he had put the carton he'd brought with him from home. He got a pack out, tore it open, put a cigarette between his lips. But then he couldn't find a light. He prowled the room, finally saw a packet of hotel matches in the table ashtray.

Knocking at the door.

About time, he thought. His hands quavered as he lit

the cigarette. He sucked smoke in greedily as he crossed the room, and he was thinking of the vodka when he opened the door. But it wasn't room service waiting in the hall.

Mona.

TWENTY-THREE

IF he had had his head together, he might have slammed the door in her face. But he did not have his head together; he just stood holding onto the inside knob, staring at her.

"God, Steven, what's happened to you?"

Concern in her voice. Concern in her face, too—hazel eyes all smudged and dark, as if she had not slept much; no lipstick, the red hair wind tousled. Pearl-colored coat buttoned up to the neck and both hands tight around a small pearl-colored purse. The Gray Lady look.

"Go away," he said.

"You've been hurt. They hurt you, didn't they."

"What do you care?"

"Darling, what *happened?*"

"Don't call me darling. I'm not your darling."

"Steven—"

"It won't work, Mona," he said, "not this time."

He started to close the door, but she came forward at the same time, in that aggressive way of hers, and put her shoulder against the panel. Her eyes probed his. He could not hold her gaze; he pivoted, went across the room. The cigarette was still in his mouth, wreathing his head in smoke, so that he had to squint sideways to see her through it.

She remained in the doorway, watching him. And behind her, just then, a uniformed busboy appeared with the vodka and ice bucket on a silver tray. Mona heard him, glanced around. Giroux called, "Come in, put it on the dresser," the hell with Mona. The busboy did as he was asked, silently. Giroux signed a chit, gave his attention to the bottle of Smirnoff. He had the cap off and three fingers poured when he heard the door close. He added ice, picked up the glass in both hands, and drank. Then he lowered himself into the chair and sat slumped there, looking at one of the walls.

Mona had not gone out with the busboy. She said from near the closed door, "Where did you go last night? What made you leave the way you did?"

"Why don't you answer the same question?"

"You woke up and found me gone—is that why you left?"

He drank again, by way of an answer.

"I knew I shouldn't have left you," she said. "But I was hungry, starved, I hadn't eaten since noon; and there's no room service at the Mason House after eleven o'clock. I went downstairs to the coffee shop to get us some sandwiches."

"Sure you did."

"But they were busy and it took longer than I thought. I should have written you a note, or woke you to tell you I was going. But you were sleeping so soundly . . . I thought it would be all right. Steven, where did you think I'd gone?"

The vodka had a relaxing effect on him, but it also made him feel incredibly tired. He did not want to listen to any more lies. He did not want to act out any more cosmic farces. He said, "I found the tickets, Mona. I was out of matches and I looked in your purse for some and I found the goddamn tickets."

"Tickets," she said.

"Quit playing innocent. You know what I mean."

"Your airline tickets."

"That's right."

She opened her purse and took out a familiar blue-and-white folder. "These," she said.

He sat up. A memory swirled out of the mist inside his head: he had taken the folder last night, put it into his jacket pocket before leaving her room. He jabbed out his cigarette, got to his feet and went to her and took the folder from her hand. The United Airlines tickets inside were his.

Turning, he threw the folder down on the dresser. He still had the glass in one hand; he splashed more vodka over the ice.

Mona said, "They were waiting for me when I came back from lunch today. In an envelope at the hotel desk— no message. I didn't know what to think, because you told me they'd been stolen from your room."

Lies. "She gave them to you, didn't she?" he said. He drank. "She left the bayou house early; she probably drove straight back here and the two of you had a conference."

"You're not making sense. Steven, I never saw those tickets until this morning."

"No? Then what were they doing in your purse last night?"

"Someone must have put them there."

"Sure. When?"

"While we were together in the lobby, before we went up to my room. That has to be it. I looked in the purse before I went downstairs and met you."

He shook his head: Lies.

"When you went to buy cigarettes and I was waiting at the elevator," Mona said. "A man bumped into me—I didn't pay much attention to him—and that must have been when it was done."

He said it aloud this time: "Lies."

Her mouth tightened. She came over to him, took the glass out of his hand like a mother taking something away from a difficult child; again he was aware of the strength of her, the aggressive will. She set the glass down, stared so hard into his eyes that he could feel a kind of optokinetic force.

"You think I'm involved in what's been happening to you, don't you?" she said. "You think I'm mixed up with Chalmette and the others?"

He averted his gaze. "Aren't you?"

"No, I'm not."

He didn't speak.

"Look at me, Steven. Look at me!" And when he obeyed, "I'm not involved, I don't know who those people are, I had nothing to do with stealing your airline tickets and I did not put them in my purse. That's the truth."

"Then why would they do it? Why steal them and put them in your purse? Why take them away from me again last night and give them back to you?"

"To turn you against me. That's the only thing I can think of."

"Why?"

She put her small hands on him—cool fingers on the sweaty flesh of his upper arms. "All I can tell you is that I'm Mona Jensen, I'm a teacher from Milwaukee, and I've never been in New Orleans in my life until I came here for Mardi Gras last Thursday. If you want me to, I'll give you a dozen references in Milwaukee and you can call them and ask them about me. They'll verify what I say."

Her eyes were like they had been last night in her room: bright, hot, all green with emeraldfire. Magnetic—pulling at him, commanding him, so that he could no longer look away even if he wanted to. And he did not want to, now. He felt himself weakening, losing some of his conviction against her, the sense of betrayal.

"You came to me on faith yesterday and asked me to believe what you told me," she said. "Well, I did believe you; I still believe you. Now I'm asking you to believe me, on that same faith. I'm not one of them, Steven."

The last of his defenses crumbled; bewilderment swept away the debris. He was alone and empty, eviscerated, and he wanted to believe in something again, and so he believed in her. Blindly—like a whipped dog groveling at the feet of a stranger, laying itself open to another beating. He put his arms around her, and she came in tight against him, and the warmth and strength that funneled into him was infinitely better than that which the vodka gave him.

"I've been frantic ever since I came back last night and found you gone," she said. "I tried calling you a dozen times; I stopped by here twice before this to see if you'd come back. I thought . . . God, I thought they might have killed you."

"They almost did."

She drew back from him, touched his face. "What happened? What did they do to you?"

"Kidnapped me. Took me to a place in the bayou country. Mona, you were right: it's some kind of crazy voodoo cult."

"You mean they—?"

"No, they didn't do any blood rites with me. But I saw them dancing naked, and Juleen had a snake and she cut off the head of a chicken and drank its blood."

Mona grimaced. "Then she is alive."

"Yes. She's one of them."

"How many others?"

"Two that I saw, two men. They're on drugs, all of them—hard drugs. That's part of it, too."

"You'd better tell me, Steven." The emeraldfire was brighter, fueled by anger. "Everything that happened."

He lit another cigarette, took a small sip of vodka, and relived it for her in detail. But it was as if it had happened to someone else, and he had stepped in as an *ex post facto* surrogate: he felt removed from it, as though his mind refused to credit an involvement in that much terror. Mona's mouth twisted into an expression of disgust when he recounted what had taken place in the swamp clearing; and twice—when he told her about the beating, then about the interrogation inside the house—she bit her lip. Otherwise she stood expressionless, her gaze never leaving his face.

When he was done she said, "Are both of the men young? Juleen's age?"

"They were masked the whole time. But their bodies looked young, and they sounded young. Mid-twenties."

"Did they say anything about the photograph? What it might be of?"

"No, nothing."

"It might have something to do with drugs."

He nodded. "But then there's no possible connection to me. I don't do drugs, I don't even know anybody well who does. What would I be doing with a drug-related photograph? Or a voodoo-related photograph? Or any goddamn photograph that would interest their kind?"

"Tell me again what they said to you. In the house and in the car."

He told her, omitting only the obscenities.

She was thoughtful for a time. Then she asked, "Did either of them have a gun?"

"No. The knife was all I saw."

"Well, that gives us one potential advantage."

"What?"

"I *do* have a gun, Steven."

"Are you serious?"

"Of course I'm serious."

"But where would you—?"

"I brought it with me from home." She put a hand into her coat pocket, took it out again and showed him the weapon. He stared at it. Small and silver-plated, with a white grip—but it looked enormous in the tiny curve of her hand. "There's so much crime these days," she said, "everywhere you go, and it's even worse for a woman alone. I don't feel safe unless I have it nearby."

"You carry it around with you all the time?"

"No, of course not. I usually keep it in my nightstand at home, in the hotel nightstand whenever I travel. But I wanted it with me, after all you've been through." She put the gun away in her coat. "I have a permit for it. And I know how to use it; my late husband was a very good instructor."

"Mona, what are you suggesting?"

"The only thing we can do, under the circumstances. Take matters into our own hands."

"How? Do what?"

"Track them down, find out who they are and what they want, and put an end to it."

"That's for the police to do, not us."

"But the police won't do it"

"Why won't they?"

"You have no evidence to convince them, that's why."

"Look at me. Aren't these cuts and bruises evidence?"

"Not of anything conclusive. You don't know who Juleen and the two men are; you don't know Juleen's address or where the bayou house is located; you don't even know what sort of photograph they're after. What could you tell the police that would convince them you're not a crank? This is Mardi Gras—the police are probably swamped with crimes and drunks and cranks. They wouldn't do anything,

Steven, at least not quickly enough to protect you. You must see that."

He didn't know what he saw. Maybe going to the police was the right thing to do; but maybe it wasn't. Maybe Mona was right. What if they treated him like a crank and threw him out? Chalmette would know he'd gone and Chalmette would kill him. Sooner or later. Except that Chalmette was going to kill him anyway, sooner or later. Wasn't he?

If only he could believe, really believe that the police would help him. Mardi Gras lunacy, hundreds of incidents, dozens of wild stories . . . would they listen, would *they* believe? Would they assign men to protect him, men to search for Chalmette and the dragon? Or would they just send him back into chaos?

"I've *got* to go to them," he said aloud. "It's the only way. I'm not a hero Mona and neither are you. We can't go running around with a gun—"

"Of course we can."

"It's too dangerous."

"Desperate situation, desperate measures."

"I don't want you to get hurt."

"Darling, I'm not a shrinking violet, you know."

"I know that. But you could still get hurt."

"You've already been hurt."

"That's not an answer."

"Yes it is."

"Why do you want to take a risk like that? Why do you want to commit yourself to me?"

"Don't you know?"

"No, I don't know—"

"I love you, Steven," she said.

It jarred him. And it should not have, he realized in the aftermath, because all the signs had been there: the way she looked at him the past two days, the things she said, the giving of herself in bed. He had just been too frightened and too self-occupied to read them for what they were.

"Mona, I—"

"You don't have to say anything. It's all right. I didn't expect it to happen that way for you; I never thought it would happen so fast for me. But it has. And it's not infatuation; I'm not a frivolous woman. I love you. I knew it last night, after we made love. It was never like that for me before, not even once in all the years I was married to Ralph. It really was making *love*."

He felt embarrassed, confused. He didn't know what to say, how to handle this. It was important, and yet it was not important; it was something as removed from the person he was at this moment as the chain of events in the bayou swamp seemed removed in retrospect. How could he deal with love, when he was still trying to deal with voodoo and terror and the threat of death?

Mona said, "Does it upset you?"

"What?"

"That I love you. My being so frank about it."

"No. It's just that . . . I can't deal with it now."

"I understand. Believe me, I do. I won't say anything more about it; I won't put any pressure on you. When this is all over, we can talk about us. We can make arrangements to see each other in Milwaukee or San Francisco—get to know each other better, find out if you could learn to love me too. I wouldn't ask anything more of you than that."

"All right." It was something to say; it tabled the matter. But there was no objection in him, no underlying sense of disaffection. She was so strong; maybe he could learn to love her. Maybe. "When this is over," he said. "If I'm still alive."

"You mustn't worry any more. Nothing else will happen to you."

He lit a cigarette, wordlessly.

"I have a plan," she said. "I couldn't sleep last night,

thinking about you, and I worked it out then."

"What plan?"

"A way we can find out who they are. Do you think you can face Mardi Gras tonight, alone?"

"I don't know what you mean."

"Go out into the crowds, watch the Comus parade— just wander around the French Quarter for a while."

From outside he heard the muted sounds of merrymaking; the thought of going back into the climactic midst of it was repulsive. He asked, "Why?"

"They said they'd keep on watching you; and they haven't lied about that before. One of them is bound to follow you wherever you go. And if you point him out to me, then I can follow *him.*"

"What are you thinking? Just go up to him, put your gun in his back?"

"If it comes to that, yes. But he might just lead me to the others."

"They know who you are," he said. "They'd recognize you, even in the crowds."

"No they won't. I'll rent a costume; I'll be masked."

He scrubbed out his cigarette, reached for the vodka again. But Mona caught his wrist, gently; and with her other hand she pushed the glass to the far side of the dresser.

"Don't drink any more, Steven," she said. "You have to keep your wits, no matter what."

Even though he had no desire for it, he lit another cigarette: something to do with his hands. "Okay. No more liquor."

"Will you do it? Leave here when the time comes, point out whichever of them you see so there's no mistake?"

". . . I don't know."

"Just that much. If the plan doesn't work, then you can go to the police. There'll be enough time; Chalmette gave you until midnight. And I'll be there to make sure nothing happens to you."

God, she was persuasive. Strong and persuasive—and so positive. That was what he needed now, a sense that everything would be resolved by a definite course of action. He knew he was weakening again; feeling the force of her will, the power of that positive certainty.

"Steven? Will you do that much?"

"All right," he said. "All right."

She leaned up and kissed him. "It's the right thing, darling. You'll see. There won't be any more terror after tonight."

"No more terror," he said, tasting the words.

"I'd better go now, before it gets any later. The costume shops will be mobbed as it is."

"What if they see you leave? What if one of them decides to follow you?"

"I'll be careful."

"What kind of costume will you rent?"

"Whatever is available. I'll call you from the shop after I pick something out."

"Then what?"

"I'll come back here and wait for you outside."

"How will I let you know when I see one of them?"

She thought for a moment. "Run both hands through your hair," she said. "I'll come up close to you, just long enough for you to tell me what he's wearing."

He nodded, blew ragged jets of smoke through his nostrils.

"It shouldn't take much more than an hour to find a costume," Mona said. "You'll be all right until I call?"

"Yes."

"And you'll leave the liquor alone."

It was not a question. He said, "Yes."

She kissed him again. "It'll all be over soon, darling.

Just keep saying that to yourself. And keep believing it."

When she was gone the room seemed empty and too small; the scent of her lingered in the smoky air. Doubts moved in on him. What if her plan didn't work? What if something happened to her? Yet he'd committed himself; he *had* to go through with it. It was positive action—no less uncertain than putting himself at the mercy of a harrassed and skeptical police force. It was hope enough to sustain him over the next few hours.

He went about the task of dressing himself. No mask for him tonight; no elaborate Mardi Gras costume. Just slacks, sports shirt, sports jacket—the conservative look, reason in the midst of chaos. But it was reason without identity, because *he* had no identity. They had stolen his wallet, his papers, his money, his self-respect, and all but the shadow of his courage. He was functioning not on his own will or initiative, but on those of a woman he had not even known existed three days ago. He was nothing trying to become something again, a cipher trying to become a man.

He looked at the bottle of vodka on the tray. *Don't drink any more, Steven. You've got to keep your wits, no matter what.* Lara wouldn't have been content with that. Oh no, she'd have made an issue of it; she'd have yelled at him, called him names, told him he was a damn disgusting drunk. But not Mona. Just a firm Don't drink any more, Steven, and that was all. Why couldn't he have met someone like Mona fifteen years ago? Married *her,* had a child by *her?* His life wouldn't have crumbled on him then, would it? Or would it? Maybe he was just one of those people born to screw up, be unhappy, suffer indignities—a loser who didn't even know he was a loser until half his life was gone.

Self-pity again. Cut it out, Giroux. *You've got to keep your wits, no matter what.* All right. Hang on, then, and pretty soon it'll all be over. No more lunacy. No more terror. No more *losing*.

He looked at himself in the mirror. And realized he hadn't shaved. Put his clothes on, got himself all set to go out, and he hadn't even shaved. He took off the sports jacket, the shirt, and went in and scraped off the stubble of whiskers on his cheeks and chin.

When he was finished he turned on the television, to have some sound in the room and to override the Carnival charivari that penetrated from outside. Then he sat in the chair, lit another cigarette and stared at the flickering images on the TV screen without seeing them.

He was on his fifth cigarette, chain-smoking, when the telephone rang. He hurried to the nightstand, snatched up the receiver. "Mona?"

"Yes darling," she said, and the sound of her voice was like a lever releasing the tension inside him.

"Did you get a costume?"

"Yes. Lady Guinevere, with a green mask with gold sequins. It was the only one I could find that was distinctive enough without making me too conspicous."

"Lady Guinevere," he said. "I don't know what that is."

"Old England; King Arthur's time. Long purple gown, a gold cloak, a pointed hat with purple and gold streamers. And the green sequined mask. Can you visualize it now?"

"I think so, yes."

"I should be able to get back there in about fifteen minutes; I'm on Royal Street now. But you'd better give me a half hour, just to be safe."

"Where will you be?"

"Somewhere near the hotel entrance. Don't look for me. I'll show myself to you."

"All right. How long should I stay out?"

"As long as you can stand it. A couple of hours, at

least, whether you see me anywhere or not. Then go back to the hotel and wait for my call. I'll call as soon as I find out anything."

She rang off. He looked at his watch, saw that it was a quarter past six, and then returned to the chair. To smoke another cigarette, to stare at the TV images and at the darkening sky beyond the window embrasures, to wait for thirty minutes to crawl away. And to think, over and over, until the words were like a silent prayer: It'll all be over soon, it'll all be over soon, it'll all be over soon . . .

TWENTY-FOUR

It was dusk when he came out through the front entrance of the Pirate's Head. The sky, swept free of clouds, was stained a rich purplish hue and studded with rhinestone stars, as if the heavens, too, had masked for the final hours of Mardi Gras. Streetlamps, building lights, strings of Rex-colored bulbs put streaks and daubs of brilliance on the velvety dark, gave the banners a luminous sheen here and there along the packed streets. Firecrackers rattled and popped like artillery fire. Trumpets and drums, noisemakers and raucous singing, created such a vibratory sound that he imagined he could feel tremors in the pavement beneath his feet.

He looked for Mona, didn't see her. Even here, blocks removed from the hub of the Quarter, the crowds were thick—a tide of weirdly costumed humanity, ebbing and flowing along the *banquettes,* spilling over into the streets. Creole queens, princesses, giant flowers, witches, Annie Oakley, even a walking Sazerac cocktail; but no Guinevere. No dragon, either. And no voodoo devil. Just the writhing, alien gaiety of the masque congealing around him, stretch-

231

ing on endlessly into the purple and gold darkness.

His resolve faltered. I can't do it, he thought. I can't become part of this . . .

He saw Mona.

She came across Ursuline toward him, moving with half a dozen others, gold streamers fluttering from her pointed hat. A short veil, and the green sequined mask, covered most of her face. He stood still, watching as she stepped onto the *banquette,* hesitated for a moment, and then put her back to him and crossed Burgundy. She gave no sign that she knew him or had even seen him.

The resolve came back, solidified. He could do it. All he had to do was walk around; it was Mona who was taking most of the risk. On his behalf—risking her life for him. And it was *his* life that was at stake here, wasn't it?

One of the singing group, a woman dressed as a masked nun, with a go-cup full of beer in one hand, plucked at his arm. She sang at him invitingly in a whiskey contralto, spattering his face with moist beer fumes.

> *"If ever I cease to love,*
> *If ever I cease to love,*
> *May the moon be turn'd*
> *To green cream cheese,*
> *If ever I cease to love."*

He shoved away from her, into the street. He could no longer see Mona, but she wouldn't lose sight of him, no matter how thick the crowds got. He had to believe that much. He went down Ursuline—one block, two. The smells came at him again in a choking miasma. Jazz music hammered the night; he heard snatches of "Basin Street Blues" and "Oh Sister Ain't That Hot?" Bourbon Street was a river of maskers dancing, yelling, throwing confetti from party-lit balconies and galleries; of vendors hawking bal-

loons and popcorn and cotton candy; of combos and solo-
ists jamming on every block.

He stopped on the corner, let the crowd flow around
him while he scanned the masked faces. Mona was behind
him; he could see the pointed hat and the gold streamers.
But there were still no dragons, still no devils.

A black woman dressed as a panther sidled up to him
and made deliberate purring sounds. "Mardi Gras date,
honey?"

"No," he said.

"It'll be a party you won't forget."

"No."

She made a claw of one hand and scratched him lightly
across the chest. "Go screw yourself then, honey," she said,
and purred again, and went away.

He walked down to Royal. Another river here, and one
he couldn't ford: both sides of the street were packed solid
with maskers waiting for the start of the Mystick Krewe of
Comus. Down Royal, up Orleans, out of the Quarter to
Beauregard Square and the Municipal Auditorium—that
was the parade route. He turned around, headed back toward Bourbon. Passed Mona and did not look at her.

He pushed his way up this street, struggled down that
block, making each turn mechanically. Now and then he
stopped to peer at the surrounding masks. Mona was still
following, still nearby. He saw dragons, he saw voodoo
devils, but they were the wrong size or the wrong shape or
the wrong sex. Maybe, he thought once, they weren't
watching him tonight after all. Maybe they had given up,
gone away. But he did not believe it; it was false hope,
another lie. At least one of them was there in the crowd,
somewhere close by. He could almost feel the eyes on him
—dragon's eyes, devil's eyes.

He made himself think about other things. He thought
about Marcie, and wondered how something so good and

sweet could have come from a union between him and Lara. Not a mean bone in her body. She'd found a baby mouse once, half-dead, mauled by a cat, and nursed it back to health, and then let it go when it was well enough and old enough to fend for itself. She'd stood up to a boy two years older than she was for antagonizing a playmate, and broken her thumb in the fight that followed, and Lara had been appalled and tried to discipline her, but he'd stepped in on the child's behalf. One of the few times he'd shown any guts, paternal or otherwise. Stepped in and praised Marcie for caring, and refused to punish her, and Lara had jumped him about it later and wouldn't let him touch her for two weeks afterward—God, what a bitch she was. But Marcie . . . Marcie was a wonderful kid. Smart as a whip, too, especially when it came to math. The new math they taught kids these days bewildered him, he wasn't sure he even approved of it, but she loved it. Said she wanted to be a computer technician when she grew up. Eleven years old, for God's sake, most girls were still playing with dolls, or getting ready to play with boys, and she was already talking about a career in computer science . . .

Another corner, this one claimed by harlequins with banjos and fiddles playing bluegrass music. He dragged a cigarette out of his pocket, his mind still on Marcie . . . old memories, good memories. Stepped back against a building wall to strike a match. Glanced behind him as he did, at the maskers nearby.

And the dragon was there.

Standing ten feet away, implacable as ever, staring straight at him.

The matchbook slipped from his fingers; he did not pick it up. Near where the dragon stood was a lamppost wrapped in purple and green and gold lights, and the radiance bathed him in a surreal glow: he looked less like a masker than a mythical being come to life. Giroux resisted the impulse to look for Mona. Instead, he moved away from the building, away from the bluegrass musicians, and crossed the street. On the far *banquette* he stopped again, ran his hands through his hair. Patted his pockets, found more matches. Ran his hands through his hair a second time.

He had the cigarette lit, and was shaking out the match, when the figure of Guinevere came up beside him. "Don't look at me," Mona said. "He's just across the street."

"You saw him?"

"He's been following you for the past ten minutes. Probably all the way from the hotel, without the mask."

"I didn't see him until just now."

"He's coming across. Don't say anything else. Just start walking again."

His legs worked, obeying her, and carried him along with the revelers. He was afraid to look back, afraid he would do something to give Mona away. The smoke from the cigarette made his throat burn, made him cough. He pitched the butt into the street.

He was nearing Bourbon Street again. The noise level had picked up: blaring jazz, the shill for a topless club screaming at the top of his voice, a woman's hysterical laughter. He saw a war-painted, half-naked Indian riding a white mule, and three black women in blonde wigs and whiteface singing Al Jolson's "Mammy," and two cowboys staging a mock gunfight, and an Arabian shiek pouring beer over the head of Blackbeard the Pirate, and Little Miss Muffett drunkenly trying to peer under Tarzan's loincloth while he imitated a jungle yell and a group of onlookers howled with glee. It was all a seething mass of light and color and noise and confusion—an unreal world, a distorted version of the wonderland Alice found when she tumbled down the rabbit hole. It assaulted his senses, slashed at his nerves, drove him away at an angle across the street and back the way he had come.

He saw the dragon once more, but not Mona. What if she'd got lost in the throng already, or got lost in it later on? He shook his head. No, don't think that way. Don't think at all. Just walk.

Time passed in swirls of purple and green and gold. He saw Mona again. Didn't see the dragon. Saw the dragon. Didn't see Mona. Hide-and-seek. Now you see them, now you don't. Peekaboo, I see you, hiding in the middle of Mardi Gras. The phrases repeated themselves inside his head, like whispers, and were joined by others: If ever I cease to love, all twisted in the hole I'm in, there'll be a hot time in the old town tonight, mystick krewes and no booze, *laissez les bon temps rouler,* the old *joie de vivre,* bleeding dolls and conjure balls, and headless chickens and hornless goats, and Rex colors, and blood colors, and on and on and on . . .

He found himself on Governor Nichols Street, down near Royal again. The Comus parade was underway; he heard the martial beat of band music, caught glimpses of a group of flambeaux carriers—big dusky men, masked and stripped to the waist, torches held aloft and waving like batons in time to the music. Torchlight shone off their ebony skin, smeared flame against the dark sky above, cast bizarre shadows off the crumbling walls and wrought-iron balconies and costumed bodies that flanked the narrow street.

He turned away from that, too, and more time passed, and the hide-and-seek went on, and then the krewe was in front of him once more, on Orleans Street this time. Huge floats, waving maskers, showers of doubloons and glass beads, a continual multivoiced shout of *"Throw me something, mister!"* that ululated above the throbbing beat of the drums and the brass. Released balloons bobbing and weaving on currents of air, drifting skyward. Horses, policemen on motorcycles, more flambeaux carriers; giant serpents made out of flowers, the King and Queen of Comus with scepter upraised and bejeweled crowns glinting in the torchlight. Creeping along, creeping along, like a medieval funeral masque on its way to the cemetery.

He backed into a doorway, lit a cigarette. Threw it away almost immediately. Back to the corner, turn right, walk a block, turn left. No sign of Guinevere. No sign of the dragon. Another half-block, and a tree-shaded courtyard appeared on his left, and then a sign on a decaying old building with bricks showing beneath its broken-cement facade: *Lafitte's Blacksmith Shop.* Jean Lafitte, pirate and patriot. Supposed to have operated his "black gold" trade in slaves out of this shop. Supposed to—

He felt eyes on his back, someone watching him. There was a sudden crawling sensation on his neck, as if something with many legs was moving through the short hairs. He twisted around.

The voodoo devil, Chalmette, was leaning against the courtyard gate.

He faced the sign again, jerkily; he seemed, now, to be having trouble with his motor responses. He walked to the corner, crossed the street to where more maskers clogged the *banquette.* Ran hands through his hair. Repeated the gesture as another mindless verse of "If Ever I Cease to Love" blared down from a nearby balcony. Come on, Mona. Where are you, for Christ's sake?

Someone beside him—but it wasn't Mona. Chalmette. "You've only got two hours left, Giroux," and the devil mask seemed to leer at him, and the knife Chalmette took from his pocket shone purple and gold and green in the instant before it disappeared again.

He wanted to run. Might have run if Chalmette had not moved first, glided away into the crowd and was absorbed by it. He stood still, with dark-hour feelings tumbling through him. Thinking: Mona, where are you? Where did you go?

The music swelled around him, lyrics speeding up in his perception until they were gibberish: "If ever I cease to love may fish get legs and cows lay eggs if ever I cease to love may dogs refuse to eat fresh meat if ever I potatoes grow on a mulberry mow cease to love may all the seas turn into ink love love if ever I cease to love . . ." A group of maskers went by waving sparklers that seemed to turn into pinwheels, whirling, blending with the other lights and the spectrum of colors. He shut his eyes, leaned against a gallery pole. A voice floated to him, disembodied: "Take it easy, fella, it's not even midnight yet. Mardi Gras's still got hours to run."

Hours to run.

But it'll all be over soon . . .

He took deep breaths to ward off the dizziness. His legs felt wobbly; fatigue was heavy in him. How long since he'd slept? Unconscious part of last night, chloroformed— but that wasn't sleep, wasn't rest. Two days? Too much strain, mental and physical. He was ready to collapse, functioning on bare reserves.

He just couldn't take any more of this. Two hours until midnight, Chalmette had said. He'd been out in the midst of Mardi Gras for three hours now, and Mona was gone and Chalmette was close by and *he* was vulnerable, and he had had enough. Go back to the hotel, where it was quiet and there was at least the illusion of safety. Maybe that was where Mona was; if she had lost him in the crowds, that was where she'd go, wasn't it? To the Pirate's Head to wait for him? And even if she wasn't there now, she'd come soon. Or call. He'd give her until eleven o'clock or a little after. Then he would call the police, no matter what.

He shoved away from the pole, recrossed the street.

Two blocks up St. Philip and then a turn down Burgundy. He tried to think about Marcie as he went, to keep himself calm, but he couldn't. His mind would not concentrate.

There were not as many people near the Pirate's Head as there had been earlier. The bulk of the revelers had drifted away to the clubs and topless bars on Bourbon Street, or were following the Comus parade up Orleans. Those left in the area were dancing on the *banquettes* and in the streets, spilling out of the hotel lounge and another bar just down the way. Smoky hot Dixieland poured from the bar, pulsing and shimmering in the cold night air.

He saw Lady Guinevere.

She came out of the shadows on Ursuline and hurried toward him, the pointed hat cocked sideways and the green sequined mask winking with pinpoints of reflected light. He came to a standstill, relieved, and waited to see if she would acknowledge him. She did: she came straight to where he was, put her hand on his arm.

"Mona," he said, "I couldn't take the crowds any more. I had to come back."

She didn't speak.

"What happened? Did you—"

He quit talking in mid-question, because her other hand had lifted and was tugging at the green mask. She pulled it up and away from her face—just a little, just enough.

"Where's the photograph?" she said.

It wasn't Mona; it was Juleen.

TWENTY-FIVE

HE reeled away from her, collided with someone and spun off against the hotel wall. He clutched at it, held himself upright. For a few seconds everything seemed to tilt again, combining vertiginously with the light behind his eyes; then the night and the street righted themselves, and he was blinking at an empty expanse of *banquette*.

Juleen was gone.

Two other maskers stood a few feet away, staring at him; one of them, a steamboat captain in gold braid and a Mark Twain mustache, was rubbing his arm and scowling. Giroux stumbled over to them. "Lady Guinevere," he said, thick voiced. "Where did she go?"

"Damn drunk," the steamboat captain muttered.

"Did you see where she went?"

The captain sidestepped him. "Up yours, buddy," he said.

Giroux spun off to the corner, but it was too late by then, she had vanished. He stood for a moment, looking up and down Burgundy, hearing somebody's gutbucket horn climb through a series of shrill riffs. Then he lurched to the hotel entrance and pushed through into the lobby.

Moments later he was in the elevator, and moments after that he was in his room with the door shut behind him and his hands fumbling the chain lock into its slot. The vodka bottle winked at him. *Don't drink any more, Steven. Damn drunk. Up yours, buddy. Damn drunk. You have to keep your wits, no matter what. Damn drunk, damn drunk.* And the thought of how the vodka would taste made his gorge rise, repelled him from the dresser and sent him to the bed. He collapsed on it, folded his arms over his face.

His thoughts settled like stirred-up dust. Mona's image came to him; the sound of her name seemed to echo, ghost-like, in his ears. Was she one of them or not? Had she given Guinevere to Juleen? Or had they taken it from her—abducted her like they'd abducted him, done something to her? He couldn't deal with it either way. He'd had enough. The time had come, the time was long overdue, for the police.

He sat up, looked at the phone.

And it rang.

He listened to it ring again, then stretched out a shaky hand and dragged up the receiver. A voice that did not sound like his said, "Hello?"

"You've got one hour, Giroux. Then you bleed like the doll. Then we cut off your fucking head."

Click. And silence.

An impulse came to him to rip the phone out of the wall, kill it so it could never shriek at him or threaten him again. But he thought: No, the police. He dropped the handset, clattering, into its cradle.

Blow after blow after blow. They knocked you down, you got up, they knocked you down again until you were punchdrunk and reeling. But just when you thought you'd reached the limit of what you could stand, and the next punch was sure to knock you out, that next punch came and you found you could take it and you realized you hadn't reached your limit after all. How much more could he take, then? How many more shocks?

Going to find out, he thought. Oh yes, I'll find out.

He picked up the receiver again. The pad on which he had written the number of the New Orleans Police Department was still on the nightstand. Steeling himself, he dialed the number.

The line was busy.

He took the handset away from his ear and stared at it. Busy, for Christ's sake? The goddamn police department's service line was *busy?* He could hear the cosmic laughter again, feel the intimations of mockery and manipulation. He slammed the receiver down, jerked to his feet as if on invisible wires.

His mouth was caked with dryness. He went to the dresser, caught up the ice bucket, drank the cold water in it in gulping swallows. Stuffy in there; he must have shut off the air conditioner earlier. He went over and switched it on. And then returned to the telephone.

The police number was still busy.

He lay down on the bed, got up again almost immediately and paced the room. Sat in the chair. Went into the bathroom to refill the ice bucket with tap water because his thirst still raged.

The telephone bell cut shrilly through the quiet.

The bucket slipped out of his hand; he heard it thud on the formica top of the sink cabinet. All right, he thought as the jingling repeated. But this is the last time. The last time. He went out and answered on the third ring.

"Steven? Is that you?"

Mona's voice. But he felt nothing, not yet. He sat down on the edge of the bed. "Yes," he said, "it's me."

"You sound strange. Are you all right?"

"No, I'm not all right."

"God, has something else happened?" Urgent, solicitous.

"I came back to the hotel," he said, "and Guinevere was waiting for me. Pointed hat with gold streamers, and a green mask. Only it wasn't you. She pulled up her mask and it was Juleen."

"My God." And then silence.

"How did she get to be Guinevere, Mona? Did you give her your costume?"

"Of course not. I'm still wearing it. Steven, you're not doubting me again?"

"How did she get to be Guinevere?"

"I don't know. Unless . . ."

"Unless what?"

"Unless she followed me to the costume shop after I left you. I was careful to look for men in dragon or devil masks, but I just didn't think to watch for a woman."

He said nothing.

"That must be it," Mona said. "Don't you see? She followed me and saw the kind of costume I rented. So she managed to get a duplicate for herself, and then went back to the hotel to wait for you."

"Why would she do that?"

"To frighten you. Did she say anything?"

"Just 'Where's the photograph?' Then she disappeared."

"I see. Steven, you haven't called the police yet, have you?"

"I tried to," he said. "But their line was busy. Can you believe that? Their line was busy!"

"It's Mardi Gras, that's why. I'm glad you didn't get through."

"Why?"

"Listen to me carefully," she said. "I know where Juleen's house is."

He sat there. The embryo of something that wanted to become hope formed inside him, wriggling. "How do you know?"

"I followed the man in the dragon mask. He met the other one, Chalmette, while you were watching the parade on Orleans Street. They talked for a minute or so, and I got close enough to hear part of what they were saying. The dragon said he was tired of following you and wanted to go to the house. For some sort of drug fix, I gathered. Chalmette said he would take over and meet him there later. After that, the dragon led me straight to the house."

"Where?"

"On Race Street. In the Irish Channel, not far from the park on Tchoupitoulas. It's the same house you were in; I'm sure of it."

The hope grew, fetuslike, and began to bulge within him. "You're not lying to me? You really know where this house is?"

"I swear it to you."

"What's the address?"

"I'm calling from an all-night cafe on Magazine Street, not far away from there," she said. "What I want you to do is take a taxi and meet me here."

"Why? What for?"

"So we can go to the house together. So we can confront them. Chalmette and Juleen should have arrived by the time we get there; we'll make them admit what they've been doing to you, and why."

"We can't do that."

"Yes we can. I have my gun, don't forget that."

He said, "The police—"

"The police won't help us, Steven."

"Why won't they? Now that we know where the house is—"

"We've been over this and over this," Mona said. "We

still don't have evidence to incriminate Juleen and the others."

"There has to be evidence in that house."

"Yes, but the police can't enter it without a search warrant. And they can't get a search warrant without reasonable cause. We can't give them reasonable cause, Steven. There's just nothing they'd be willing or able to do on our say-so."

He tried to think, to weigh the two alternatives. But his thoughts kept sliding off each other, like ball bearings in a pan of grease.

Mona said, "I'm furious, I really am, and you should be too. You should be enraged. Don't you want to see their faces, hear them confess the truth?"

"Yes, but—"

"Then come meet me and we'll go together. Otherwise I'll go alone. I mean that. I'm at the Green Wave Coffee Shop on Magazine near Orange. If you're going to come, you'll have to take a taxi."

"I don't have any money."

"I do. I'll pay the driver when you get here."

"What if Chalmette is still outside when I leave? And follows me again?"

"You'll have to try to lose him. But I don't think he'll be there. Nor Juleen. It's almost midnight."

"Midnight?"

"Hurry, darling," she said, and rang off.

He rubbed at his face. It felt hot, swollen. He was going to meet her, he knew that; how could he not meet her? And he *was* angry—furious. He could feel the rage smoldering in him, and the hope thickening in its center, fed by it, supported by it. Confront them? Oh yes, he did want it that way. With a weapon on his side this time, and some of the fear on theirs.

He pulled on his jacket—he could not remember having taken it off—and went to the door. Something made him look at his watch as he let himself out. Sixteen minutes to twelve.

Almost midnight.

It'll be over soon, he thought.

And he believed it now. One way or another, it would all be over soon.

PART V

ASH
WEDNESDAY

And Darkness and Decay and the Red Death held illimitable dominion over all.

—EDGAR ALLAN POE
"The Masque of the Red Death"

TWENTY-SIX

WHEN the taxi pulled up in front of the Green Wave Coffee Shop he saw Mona appear almost immediately, as if she had been watching and waiting just inside the door. She still wore the Guinevere gown and cloak, but the pointed hat and the mask were gone. She was carrying her little pearl-colored purse in one hand.

He glanced across at the meter as the cabbie threw the flag. Then he opened the door and said to Mona, "It's five dollars even."

She gave the driver a five and some change, and Giroux got out, and the taxi went away. The night wind blew cold down Magazine Street, swirling papers, rustling leaves on a live oak that grew nearby. Streetlamps gleamed dully, creating puddles of light on the dark street. There was no one abroad and no traffic at the moment; the dominant sound was the low shushing of the wind. It was like an unguent on raw nerve ends, all that quiet, after the endless cacophony of Mardi Gras.

Mona said, "What took you so long? It's almost two o'clock."

251

"I couldn't find a cab. I had to go all the way over to Canal Street."

"You weren't followed?"

"I don't think so. No."

"They must all be at the house by now. Drugged out of their minds, probably—the filth."

She took his arm, prodded him away from the coffee shop. There was a forcefulness in her grip, like the grip of a man. And there had been a forcefulness in her voice, too, different from any timbre he'd heard in it before—a grim sense of purpose, steel-ribbed, angry, locked on a single objective. She wouldn't be deterred, she wouldn't be argued with. Not by him, anyway. And that was fine, because he no longer doubted her; the doubts had disappeared as soon as he saw her come running out of the cafe. Her strength was his strength, as before, and her purpose would become his purpose. He did not even have to think anymore: Mona would do the thinking for both of them.

It'll all be over soon.

They went past a darkened antique shop, a musty looking secondhand bookstore, and turned onto Race Street. Their shoes made hollow clicking noises on the empty sidewalk. A car whispered past on the cross street ahead of them; shadows shifted and changed shape as the wind bent tree branches, ruffled shrubbery. The houses were like those he had seen on his wanderings Monday afternoon: small, some in need of repair, some half-hidden by vegetation. Most were lightless and all had a grayish sameness in the night, features indistinct and blurred together, like stereotypes poured and pressed from the same matrix. None of them struck a familiar chord in his memory.

They crossed three intersections, walking in silence. His legs were holding up; most of the heavy fatigue he'd felt earlier had vanished along with the doubts. Getting through the rest of this physically was not going to be a problem.

Toward the end of the fourth block, Mona's grip on his arm tightened. With her free hand she pointed diagonally across the street. "That house over there," she said. "The one showing light."

It was a small cottage-style house with a pillared porch, raised up off the ground on a cement-block foundation and set behind a square of untrimmed lawn. A magnolia tree shaded the near side of it, and a live oak grew between the sidewalk and street in front. The front windows were dark; the only visible light shone in a side window near the magnolia, so that some of the blossoms were illuminated and stood out whitely against the darkness. He shut his eyes and tried to dredge up images from Saturday night and Sunday morning. The elevated porch, yes—and the lawn, and the fence, and the trees. He couldn't remember the contours of the house itself. But the fact that it was built on cement blocks was significant; only a house built that way could have a cellar in New Orleans, with the water table being just a few feet below the surface of the ground.

"Familiar?" Mona asked.

"I think so. Maybe."

"It's Juleen's house. It has to be."

"What do we do? Just go over there and knock on the door?"

"No. I'll show you."

She led him to the corner, across Race and half a block along the intersecting street. What looked like an overgrown driveway appeared between two trees; then he saw it was an alleyway that bisected the block, abutted by the rear yards of the Race Street houses on one side and those fronting the next parallel street on the other side. One of the Race Street houses would be Juleen's.

The alley was unpaved, rutted, grass choked in the

center and along the edges. Rear fences of different sizes and shapes flanked it. They picked their way along, Mona leading. A dog barked somewhere nearby and then was silent; the only other sounds were their shuffling steps in the grass. The backsides of the houses stood dark and bulky against an immense sky patched with stars and shifting clouds. None of the houses showed light except Juleen's: a yellowed rectangle in the rear wall, to the left of a flight of stairs.

Near where a flowering dogwood shrub separated Juleen's property from that of her neighbor, Mona stopped and crouched down in the grass. He did the same just behind her. He was not afraid. Mona was there and Mona wasn't afraid, and he was close to the truth now, close to the end. He just wanted it to be done, a dying memory, so he could begin to live again.

The fence here was the same as in front: rusted iron stakes, fashioned in the shape of spears, with a gate farther down. Over Mona's shoulder he could see another stretch of untrimmed lawn, a small kiln of some kind, a budding fruit tree, the pyramidal shape of a big pine that spread shadow over a minijungle of flowers and bushes.

And in the stillness he thought he could hear the faint throb of drums coming from somewhere inside the house. He strained to hear. Yes. Boudoum boudoum, boudoum boudoum. It made him shiver.

He whispered, "Do you hear that? Drums."

"I hear it," she said. "That lighted window is probably the kitchen."

"It's not coming from in there, is it?"

"We'll find out."

She rose up, moved ahead to the gate. Following, he saw her open the latch and ease the gate inward. Rusty hinges made a low squeaking noise, set the unseen dog to barking again. Mona slid through the opening, ran into the shadows beneath the pine. When he joined her he saw that she had taken the little gun out of her purse. The silvered metal of its barrel gleamed as she lifted it, turning, and her hand came out of the shadows.

He kept staring at it. It had an alien look, like some sort of deadly silver spoor that had taken root and grown in her flesh. A sense of unreality touched him. But then Mona took another grip on his arm, and he became an extension of her again, like the gun.

"We'll go over to the stairs and look through the window," she said against his ear. "If there's no one in the kitchen, I'll go up and try the rear door. You wait. If it's unlocked, then you can follow me inside."

The dog was still barking, but in a desultory way; and as they left the pine and crept ahead to the stairs, the barking stopped altogether. Then he could hear the drumbeat again: boudoum boudoum, boudoum boudoum. But muffled, hollow, as if it were coming from somewhere underground.

The cellar, he thought.

They reached the stairs, went around them, hunched over, and up against the wall near the lighted window. Mona raised up first, and when she didn't pull her head back down, he lifted himself and peered in. Not only was it the kitchen, it was the same kitchen he'd been in on Sunday morning—the same coil-top icebox and gas stove and sink set in a wooden drainboard. Juleen's house, no question now. The room was empty, but to one side he could see the cellar door standing partway open, just as it had been on Sunday.

"They're in the cellar," he whispered.

Mona nodded, made a staying motion with the little silver gun, and moved to the stairs. He watched her climb them, slowly, testing each runner before she put her weight on it; watched her take hold of the knob, then release it. She eased down the stairs, gesturing to him. When he went to her she murmured, "It's locked. We'll try the side windows . . . the front door, if we have to."

She led the way around the far corner, along the side of the house where the magnolia tree grew. The first window they came to was dark, and locked tight; the sash moved not at all when he tried to shove upward on it. The second window was the lighted one. Dirty chintz curtains were drawn within, but he could see through them and into what had been made into a potting studio: potter's wheel, shelves with finished pots and jars of paint and glaze and coffee cans of brushes, clay, other things. Juleen had told him she was a potter; that much had been the truth. He tried the sash. And it, too, was locked.

He followed Mona to the front corner. Race Street was deserted; the other houses on the block remained dark, silent. Around the corner, up onto the porch. A question formed in his mind as she reached out to try the door: What do we do if all the doors and windows are locked? But he did not have to put it into words.

The knob turned and the door opened soundlessly.

His pulse quickened. Mona widened the opening, then touched his arm as if to reassure him; he felt the heat of her anger and her purpose. And went after her into the darkness within.

Boudoum boudoum.

Mona shut the door behind him. But they were not in total darkness: a bar of light was visible at the bottom of the closed potting-room door on his left; and on his right, across the living room, the swing door to the kitchen stood open and illumination from in there stretched partway across the floor. Furniture sat in bulky outline. He saw the welter of candles jutting upward like blunt black fingers, menacing rather than phallic in the gloom. Saw the shadowed paintings on the walls, the one of the giant serpent that leered down from near the swing door, where the outspill of light brushed it and gave it a kind of gleaming clarity.

Against his ear Mona whispered, "Watch where you walk. Don't make any noise."

He nodded, and she started to thread a course through the furniture shapes toward the kitchen. Following, he watched her and watched his feet. But despite his caution, the toe of one shoe stubbed against a table leg, made it scrape on the bare floor. Both he and Mona froze. But the quality of the stillness did not change; the drumbeat went on in the same steady muffled cadence, as if the house itself were alive and the sound were that of its heart.

They covered the remaining distance into the kitchen in silence. He blinked at the blaze of ceiling light, looking toward the partially open cellar door. The drums came from down there, rolling up out of flickers of light and shadow. Something else rolled up out of the cellar, too: a heavy, dark, familiar stench.

Blood smell, death smell.

He saw Mona wrinkle her nose, knew that she also smelled it. The sweat on him was thick and greasy, like butter, and it gave him a brief wild fancy that he was melting. The tension in him was like a high vibratory note just beyond the range of hearing.

Mona moved forward, pushed the door open wider with the tips of her fingers. The restless play of light and shadow grew more pronounced. Candles—a lot of them.

And what else? he thought.

What else have they got down there?

He crowded close to Mona and they went through the doorway to find out.

TWENTY-SEVEN

INSIDE the door was the narrow landing; the railed stairs led down from there. He could not see much of what lay below because Mona was in front of him and because of the angle of descent under the floor. The candleflames were invisible until she edged down onto the top step; then he saw some of them spread out at intervals on the cellar floor. And when he pressed closer to her, ducking his head, he saw the rest of them—and Juleen and the two unmasked men.

The candles were arranged in a rough circle, inside of which a crude pentagram had been drawn with white paint. The three of them sat on points of the pentagram, cross-legged, fully clothed, Juleen and one of the men motionless, the other man thumping softly on a cask drum. Grotesque shadows clung to their faces, climbed the walls behind them. The candlelight revealed a cloth-draped altar, similar to the one he had seen in the swamp clearing, set on the floor against one wall; on top of it was the same cage, or its twin, that had contained the big speckled snake Juleen had danced with. Beyond, hanging over a narrow trough, was what looked to be the carcass of a young goat.

He felt Mona nudge his arm, but he could not take his eyes off the three of them down there, the gutted thing hanging over the trough beyond the circle of candles. He stood like that, bent at the waist, staring, even when she stepped around him and back onto the landing.

Then the cellar lights went on.

He blinked, startled at the sudden radiance from a pair of low-wattage ceiling bulbs. Juleen and the drummer were startled too, but in a belated, dreamy way; the drums stopped and their heads turned and the man made loose-limbed motions to rise. The other man continued to sit, hands in his lap, a fixed smile on his face. His lips and chin were wet with saliva.

Mona was moving down the stairs, with the little silver gun extended in her hand. Giroux went after her, clumsily, peering around the cellar. But it was not what he had imagined it would be—not some sort of charnel house, bodies lying all around, torture devices, voodoo trappings. It was just an ordinary cellar: concrete walls and floor, storage shelves, homemade cabinets, a workbench, a litter of broken furniture and boxes and discarded items in one corner. The altar and the candles and the pentagram and the snake box were the only symbols of pagan worship. That, and the carcass of the young goat, skinned and disemboweled and hung on a metal hook to drip its blood into the trough. It was no longer draining, but he could see the blood glistening in the trough, and smell it on the dark musty air.

The drummer was on his feet when Mona came off the bottom step, but he made no move toward her. He seemed to be struggling to understand the intrusion; his face revealed a kind of heavy concentration. He was in his mid-twenties, dark, wavy haired, wearing Levi's and a shirt with a serpent painted on it in crimson. Juleen was still sitting on one of the pentagram points, eyes turned up toward

Mona, the same struggling awareness in them. She wore the red robe she had worn on Saturday night, and her face was painted, and the Legba staff lay at her feet. The second man, dressed as the other one, kept sitting like a thin Buddha statue. He had lank, dirty blond hair and a hatchet face and his pupils were shrunken to the size of pinpoints. He made a low giggling noise; another. More drool came out of one corner of his mouth.

The wavy haired one said, "What are you doing here?" in a thick voice that had no inflection. Chalmette's voice. "How did you find us?"

"Go away," Juleen said dreamily. She moved as she spoke, and the robe fell away at her lap to expose one naked thigh. "It's long past midnight. Fat Tuesday is gone."

"That's right, you little bitch," Mona said. "And now it's your turn to unmask."

"No. The masque is secret."

Giroux came around from behind Mona, to stand alongside her. The tension in him had lessened, but only just a little; anger mixed with it, and relief, and expectancy, and dread. He said, "What do you mean? What secret masque?"

"Go ahead, tell him," Mona said. In the uncertain light her face had a cold hard look, like finely veined white marble. She moved the gun. "Tell him. Tell us both."

"Where's the photograph, Giroux?" the blond man said suddenly, and then giggled. He still did not move his body.

"Tell us, damn you."

"Our secret masque," Juleen said. "For Carnival. Just like every year."

"Every year, man," the blond one agreed.

"In honor of Papa Là-bas."

"Voodoo, man. Don't you just fucking love it?"

Chalmette made an appealing gesture with one hand.

"But it's over now. Why don't you go away?"

"It's not over," Mona said between her teeth. "Don't you know what you did to him, you animals? Don't you have any human feelings, any of you?"

"He was the chosen," Juleen said. "Papa Là-bas sent him to us. I knew it as soon as I saw him."

"We didn't kill him, did we?" Chalmette said.

"But we thought about it," the blond one said. "No more chickens, no more goats. Whee!"

"We didn't kill him," Chalmette insisted.

It was beginning to break in on him now, sickeningly. "The photograph," he said, "what about the photograph?"

"There is no photograph," Mona said. "Don't you see, Steven? There never was a photograph. It was only a prop in their filthy masquerade."

"The voodoo too?"

"Yes. The bleeding doll, the conjure ball, the snake's-head stick—all of it. There isn't any voodoo cult. Just these three freaks playing at devil worship."

"We aren't playing," Juleen said. "Papa Là-bas is real."

"Pagan freaks."

"We dance and sing in his honor. We offer him blood."

"Goats and chickens," the blond one said. "Far out, man."

"We offer him fear," Juleen said.

Giroux shook his head. It felt loose, broken, on the stem of his neck. "You weren't after *me*," he said. "You picked me at random. It could have been anybody in New Orleans."

"You were chosen by Papa Là-bas."

He saw it all now, and it was even more monstrous than any of his imaginings. So much terror, and yet none of it had been real. Or personal. The blood on his hands

Sunday morning must have been goat's blood; the dead thing he had smelled in the cellar was the goat; the photograph and the voodoo trappings and the threatening calls and the stolen tickets and the abduction and the physical abuse and the duplicate Guinevere had been elaborate set pieces, like the flower images and the waving pennants and the bags of doubloons and glass beads on one of the parade floats. He was Comus or Hermes or Rex; he had been selected King of the Masque of Là-bas, and swept along by its sociopathic, sensualist organizers in an improvisational krewe through the French Quarter, through the Irish Channel, all the way down into the bayou swamps. Anyone could be King of Là-bas, but *he* had been chosen this year. And they could not have made a better choice; he had played right into their hands, opening up to Juleen the way he had on Saturday, telling her about his fears, giving her all the personal information about himself that they needed to know. But if he had failed to respond, if he had balked at any time during the festivities—called the police, say, after waking up with blood on his hands, or gone all the way down into the cellar that morning and found the goat— why, they would have covered up, denied everything, and then considered him as having abdicated and crowned a new king. It was Carnival, it was Mardi Gras; New Orleans was full of men alone, vulnerable; there were suitable Kings of Là-bas on every corner, in every bar and jazz club and topless joint in the Vieux Carré.

He moved forward a step. "How did you get into my room to steal my airline tickets?"

Chalmette said, "What difference does it make?"

"We used your key," Juleen said. "In the night."

Saturday night, while he was passed out. He'd taken the key with him then; he'd forgotten to leave it at the desk. "Then you brought it back here and put it in my jacket before I woke up. That's it, isn't it?"

They just looked at him with their spaced-out eyes.

"I began to suspect the truth when you told me what happened at the swamp house," Mona said. "But I didn't say anything to you because I couldn't be sure. If they were really after a photograph, why did they bring you back to the city and turn you loose? Why didn't they keep you there and torture you?"

He nodded. And why, if they were after a photograph, had they wanted him to think he'd killed Juleen? How would that get it for them? And there had been no point in the voodoo; no need for the bleeding doll or the conjure ball. When you looked at it all in perspective and hindsight, it had been a jumble of events that had no purpose, no logical pattern. It had to be a masque, because there was nothing else it could be. Time after time he had reflected on the lunacy of it, the disconnected elements, and yet he had been too wrapped up in his own fear, too well manipulated by shock after shock, to take it the one step further he needed to see the truth. If he had—

If he had, the masque would have ended long ago and he would not be here now.

If he had.

If.

"Thrills, that's all it was," Mona said. "Cheap, sick thrills. Like the drugs they're on right now."

"Stoned, man," the blond one said. "Flying, man."

"They're vermin. They crawl in the dirt, they wallow in feces."

"Fuck you, lady," Chalmette said. "Go away. It's finished, goddamn it."

"Until next year."

"That's our business."

"Papa Là-bas must be served," Juleen said.

Giroux felt sick to his stomach; the death smell, the sight of the goat carcass and the trough full of blood, were making him nauseous. He wanted to get out of there, into the fresh air. He wanted to sleep. He wanted to go back into a world he understood.

"We'd better call the police," he said to Mona.

Chalmette said, "Go ahead, call them."

"Shut up, you. I don't want to listen to you any more."

"What do you think they'll do to us? We're stoned, but they won't find our stash. Probation, man, that's all. We don't have police records."

"Elton John records," the blond one said, giggling, "that's all *we* got."

"I'm going to press charges," Giroux said. "Harrassment, mental cruelty, kidnapping, assault."

"How you going to prove it? It's your word against ours. Prove we kidnapped you. Prove we knocked you around. Prove we did a masque with you."

Mona said softly, "He's right about that, Steven. I told you."

"How'd you get in here?" Chalmette said. "Breaking and entering. Trespassing. We'll press charges against *you.* Why don't you just get out of here. Go away, let us do our thing."

"No," he said.

"Call the police then."

"Damn right I'm going to call them."

"Steven . . ."

"No, Mona, I'm going to make the call. I'm not going to let them get away with what they did."

She looked at him for a moment. Then she said, "Yes, you're right. They mustn't get away with it. You go ahead. I'll hold them here."

He backed to the stairs, turned and went up slowly, with one hand on the railing for support. The fatigue had returned; he had never felt so tired. Or so empty. And yet his thoughts had never been clearer—a stark, dazzling clarity that was almost painful.

He reached the landing, went through the doorway into the kitchen. He didn't know where the telephone was; he could not remember having seen one anywhere in the house. He walked through the open swing door, saw the painting of the serpent and the blood-red words *Danse Calinda.* Looked away. Looked at the opposite wall for a light switch—

A flat cracking sound came up out of the cellar behind him.

Another.

Gunshots.

He wheeled around, and all the fear and tension and nightmare images came rushing into him again. *Mona!* he thought, and ran across the kitchen, slapped the door aside, lunged through onto the landing and down three steps.

And froze there, both hands clutching at the rail.

Chalmette lay sprawled across half a dozen of the black candles, so that their smoke smouldered under and around him, and Juleen lay on her side on the pentagram, and there was blood on Chalmette's head, and Juleen only had one eye and redness where the other hand been, and Mona was standing next to the blond man, looking down at him, and he looked up at her, half grinning in a kind of rictus, giggling, and extended one hand toward her, palm up, as if in supplication, and she put the little silver gun to the side of his head and she

she

she

pulled the trigger—

TWENTY-EIGHT

HE saw a spray of blood, and the blond man toppled sideways, and then he was scrambling around on the stairs, plunging upward in a frenzy. He lost his balance, cracked his knee against the door jamb. Threw himself into the kitchen and caromed off the old-fashioned icebox and looked around wildly. But there were running footfalls on the stairs, and he had nowhere to go—and Mona appeared in the doorway.

"You killed them," he said.

She was calm, almost serene, as she came toward him. But the emeraldfire was in her eyes, and it burned, and it burned, and he saw that it was not passion, not purpose, it was just a burning deep inside, like fire in a black pit.

"I had to, Steven," she said. "It was the only way. They would have got away with it if I hadn't. They would have gone unpunished. And next year they would have done it to someone else, maybe killed someone. I couldn't let that happen. You understand that, don't you?"

"You *murdered* them."

"They were filth, they didn't deserve to live. It isn't

murder when you step on vermin, is it?"

He shook his head. Kept on shaking it.

"Don't look at me like that," she said. Her voice was gentle, tolerant. "It's all right, darling. Really it is. You'll see. Nobody will ever know."

I'll know. *I'll* know.

"Nobody ever found out about Ralph," she said. "And that was two years ago."

"Ralph?"

"My late husband. He was vermin, too. I didn't realize it until afterward, but he was. He should never have left me; he should never have said all those things to me."

"Oh my God," he said.

She smiled in a way that turned his skin to ice. "Everyone thought it was an accident, that his gun went off while he was cleaning it. We can't make this look like an accident, but it won't matter. No one saw us come into the house. No one will know we've been here. We'll be very careful, darling."

Headshake. He had no more words.

She was still smiling, and the emeraldfire burned, and her shining face was the face of fear. And now he understood everything—all of it, all of it. He understood who and what Mona was beneath her controlled exterior, and how the malevolent gods had set it up from the beginning, and all the ways in which he had been manipulated, and the whole scheme of the present, and the dark shape of the future. All the masques were ended; all the participants were unmasked before him. And Fat Tuesday was gone— there would be no more Fat Tuesdays. It was Ash Wednesday now.

In old New Orleans everyone went to Mass on the morning after Mardi Gras, and the priest would put penitential ashes on their foreheads, and he would say, "Dust thou art," and smear the ashes "and unto dust thou must return," making the sign of the cross with

his thumb, and for each of them in turn the fun and the frolic were
no more.

"I love you, darling," the stranger named Mona said.
"I've never loved anyone the way I love you. I'll kill anybody who tries to hurt you . . . anybody from now on."

All the masques were ended, yes—but not the terror.
The terror was just beginning . . .